Ankush Saikia was born in 1975 in Assam in India's North East, and grew up in the US, Assam, and Shillong, Meghalaya. He has worked in journalism and publishing in New Delhi, and is the author of several crime thrillers including *The Girl from Nongrim Hills* and the Detective Arjun Arora series. Saikia was shortlisted for the Outlook/Picador India non-fiction writing competition in 2005, and was one of the recipients of the Shanghai Writers' Association's 2018 fellowships. *The Forest Beneath the Mountains* is his eighth book, and the first to be set primarily in his home state of Assam in North-East India. His articles and longform stories (mostly on North-East India) have appeared in *FountainInk* magazine, *Scroll.in*, *The Indian Express*, *The Hindu*, and *Hindustan Times*, among others.

The Forest Beneath *the* Mountains

ANKUSH SAIKIA

SPEAKING TIGER

SPEAKING TIGER BOOKS LLP
4381/4, Ansari Road, Daryaganj
New Delhi 110002

Published by Speaking Tiger Books in paperback 2021

ISBN: 978-93-90477-55-5
eISBN: 978-93-90477-64-7

10 9 8 7 6 5 4 3 2 1

Typeset in EB Garamond by SÜRYA, New Delhi
Printed at Chaman Enterprises, New Delhi

This is a work of fiction. Names, characters, places and incidents either are the product of the author's imagination or are used fictitiously, and any resemblance to actual persons, living or dead, events or locales is entirely coincidental.

In memory of my grandparents,
residents of the north bank:

Purna Kanta Saikia (1911–2004)
Durgamoni Saikia (1928–2006)
Ratna Bora (1904–1979)
Molani Bora (1916–2011)

'The thinning, changing, and elimination of forests—deforestation, no less—is not a recent phenomenon; it is as old as the human occupation of the earth and one of the key processes in the history of our transformation of its surface.'

—Michael Williams,
Deforesting the Earth

'The very thing which may usually convey a sense of purposeful intelligence—the exposition of an idea by means of a certain stylistic facility—now seemed to me nothing but an entirely arbitrary or deluded enterprise.'

—W.G. Sebald,
Austerlitz

CONTENTS

The Forest Officer's Son

One summer evening a couple of years ago, a slender man in his early thirties got down from an inter-state bus at the Mission Chariali crossroads on the outskirts of Tezpur. He stood there for a while with his duffel bag, looking around. He remembered it as a nondescript crossing with a few dusty wood-plank shops; now there were brightly-lit stores with rubbish scattered before them, a traffic circle, and people all around waiting for buses and autos, walking this way and that. The heat seemed to be magnified by the roar of the goods and army trucks, which dwarfed the cars and autos and small buses. At the corner of the old mill was a large new hotel and departmental store. A woman in a burkha followed by several children hurried behind a small man carrying two large bags. The crush of people, the exhaust fumes mixed in the hot, gritty air: it seemed like just any other part of the country. Abhijit Saikia watched the bus drive off toward Itanagar. Not for the first time, he felt a sense of apprehension. Twenty-five years was a long time.

His return was connected to his mother's death in Guwahati several weeks ago, from a stroke she suffered in her sleep. She had been only fifty-seven years old. After the rituals and formalities had all been completed, Abhijit went with his uncle one day to the ghat from where the ferries left for Umananda island and scattered his mother's ashes in the Brahmaputra, and then went back to Delhi. He was still numb with grief, and on the flight to Delhi one thing kept playing on his mind: the remark made by his uncle, his mother's elder brother, late one night when he thought Abhijit was asleep.

He had retired to her room, and then, unable to sleep, had pulled the curtains and sat beside the windows looking out at the deserted lane lit by a streetlight. Without meaning to, he had started following the conversation between his uncle, who was drinking, and his aunt in their drawing room.

'She died because of Khagen,' he had said, after a few drinks. 'When he killed himself, I knew it would affect her badly, even though she never showed it. He broke her heart.'

His wife had told him to keep quiet, saying Abhijit might hear him.

He couldn't sleep that night. What he had been told as a child was that his father, a forest beat officer, had gone alone into the reserve forest in his departmental jeep, where he had been shot by insurgents near the Assam–Arunachal border. That was what he had believed for twenty-five years. This other explanation was too monstrous for him to even consider. Why would his father abandon him and his mother? Asking his uncle would have been of no help; Abhijit noticed he seemed to be on tenterhooks around him, possibly on account of the share he had been given from the sale of the family house in Shillong. Abhijit had quietly accepted whatever he had received, not wishing to make a fuss after his mother's death. In the morning he checked everything in the room his mother had used, in the hope of finding a note or a letter, but to no avail: she had removed all traces of Abhijit's father from her life. This lack of rememberance he had always taken for granted; now however, in light of what he had heard his uncle say, it roused his suspicions.

Back in Delhi, he felt a growing disassociation with the city, with his job as an editor, and even from his girlfriend Debolina, who was from Kolkata. Things had already been strained between them, even before he went to Guwahati. She had started talking about getting married, something he felt he didn't want to get into yet, but couldn't bring himself to tell her directly. Then they had gone on a holiday to Himachal, with a detour in the hills which had seen them losing their phone network for a couple of days. It was only when they were headed back to Delhi that Abhijit found out about his mother's sudden death, after which he could only make it to Guwahati in time for the shradh on the eleventh day: the holiday, and the detour, had been her idea, and it served to further sour things between them.

Slowly the question took hold of his mind, until in time it was all he could think about. What had really happened to his father? He stopped going to work, and spent a lot of time on his laptop in his barsati room in Lajpat Nagar looking up maps and reading whatever he could find about the area where his father had passed away. At night, when it was a bit cooler, Abhijit would pace up and down the terrace, trapped in a forest of shoddy concrete buildings, and when he slept he would often dream of that immense wilderness which his father had patrolled as a beat officer. He stopped meeting his girlfriend: both of them agreed it was better if they took a break.

A few weeks later, he sold most of his meagre possessions, parcelled two cartons of books to his uncle's address in Guwahati, and bought a train ticket back to Assam, travelling the way he had on his first journey to Delhi several years back. On reaching Guwahati, he didn't go to his uncle's place, but stayed in a cheap hotel in Paltan Bazar near the railway station. Early the next morning he walked across to the ghat where he had scattered his mother's ashes in the river. His father's ashes had been scattered in the same river, but further upstream. Then he caught a bus to Tezpur.

Peak summer, and it was hot and stuffy inside the bus. The conductor kept picking up more passengers on the highway, while the sun beat down outside on the green rice fields. The bus took the south bank road, using the new Nagaon bypass, and crossed over to the north bank by the 3-km-long Koliabhomora bridge over the Brahmaputra. Abhijit tried to get used to it—the heat, the dusty seats, the different communities, the gentleness of the language compared to north India. It was evening when the bus dropped him off at the crossroads outside Tezpur.

On the road that led to the army's 4 Corps headquarters, conductors outside their buses beyond the old railway line were shouting 'Dhekiajuli, Dhekiajuli!,' even as a couple of men were pissing by the railway line. Abhijit walked around the traffic point toward the large autos waiting by the wall of the old mill and got into the back of one of them, stuffing the bag among the other passengers' feet. Once there were enough people on board it moved forward with a jerk, headed for Tezpur town. The auto went past the market, the Mission Hospital opposite, and new showrooms and a petrol pump. He got down near the old aahot or ficus tree at Ketekibari, and walked down the gravelled road next to the large tree.

It was the first house to the right after turning left on the inside road: he recognized its silhouette beyond the brick wall. The rusted iron gate, the grassy patch where he played cricket with a couple of the village boys, the guava tree beside the house which he used to climb, the tops of the betel nut trees in the backyard rising above the sloping tin roof: it was still the same. He opened the gate and walked in. By the dim light in the veranda he saw the old wooden bench, now painted blue like the closed front doors. An equally dim light came from the bedroom through its open wood-frame windows. The left side of the house was in darkness. Stepping up to the veranda he pressed the calling bell fixed to one of the columns and heard what sounded like a lizard's *chik chik* from inside the house. The door was opened by a balding, elderly man wearing glasses and a worn grey long-sleeved shirt. His father's younger brother, Hiren, who nodded at his introduction and stepped aside to let Abhijit enter, as though people regularly showed up at the house after an interval of a quarter century.

The yellow light from the 60-watt bulb, the cane sofa set with the embroidered green and red cushions, the faded whitewashed walls—nothing had changed inside as well. The same number of framed black and white photos hanging on one wall, no additions or removals, including the one that showed his grandfather in a dhoti and a coat standing with a few other men, all looking straight at the camera without smiling, one man with a rifle in his hands and one foot on a dead tiger spread out on the ground. As a child the sight of this photo had always given him a vague feeling of having been born too late; he was surprised to feel the same emotion in himself as a grown man—if anything it was even stronger now, the feeling that he had missed something important by not being born forty or fifty years earlier.

The rest of the house too seemed the same. At the end of the corridor his grandmother was in her usual place, in a heavy wooden chair by the table in the rear veranda, keeping an eye on the helper in the half-open kitchen just behind the house, a middle-aged woman tending to the fire in an earthen souka or fireplace. The table was overflowing with newspapers, pickle bottles, old batteries, and other household odds and ends which he had found so fascinating years ago, when he and his mother had still lived here. His grandmother was dressed in an old white sari, her grey hair oiled and pulled back, a lifetime's fine wrinkles on her nut-brown face. She looked up at him and held his hands when his uncle said it was Khagen's son, Abhijit, but he could see there was no recognition in those eyes. She smiled and asked him to sit and kept smiling at him.

The dheki under the kitchen roof that had been used for pounding grain looked unused. Perhaps it had been a while since the ripe paddy had been brought to the house from the fields and placed in a circle near the well to be threshed by a pair of cows. A bamboo pole on a frame, with a rope tied to it for the tin bucket, still hung at an angle over the well. At the other end of the rear veranda, under the eaves, was his uncle's old Bajaj scooter. His uncle nodded when Abhijit mentioned the scooter; he said it was still in good condition. They had black tea with Krackjack biscuits, his grandmother looking at Abhijit all the while with her sad, confused smile.

'What actually happened to my father?' he asked his uncle. 'Who pulled the trigger?'

His uncle looked out into the darkness of the backyard for a long time before replying.

'The insurgents fighting for Bodoland had their hideouts in that forest then. They killed him. And now that forest has almost disappeared.'

'I'm thinking of returning to those areas,' Abhijit said. 'To find out more.'

His uncle looked at him, and said, 'Those areas are even more dangerous now.'

There was a power cut, and when the lights returned, they ate rice and a curry made with medium-sized bhagun fish and green bananas off kahi or brass plates in the dining room. To one side was his grandmother's room, while his uncle's room was at the front of the house. Before dinner he had spent some time in both the rooms, sitting in silence by the harsh brightness of an emergency light, watching his uncle fiddle with the parts of an old transistor radio (it was a hobby of sorts, opening up electrical appliances, especially old ones), and then watching his grandmother fold and refold the day's Assamese newspaper while talking about an uncle who had come to visit them from Sootea just after her marriage. In one corner of her room on a small, low table with a gamusa on it were a couple of religious texts, like Sankardev's *Naam Ghoxa* and an Assamese *Bhagabad Gita*, and two framed black-and-white photographs—of her husband Jogeshwar Saikia and their late son Khagen—with a brass plate before the photos on which was an earthen lamp with a wick and some mustard oil.

The house and the grounds had the feel of a place where things had ground to a halt—one could feel everything important here had taken place in the past, and in the mood he was in, this comforted Abhijit. At the same time, he could see how his father's death and the abandonment of this house by his mother had contributed to that decline, along with the behaviour of his two eccentric uncles (they had not always been that way though, especially when his father was alive), the younger one with his room full of transistors and watches, and the elder brother Romen, an engineer in Mumbai, making only one trip home a year to see their mother.

Hiren Khura opened up the room beside the sitting room for him. It had been his grandfather's room, and was more like a store room now, with suitcases, cartons, an old cycle, a step ladder and other sundry items, but there was also a single bed (above which a mosquito net had been strung), and a simple wooden desk and a chair. It suited Abhijit just fine. As he lay in the darkness under the net with the fan whirring above, the musty old smell of the room reminded him of the time when he would lie awake beside his mother at night and ask her when his father would be back from the jungle. He was always worried about his deuta falling in the path of a rogue elephant, a man-eating tiger or a wild buffalo; but in the end it was a gun that had killed him.

'Animals have limited wants, unlike us humans, whose wants are never-ending,' he remembered his father saying as they sat before a burning log at the Gabharu forest beat office, on the last night Abhijit had spent with him. Then his father had started the jeep and they set out for Foothills, driving past Lama Camp, stopping at the Kolamati forest gate where Khagen Saikia had a word with one of the forest guards, and then they entered the wall of forest looming ahead of them in the dark. The jeep's headlights flooded the narrow road between the high trees, showing the tangled undergrowth below, with the damp smell of rotting vegetation in the air. Abhijit felt a child's fear of the dark, the unknown, but there was also a sense of adventure and wonder: at this primeval world which his father looked after.

They came to a wooden bridge over a small river, more like a stream now in the dry season. To the left of the bridge was a muddy clearing bordered with undergrowth. Khagen Saikia brought the jeep to a halt, killed the lights, and pointed through the windscreen to the left. It took Abhijit a while to see the shape at the far end of the clearing, which his father whispered was a tiger. Terror gripped him and he was painfully aware, over the low rumble of the engine, of the open door at his side. After what seemed like several minutes, his father switched on the lights and took the jeep forward over the small bridge; the wooden planks clattered, and he heard a growl and saw the shape moving away into the undergrowth. His father said it had come out to hunt. He could feel his heart thudding for a long time.

Further ahead the road bent to the right and then continued arrow straight for several kilometres through the forest. His father lit a Charminar, and Abhijit kept a hand on his father's .315 rifle propped up on the front seat. At a slight right on the straight road, which further ahead took a few turns and then climbed up into the hills of Arunachal Pradesh, a dirt track went straight ahead and then curved left toward the Belsiri river. They passed the supposedly haunted ximolu tree, the Nepali basti with its few tin and mud huts, then the field and the whitewashed posts and the huts of the army's khachar or mule camp, and then ahead a right turn to the MES pump house, beside which was Pradip Deka's camp, with the familiar green Gypsy and a fire burning before the two-roomed house with a netted veranda in front.

Abhijit knew Pradip Deka as an army contractor from Tezpur who had been with his father in college. He was a tall, well-built man, liked a bit of shooting and fishing with his friends, and that evening there were a couple of them around the fire, drinking and singing old songs. His father took one of the chairs and was poured a drink by Pradip Deka (the bottles were set out on the Gypsy's bonnet) while Abhijit sat on a moorah beside his father. He liked being part of this rough group of men, the firelight glowing on their unshaven faces, and in a while even his father seemed a different person, laughing, singing part of Bhupen Hazarika's *Kohuwa Bon*, and protesting when for some reason Pradip Deka started ribbing him about going up to Dirang in Arunachal Pradesh.

But soon he was bored, the men's talk about demand notes from the 'organization' (as the ULFA was referred to) and the fight for a separate Bodo state going above his head. His father told him to go and eat, so he went inside and through one of the rooms to the kitchen at the back, where a youth named Biren who stayed at the camp served him rice, vegetables and chicken curry. He ate in one of the rooms by the light of a kerosene lamp, and as he ate, became aware of the shotgun and rifle propped up in one corner, the cartridges and bullets lined up on a shelf, and two searchlights with lengths of wire lying on one of the two single beds.

He had then asked his father if he could stay back, as he had done before, to accompany the men when they went hunting, but his father reminded him that he had to return to Tezpur the next morning. They left sometime after that, his father telling Pradip Deka that he would have his dinner back at the beat office. On the return journey, Abhijit heard the hoarse trumpeting of a wild elephant ringing out from somewhere within the forest.

'How come you never stop them?' he asked. 'Are they allowed to go hunting?'

'I can't stop everything,' his father said, and then, with a note of sadness in his voice, added, 'Anyway, these forests will also be gone one day.'

He was too sleepy to ask any more questions, and his father had to wake him up by the time they reached the beat office. He thought his father might have been humming

Kohuwa Bon in the jeep as well. The next morning, he awoke on the bed he shared with his father to find him sitting on the easy chair looking at Abhijit with a strange, sad smile, a notepad and a pen in his lap, smoke curling up from a lit Charminar in one hand. He asked his father what had happened, but Khagen Saikia just shook his head, stubbed out the cigarette, and went to the bathroom and started shaving. Later that morning he dropped off Abhijit and a forest guard going to the Tezpur DFO office at the Missamari bazar from where they caught a line bus. As he climbed up into the bus he looked back at the jeep, and saw Khagen Saikia—wearing the dark-brown uniform sweater which made him look so handsome—wave at him, and he waved back and climbed aboard. It was the last time he would ever see his father.

The Camp at Foothills

In the beginning were the hills and the mountains, with rivers running down from them to the forests and the plains. Wild animals roamed the land and man was nowhere to be found. In the midst of it all a vast body of water, raging down as several rivers from high mountains in a corner of this land and then flowing deep and wide on its journey westward. The first people who came down from the mountains and set eyes on this immense river wouldn't go too close to it, out of fear. Whence did it come from, whither did it go? Later, they wouldn't settle near its banks, because of the seasonal floods. In time, more people came, from west and east (and even north and south) and settled above this great river; it was from among them that Abhijit Saikia's ancestors came, part of this mixture of peoples and races on the north bank of the Brahmaputra river in north-east India.

Khagen Saikia, Abhijit's late father, was a stocky, brown-complexioned man, and anyone who saw the family realized that Abhijit had taken after his mother, as he was slim and almost pale in appearance. As for the family name: Saikia is a common enough upadhi or surname in Assam, which was given by the Ahom kings to people controlling a hundred or xo soldiers (hence xoikia or Saikia). In the north bank region of Assam, above the Brahmaputra, people who have this title are not usually Ahoms but belong to other communities.

Khagen Saikia came from an old family on the outskirts of Tezpur town, the second of three brothers. He entered the state forest department a few years after doing his Masters from Guwahati University (before that he had graduated from Tezpur's Darrang College), and was posted during the late 1980s at Chariduar reserve forest to the north of Sonitpur district, along the border with Arunachal Pradesh. Those were troubled times, and Assam was up in flames. Khagen Saikia was an upright and efficient forest officer, even if occassionaly harsh in his behaviour. One afternoon he drove into the reserve forest, and never came back. His body was later found inside his departmental jeep with a gunshot wound. There was no suicide note, and later there were rumours about the involvement of armed men in the area. His only child Abhijit had spent a few days with him at the beat office hardly a week before the incident. Abhijit and his mother had been staying at Khagen Saikia's parents' house, and after the incident she took Abhijit with her to Shillong, where her parents lived, effectively cutting off all contact with her late husband's family. The boy was told that his father had died at the hands of the insurgents.

Abhijit went to school and college in Shillong, and then left for Delhi, where he did a vocational course or two before getting into journalism, which he later left for publishing. How had his father's disappearance from his life affected him? It gave him, he came to realize as he grew older, a certain hesitancy in all matters, as if the absence of a father had robbed him of a certain masculine aggressiveness. And his mother's love was, by the time he was in college, something suffocating he needed to get away from. He did have a certain stubbornness, possibly born out of a feeling that he had been in some way cheated by the family tragedy. As for the insurgents who were said to have killed his father, he felt no hatred for them, rather a sort of pity; he wouldn't have been able to articulate it if asked, but he felt that those men would have had their own compulsions.

He wrote and then published a slim volume of short stories after he had been in Delhi a couple of years (*The Village by the River and other stories*, Bracket Books, Delhi, 2010), simple sketches of a character during different time periods in Assam, Shillong, and Delhi. When his mother passed away in her sleep in Guwahati, she was staying with her younger brother and his family, after they had sold the family house in Shillong. His mother's share from the proceeds of the sale of the family house in Shillong's Motinagar locality had come to him (there were some savings of his own too), freeing him for a while from the necessity of working. In an effort to find out what exactly had happened to his father, he decided to return to Foothills, and look up people from the old days.

Of that great forest all he possessed were memories, which was also why he wanted to revisit it, to see if the reports of settlers having spread there were true. Among the short stories he had written (which were about a couple and their sensitive only son), was one set in an unnamed location in a forest along the Assam–Arunachal border: the boy sees a deer being shot, and later watches the hunters, who are drinking army-issue rum, gutting and skinning the animal. Abhijit had written: 'He senses indistinctly the timelessness of such things; men, fire, animals, blood.' What that boy (or the young Abhijit) wouldn't have known then was that it was the end of an era: larger forces were sweeping the region, and a small place like Foothills couldn't stay isolated.

The detail about the hunters (the entire story in fact) came from Abhijit's own experiences. His father sometimes took Abhijit to Pradip Deka's house, which was also on the outskirts of Tezpur town (in the old days, those from the so-called lower castes were expected to stay away from the more 'civilized' areas of town). Pradip Deka, or Pradip Khura as Abhijit called him, was a contractor with the MES or Military Engineering Service, and had set up the camp at Foothills towards the late 1980s as a carpenters' workshop and storehouse for his 'periodical' or annual maintenance work at the nearby Missamari army base. Foothills was the actual name of the place, dating back to when an AR or Assam Rifles camp came up there after 1947, when India sent up people to claim the Tawang tract as its own (Bob Khathing, a Tangkhul Naga from Manipur, had led the first expedition). The AR camp had occupied the area taken up later by the khachar camp. Abhijit had a faint memory of watching the mules with their docile, long-suffering look being made to walk around a mini-obstacle course on the field with small bridges and water pits. Sometimes there were sirens and explosions nearby to get them used to war conditions (they were trained to carry loads for the army up on the border with China).

Pradip Khura's house was an old one, made of plaster and timber with a tin roof, falling apart in places, and had been built by his grandfather, his father's father, who had done some trading with the British in his day. It had a cemented forecourt and inner courtyard (with moss stains from the rains), and in the semi-wilderness of the large bari or garden behind the detached kitchen were betel-nut and starfruit trees and a pineapple patch. Pradip Khura was a heavy drinker, like so many of those around him.

Pradip Deka passed away about a decade after Khagen Saikia's death. Many years later, watching *The Grand Budapest Hotel* in Delhi, Abhijit would remember both men when the narrator said: 'His world had vanished long before he entered it. But he sustained the illusion with a marvellous grace.' The effects of change upon tribal societies in the hill states of north-east India is a topic of interest among academicians, but it is unlikely anyone will study the inner contradictions of people such as Khagen Saikia and Pradip Deka (and their friends), caught as they were between the British-ruled society of their parents and the mutations of democracy in a distant corner of a newly-independent country.

Abhijit had visited the Foothills camp a few times during his holidays, with his father dropping him off there or Pradip Khura picking him up from the beat office in his Gypsy. Abhijit liked the man, his sense of humour, the way he spoke to him directly, as if he were an adult. Sometimes there would be Khura's companions in the vehicle, or a few labourers taking a lift to his camp, at other times there would be supplies in the back, from a hardware store in

Tezpur: paint tins and brushes, latches and hooks, rolls of wire mesh. His experiences of that great forest with Pradip Khura had been of a more elemental sort than those with his father.

In his later years in Shillong and Delhi, Abhijit could return to that winter landscape of Assam by just closing his eyes: the morning mist hanging over the yellow paddy stalks in the harvested fields, stands of trees and bamboo groves beside them, ducks in ponds, warm sunshine, the odd village: huts with thatch or tin roofs under betel-nut trees, paths white with dust. Back then, he was incurious about what he saw, because there was still a rural connection to Tezpur; paddy from the family fields arriving at his father's house to be threshed, the cows in the guhali or cowshed, their dung used in the garden as fertilizer and in the pakghor for fuel.

They would cross the wood-plank bridge over the Gabharu river in his father's jeep, and then further ahead, past the tea garden at Kolakuchi, was the cantonment area at Missamari—a few structures scattered about in a vast area, the low white-washed Garrison Engineer's office where his father would sometimes stop, the storage tanks of the oil depot and the small bazar on either side of the train tracks, the South Indian dosa shop near a block of quarters, the World War II era runway, hidden by the tall grass at the sides. Past Missamari there were a couple more villages, some of them Bengali Muslim, recognizable by the faded orange and red saris of the women and the blue lungis and white skull caps of the men. The broad, shallow Gabharu river ran close to the road at one point, near the forest beat office. Past the beat office was Lama Camp, which was another army area, and some distance ahead was the Kolamati forest gate. Somewhere in between was a house belonging to a mouzadar or revenue collector who lived there alone and whom his father and Pradip Deka knew. Abhijit remembered rooms with dust-covered furniture like on a film set, and lemon trees around the house. Left from the forest gate at Kolamati was a kutcha road that led to a forest village called Ramnathpur, and straight ahead was thick, dense forest, with towering trees and creepers draped over the undergrowth and a damp, earthy smell even in winter.

His heart would beat slightly faster as Pradip Khura drove down that narrow road. He knew animals generally avoided the road during the day, but he had seen wild buffaloes and elephants crossing it. The trumpeting of elephants could be heard from within the forest, and sometimes the heavy flapping of a hornbill taking off from a tree at the approach of the vehicle. As they went deeper, he had the sense of entering a more primal world—Abhijit would remember that great forest many years later, while studying *Heart of Darkness* in college, feeling, like Marlow, that he had been 'travelling back to the earliest beginnings of the world'. A few kilometres ahead a dirt track branched off the road toward the river, and the Gypsy would pass the Nepali settlement and the mule camp and come to the turning to the MES pump house and Pradip Khura's camp. There were a few huts at that place, where some labourers' families stayed, babies crawling in the dirt outside and the wives looking blankly at the vehicle. If you carried on straight the track would take you to the Monpa village beside the Belsiri river, a migratory dwelling where the Buddhist Monpas would come down during the winter from Rupa in the hills above (Abhijit would find out that they now preferred to call themselves Sherdukpens).

Pradip Khura would drive over to the Monpa village, where he had got friendly with the inhabitants. Rice or maize beer brought out in jugs might follow, sitting in someone's house or ramshackle shop. Abhijit liked going down to the river, which receded during winter, exposing the large boulders brought down from the mountains yonder. Sitting by the river he was aware of the clean air, the dust raised from the fine sand, the winter sun, the cold river water, the creeper with flowers known as Germany bon (some said it had been brought from there during World War II) growing wild, and it all made him feel strangely alive.

In the village were the women with their dark, shapeless garments, the yelling, runny-nosed children playing with mongrel dogs, and the sinewy men, a dao or machete always strapped to their waist. Abhijit and Pradip Khura's two daughters Pori and Tani would be given oranges from the Monpa villages way up in the hills, and they would eat the small, sweet fruits listening to the laughter of the men in those smoky rooms with deer and hornbill heads stuck up on the split-bamboo walls. The sun would glow a dull red as it sank towards the trees across the river and a chill wind would pick up. Once, at sunset, Abhijit saw a flock of hornbills, twenty-five to thirty of them, flying from the direction of the forest, alternately beating their wings and then gliding: as they crossed the river, headed for the hills above, the slow, heavy flapping of their large wings going *whup whup whup* seemed like a link to something ancient and prehistoric, to the time of the dinosaurs, when man hadn't yet appeared on the earth. The Gypsy's headlights would pick out the white, dusty track as they drove back to the camp.

The camp was a modest two-room structure, with a netted veranda in front and a small kitchen and bathroom behind the rooms, constructed in the functional army style; at the back, Lokhi, a relative of Pradip Deka's who looked after the camp, had cleared the scrub and planted some vegetables and put up a bamboo fence. The hills rose up from behind the camp, and there was a path that led to a village above. In the front yard was an open work area for the carpenters with a wooden ghora and a thatched roof; opposite to it was the storehouse with a tin roof and split-bamboo satai walls, and a kitchen with two earthen stoves where the labourers sometimes cooked their food.

In the late afternoon a fire would be lit in the kitchen beside the storeroom—wood was something never in short supply—and Abhijit would raid Lokhi's small kitchen for tea leaf and sugar and glasses. Sometimes there would be a can of condensed milk which Pradip Khura had bought. Abhijit would help Lokhi make tea, while looking at the way the afternoon light would come in through the cracks of the split-bamboo wall, creating swirling white cross-sections in the smoke rising up from the fire. Abhijit would feel very grown-up sitting outside and drinking that tea as the light faded. There was a man with bloodshot eyes and a bristly moustache called Karuna whom he found scary; once he was given a glass of tea Abhijit had made, and he took a mouthful and spat it out, saying he didn't know how to make tea (he drank the rest though).

Abhijit would hear the men talking about the 'organization'. He had already heard stories from the village boys about youths joining what was euphemistically termed 'the organization', or ULFA: the 'United Liberation Front of Asom'. It was said that they would fight the Indian army for Assam's independence. His father would say, 'What are they trying to do? We don't grow enough rice to feed ourselves and they want independence?' Pradip Deka would agree with him, but Abhijit wasn't as dismissive of 'our boys'. Indeed, there was something romantic about it—finding out about rice production figures, or even the exact concept of 'independence', didn't at that age have the same appeal.

There were stories too about politicians and tea garden owners and staff being shot, but that was mainly in upper Assam, in the areas around Jorhat, Dibrugarh, Tinsukia. In the north bank, in the tea gardens beyond Tezpur, the stories that came out were of demand notices and extortion money. Things were getting bad, people would say, shaking their heads. But Tezpur carried on as before: the sleepy life of a small town. Years before there had been the Oxom Andolon, the Assam Agitation, and Abhijit remembered listening to grown-ups talking of the incidents at that time, people being killed, mobs attacking villages. There had been the shock of seeing the old magazine cover with the grainy photo of the lines of dead children killed at Nellie, awaiting burial along with their parents. Abhijit listened to his father and his brothers arguing over what had happened—the two other brothers were on the side of the students—but then he would go out of the house to play cricket with his friends. Whatever was happening seemed remote from his life then.

There was one incident Abhijit remembered from that time, from the year 1989, a few months before President's Rule was declared in Assam and the army was finally called out. There was a local tough, an Assamese Muslim boy, who used to move around Tezpur town on a Hero Honda motorcycle. Abhijit first heard about his abduction, supposedly by the 'organization', and then a few days later a gunny sack had been found in a field near Darrang College with his severed head in it. There were burn marks on it and some teeth had been removed, maybe with pliers. The village boys whispered about how his eyes had been mutilated too. But it would be years before Abhijit would connect that incident to the larger events back then.

A Memory of Elephants

On his second day in Tezpur Abhijit got up late. He woke to what felt like an unnatural silence, and it took him a few moments to realize where he was. He had planned to head toward Foothills, but decided to wait a day. Now that he was in Tezpur, with Foothills just some 60 kilometres away, he finally acknowledged something he had tried not to think about in Delhi: how safe were those areas now? The idea came to him that he could move around as a reporter: he still had his old press card with him. It would give him a cover of sorts while he went around trying to find out more about his father. But what would he report about, and for whom?

As he was having his breakfast of chira with milk and gur, sitting by the table in the rear veranda, his uncle came and sat nearby on a moorah with a cup of red tea. His grandmother liked to sit on the bench out in the front in the morning, before the sun got to the veranda. The helper, a lean, dark, self-contained Adivasi Christian woman called Julie, had taken the morning's dishes to the well for washing. She called his grandmother ma, and his uncle dada. Abhijit felt as though he had come and merged into this small community of three people in a matter of hours.

He asked his uncle about the old characters from when his father had been posted at Chariduar. Most of them were dead, his uncle told him, like the contractor Pradip Deka. Others had moved away or were housebound with various ailments. One person who was still out and about was a man named Karuna, who lived somewhere near Dipota off the highway that went west toward Dhekiajuli and Orang. The contractor Dulu da, as everyone called him, a relative of Pradip Deka's, was still around. His uncle asked him if he remembered Mohen Doctor, whom his father had been friendly with and Abhijit was able to recall a bespectacled man with a neat French beard, a homeopathic doctor from somewhere in upper Assam who for some reason had moved to Tezpur and set up a small practice, and had then become, improbably, a sort of overseer for a couple of projects Pradip Deka had done up in Arunachal Pradesh. His uncle said he had seen him briefly a few months ago, in an auto passing through Mission Chariali. Mohen Doctor had known his father well, his uncle said, but who knew where he was now? His uncle wasn't a very social person, Abhijit reflected, and was unlikely to find out where the former doctor had gone.

He returned to the topic of his father's death. How did people know he had been shot by the insurgents? He had stayed with his father at the beat office just before the incident and hadn't noticed anything untoward.

'You were a child,' his uncle said, 'how would you know everything that was going on then? They wanted all of that area for their Bodoland, so they sent villagers from elsewhere to go and cut the trees and settle down.'

His uncle got up and put his cup on the table, saying he had to go to town for a while. Abhijit spent the rest of the morning sitting near his grandmother in the rear veranda, reading a book. She asked him several times what he was reading, *ki podhisa?* using the more formal interrogative, and smiled when he took a photo of her with his phone and showed it to her. The things that have come out nowadays, she said to him. When he asked about Khagen, his father, she said he was the naughtiest of her three boys, and loved to climb trees and to throw stones and get at any fruit: jolphai (olive), teteli (tamarind), modhuriam (guava), bogori (jujube). Then she fell silent, and looked at Abhijit fixedly, as if some faint recollection had come to her of her son's death and her daughter-in-law's desertion. He walked through the empty rooms of the house—ancient and silent and comforting spaces.

In his grandmother's room, with its smell of talcum powder and coconut oil and camphor, he bent to have a look at the photos of his father and grandfather; of the latter he had only a faint memory, a tall gruff man with a white moustache, while of the former, he admitted grudgingly to himself, most of his memories were fading. Beyond that sharp clear picture of the last day and night at the beat office and at the camp it was a bit of a blur: being dropped to school by him sometimes, going with him to the garage to get the department Gypsy fixed, a theatre show once, Bihu functions from which his mother would bring him back early while his father would stay on, the small things his father would bring for him from the forest: a hornbill feather, dried seeds of the rudraksha tree, a piece of driftwood from the Belsiri river. Abhijit felt a deep heavy pain in his heart that he almost never allowed himself to feel. After lunch he went to his room, drowsy from the heat and the rice he had eaten. He lay down on the bed and fell asleep. He woke in the late afternoon, his pillow damp with sweat, and after making himself a cup of tea, went out for a walk.

It was a short distance to the main road, and now, in the light of day, Abhijit saw new houses along the gravel path, and several shops and two-wheeler showrooms on the main road, in front of people's houses, as a constant stream of traffic went past: autos, cars, buses, rundown pick-up trucks filled with sand, motorcycles and scooters. The sleepy village neighbourhood he remembered seemed to have disappeared. He had taken a left on the main road, and here and there he saw reminders of the past: an old gelamal or provisions store, a bamboo fence before a small house. A dirt track on the other side of the road, after the now defunct train line, had turned into a metalled road with an ATM beside it.

He remembered the dip in the road, with paddy fields on either side, and then the slight rise to the BRO's Project Vartak complex, the temple just beyond the train line where they would play Hindi bhajans in the morning. On he walked, along a rough covered drain that seemed to have been constructed recently beside the road. Here and there all sorts of plastic rubbish lay in the dust. The old petrol pump was still there, as was the curious lone bent tree in the middle of the paddy fields across the main road from the pump. At Hatipilkhana the roadside garages were still working on trucks and vehicles with AR04 Arunachal number plates. There was a particular workshop his father used to visit to repair the department jeep, but he couldn't recall which one. A new apartment building rose up from behind a cluster of tin-roofed shops and houses.

Tribeni Hall at the traffic point crossroad was now a commercial complex. Abhijit took the straight road that went past a glitzy new hotel and old Assam-type houses, cars and buses choking the narrow lane. He kept walking till he crossed the two large ponds and the state transport depot and sundry government offices, and came to the old ferry ghat by the Brahmaputra with the boarded-up remains of the former train station. It was part of the Tezpur–Balipara line built by the British to transport tea from the tea gardens toward the north down to the ferries.

The river flowed deep and wide, a frightening power suggested by its sheer size, and the sun going down diagonally to the west seemed to set the brown-green waters aflame from afar. The edges of the ghat were eroded, with a ferry anchored below in the water, and there were a couple of goods trucks parked on the bare earth. A couple of men, truck drivers and handymen probably, were hurriedly bathing at a spot ahead of the green-and-white painted ferry. Abhijit was reminded of an old photo he had come across somewhere on the internet, after he had stopped going to office and spent most of his time at his laptop. The photo dated back to 1835, when the British had set up camp in Tezpur, and showed a view upriver from where he now stood—more or less the same thing, the river and its banks, but in the sepia-tinted photo the banks sprawled down and there stood a jungle above the near bank, giving the photo a touch of wilderness. In his stuffy barsati room in Delhi, the photo had reminded him of Conrad's *Heart of Darkness*. He turned the question over in his mind again: murder or suicide? Had he known the answer all along without being aware of it? The horizon turned orange as the sun sank below the river and the sky turned from a dark blue to black.

He walked back the way he had come, past the statue of Subhash Chandra Bose with an outstretched arm, then carried on straight past Church field and took a left turn from the DC office toward the town, cars and people thronging the main street with its lighted shop fronts as a slight coolness came with the dark. A mud-spattered Sumo without number plates came to a halt before the Sadar thana opposite the old pond, and Abhijit watched a couple of fit-looking policemen, black bandanas on their heads and khaki trousers tucked into camouflage canvas boots, getting down with their AK rifles. There was a camaraderie among them that he himself had never felt in any group.

He walked the length of the main street, past the pharmacies and sweet shops and cycle shops, past the Chowk bazar complex and Delight and Diamond bakeries and BK Enterprises, Bengali and Marwari shopkeepers attending to Assamese and tribal customers, and entered an old tea shop where he asked for a cup of tea and a kachori. It was another place he remembered coming to with his father. He drank his tea and watched a tired-looking Bengali Muslim man breaking a rosogolla into pieces and feeding it to his small daughter. When he got up to pay, he asked them to pack a couple of rosogollas for him.

He took a left after the Laxmi temple, and then walked

along the road which sloped up and down till he came to the Tribeni Hall traffic point once again, and from there he caught one of the shared autos headed for Mission Chariali. On the slow, noisy return journey he turned around in his mind the idea about reporting that had come to him in the morning. He had his contacts in Delhi; they could be approached for stories. And what better story, considering where he was planning to go, than about deforestation and the plight of wildlife?

The rosogollas he had bought were appreciated by all at home, and Abhijit reminded himself to buy them again. After dinner they sat on chairs in his uncle's dimly-lit room watching the news on a small flat-screen on a table; on another larger table with a powerful table lamp were the innards of radios and clocks. Hiren Saikia had once been employed by the state electricity board, but after his brother's death he stopped going to work, getting by on the rent from a couple of properties their father had owned. Gradually he had withdrawn from life, taking care of their mother and keeping to himself. Tonight, though, he was in a good mood, and Abhijit brought up the topic of the Chariduar reserve forest.

'I always remembered that forest and the river,' he said, 'and the flocks of raj dhanesh flying up to the hills from the forest.'

'Do you know, in the old days people used the oil from a gland below the hornbill's head for their aches and pains?' his uncle asked him. 'A thick yellow oil. It stains the great hornbill's white neck feathers yellow.'

'Did it work?'

'People in the villages believed it worked, besides they

didn't have things like Moov then. The old man Nana from the Monpa village told me once that if the hornbill was killed in the morning, before it flew, there was a lot of oil, but not if it was killed later in the day after it had flown.'

'There were lots of wild elephant herds in the forest then, weren't there? I'm considering writing about them. What happened to them?'

'*Ki kom aru*?' his uncle said and sighed, 'What is there to say? Those people came from all over by the trainline and cut down the forests and settled there. Now the elephants have no place to stay and no food to eat so they come out into the open, into the paddy fields and villages.'

'Have you seen elephants in the wild?' Abhijit asked him.

'Yes, in the old days,' his uncle said, meaning when he had been a more active person and the forests had still stood. 'I've seen elephants being caught too.'

His uncle told Abhijit about how he had gone with his father's brother one time to see elephants being caught by the garh method at Dharikati on the way to Bhalukpung. Now there were villages, and tourist resorts near the Bhoroli river, but then, a few years after Independence, it was all forest, like most of the state. He explained how an enclosure would be built with tree trunks and then two gates built with trees, to make the elephants think it was part of the forest, and a funnel-like approach to one of the gates made of trees as well. A wild herd would be chased in by several kunki or domesticated elephants. This was the garh method, while the other was the kheda shikar or chase method, his uncle said.

Once they were inside, the elephant catchers or phandis would snare the young calves with ropes while the larger ones were driven out of the other gate, which was then closed and a fire lit outside it to prevent the mothers from coming back—they would keep calling outside for their children for a very long time. The younger ones were chained around their middle and their legs; by the time they were taken to the training camp and the chains taken off the skin would have worn off in those places. The training process was brutal, with the young elephants being starved, shackled and beaten to break them in. When an elephant died, a pit was dug nearby and it was tipped in by another elephant. Its stomach was slit and a bag of salt poured in to make it rot faster under the ground. They would move and make a camp at another place after that.

What his uncle was telling Abhijit about were the hati mahals which existed all over the state of Assam, where businessmen hired mahouts and phandis to capture wild elephants. The animals were then tamed and sold to people, mostly for hauling logs. One of the late Bhupen Hazarika's most well-known songs was a haunting ballad of a mahout from Sibsagar in upper Assam going down to a hati mahal in Goalpara in lower Assam and wooing a maiden he sees there. The practice was brought to a close in the state by around 1980, his uncle said. The mahal or auctioning of elephant-catching rights had been started a century earlier in 1875 by the British; prior to that, a small levy was made only on those elephants sent out of Assam, which in some years in the mid-19th century exceeded 1,000 animals a year. And within the then lightly populated and densely forested province of Assam, elephants, apart from country boats, were the most efficient mode of travel, particularly for the well-off.

The capture and training of elephants was an old practice, from the times of the Ahoms, who controlled the Brahmaputra valley before the arrival of the British, even defeating the Mughals after several battles. The *Hastividyarnava*, a treatise on elephants with detailed illustrations compiled in the early 18th century under the Ahom king Siva Singha, is testimony to this tradition.

When the British took over Assam and Burma in the early part of the 19th century after the Anglo–Burmese wars, there stretched thick forest cover all across what is now north-east India and northern Myanmar, save for the rice fields in the Assam valley and scattered settlements. Elephants roamed these forests in immense herds; the ground shaking when they passed. Abhijit had read that elephants had a complex society, second only to that of humans; their family and clan structures resembling those of man before the advent of agriculture, at the hunter-gatherer stage. In the Dzukou valley stretching across present-day Nagaland and Manipur, there is a narrow pass known in the language of the local Angami tribe as the 'Elephant Pass', possibly lying on the route by which these giant animals had moved between Myanmar and Assam. As a child at the forest beat office, he remembered his father taking him close to the tame forest department elephants, making him stroke their rough, grey, wrinkled skin and offering them bananas which they would wrap up with their trunks.

Major General James Johnstone, one of the first British administrators in Manipur, in his memoirs of his time in the Naga Hills and Manipur mentions people in Samagudting (present-day Chumukedima, on the outskirts of Dimapur) telling him in 1874 that when six generations ago the present site for their village was chosen, it had been covered with the bones and tusks of elephants which had come there to die. The British cleared vast tracts of forest in Assam to establish tea plantations, and their fondness for hunting meant that tigers, rhinos, deer and elephants were shot in large numbers as sport. There were just a handful of rhinos left in what was now the Kaziranga national park in the first decade of the 20th century, and it was only the creation of a wildlife sanctuary that had saved the animal.

Uncle and nephew sat for a while in a comfortable silence. Then Hiren Khura spoke.

'You said you were thinking of going towards Foothills?'

Abhijit said he was. Would his uncle forbid him from going there?

'It's not safe. There are NDFB(S) cadres all over the place. But...if you go...try and get till Kamengbari...that place on the border. Someone told me a few people from that Monpa village by the river are there now. They knew your father. Nana, and his son Nyima.'

Abhijit was surprised. Maybe his uncle had wanted to revisit those places too?

'What about the Monpa village by the river?' he asked.

'Oh, that's long gone,' his uncle said, and then, 'The days of your father are gone.'

Abhijit went to his room after a while, but it took him some time to fall asleep. Images, both remembered and imagined, crowded his mind. He had decided he would set off for Foothills the next morning. He felt something akin to a child's dread and anticipation at the thought of the upcoming trip.

An Altered Landscape

It rained that night, and Abhijit was woken by the crashing of thunder. The rain drummed on the tin roof and he could hear the water from the rooftop gutters splashing down into the drain. By early morning the rain had stopped, and the sky was grey and overcast with a cool wind blowing. He had a few chappatis along with some sabji made by the helper Julie, and came out of the house and caught an auto till the Mission Chariali crossroads, where he got onto a Winger, a sort of large passenger van, bound for Dhekiajuli.

Passengers milled about the pan shops by the road as the bus conductors kept up a steady racket. An Adivasi boy came up pushing a cycle with a large bazar bag slung on the handlebars; the handyman stowed the cycle on top, and when the boy got in and sat down, Abhijit saw several plastic jars of honey inside the bag at the boy's feet. He himself sat on one of the single side seats, and watched as people got on and off along the way, after the handyman had succeeded in stuffing the vehicle full of passengers at Mission Chariali.

A few kilometres ahead on the highway, after crossing the army's 4 Corps HQ gate and the main GREF (General Reserve Engineer Force) workshop, they passed Beseria and then Dipota, where Abhijit looked out for Karuna's house. It started drizzling: people were ploughing their wet fields with tractors and cows, and transplanting the last lot of rice plants from their seed beds. Before Bihaguri, they crossed the old road that branched off on the right toward Missamari. It was a cool day, but Abhijit felt a sense of apprehension.

The newspaper that morning had a small item on the front page about two Bodo insurgents, supposed to be part of a larger group recently returned from the camps in Myanmar, who had been killed in a joint police and army operation somewhere close to a village above Rangapara, near the Assam–Arunachal border. After reading it, he thought of the mud-splattered vehicle without number plates outside the police thana the previous evening. Past the new medical college at Tumuki the landscape was more rural, but with enormous transmission towers running across the paddy fields. The passengers in the van, poor villagers mostly, were a mixed lot: Adivasi, Nepali, Bengali Muslim, Bengali Hindu, Bihari, Bodo and Assamese. There was even a solitary Marwari man. Among the major communities of the north bank area, only the Karbi and Mising were unrepresented.

He got down at Thelamara where there were a couple of shops and tea stalls around the junction where a road went north to the Missamari army base, and hopped into the back of an auto headed that way. Soon they were going past more villages and paddy fields, shade trees on either side of the potholed road, and then they came to a tea garden, where Abhijit again spotted a couple of police commandos, this time standing beside a battered Sumo. A signboard told him the place was Kolakuchi; he remembered the name from long ago.

The road passed a tea factory and then turned to the left, the houses of tea workers to the right, the neat lines of the plantation to the left. From the back of the auto he saw a stone crusher in a field, a vast pile of stone chips sloping away from it at one end. They passed a line of small shops and then they were at the army base's gate, where the driver stopped the auto and got down to make an entry.

'This is a PWD road,' a Nepali man sitting in the middle told his companion, 'else they would have sealed it off long ago.'

The driver came back and they set off again, soon coming to a medium-sized replica of the Red Fort's ramparts, a golf course, then the offices with undergrowth and trees behind them, and then blocks of quarters and regimental huts, with buildings of varying sizes being constructed here and there. The Nepali man spoke up again.

'In another ten years this place will become like Chandigarh,' he said.

The auto trundled through the Missamari bazar with its dusty shops. Up ahead, past a couple of villages, the road curved in an S shape, and he saw first the thatch-covered stalls, now empty, of the Gabharu haat or market to his left, the wide, flat river flowing beyond the rice fields, and the distant plantations of the Tarajuli tea garden beyond it. And, almost before he could prepare himself, he saw on the other side of the road, the bamboo fencing and signboard of the Gabharu beat office, the same small building, whitewashed now and in good shape, with a couple of new structures to either side of it. The auto stopped to drop off someone. On the other side the school was still there, and now some shops opposite the beat office. A couple of forest guards in vests and trousers were sitting outside one of the newer buildings. Further off, there was a tractor with a trailer parked in the overgrown grounds. The auto started moving again, and the office soon receded from view.

He was vaguely aware of crossing Lama Camp, and a while later the auto took a left and stopped. Abhijit got down and paid his fare. Behind the auto stood the Kolamati forest gate, now a range office, with larger buildings painted orange-brown and set some distance from the road, with a single gigantic tree before the buildings. The auto spluttered off along the dirt track that led to Dhankhana Centre and the old forest village of Ramnathpur. From the Kolamati range office (the pole of the old gate was now raised) the road carried on straight as before, but the sensation he got as he turned onto it was of a great openness. His memory of the forest looming up ahead after crossing the gate had been imprinted on his mind over the years, and what he saw now made him feel disoriented and slightly dizzy. To his left was an empty field with a hut at the far end, and beyond that was the black and green of mud and paddy, interspersed with clumps of bamboo, beside or within which were mud-plastered huts. Further up the road, again on the left, were what seemed to be a couple of shops. To the right side of the road was a stretch of green undergrowth, but it had no cover; only in the far distance did he see the silhouette of several tall, isolated trees. The wind was pushing the cloud cover away, and up ahead he could see the sun lighting up the road.

He looked back at the range office and then, without consciously thinking about it, started walking. There was a fence running ahead from the range office, three or four lines of wire with spaces between them, he had noticed it before Lama Camp as well, and it ran for a while into and above the undergrowth and then stopped; now he saw, in the distance, beyond the solitary trees, a solid dark-green haziness where the forest was. He neared the shops which were little more than huts—simple grocery shops and tea stalls, with a couple of snot-nosed children in grimy blue and white school uniforms playing near them, dark complexioned Adivasi children and fairer Nepali ones. The shops were set back from the road, and before them was a small bamboo chang or platform on which was a bloody butchered pig, a stout middle-aged Bodo woman in a dokhona standing beside it with a dao in hand. Everyone was staring at him, the children and the shopkeepers, so instead of stopping Abhijit kept walking.

The cluster of shops was soon left behind. All he could hear were his footsteps on the road. The road rose up over a culvert and went down. Very soon he was walking in the sun and could feel the sweat on his back. To his right the aspect remained the same: a tangle of undergrowth, a few solitary trees, and the forest in the distance. To his left was a stretch of undulating land through which runnels of water ran, then gave way to huts with rough gardens. Here, too, one or two Adivasis outside their houses stared at him. His apprehension had given way to confusion. Where was he? How could the landscape have so utterly changed? He approached another culvert, and then he understood—they had come up in place of the old wooden bridges; maybe it was here, with a stream flowing under the culvert, that he and his father had seen the tiger that evening long ago. But there was no forest left, just huts with thatch or tin roofs, two sometimes three of them to a homestead, a solar panel on a roof and in front by the road two or three wires strung across wooden posts like the earlier fence. These huts too were surrounded by rough gardens, with greens growing there, and patches of paddy field behind them. Here the people were noticeably Bodo tribals with weathered features, clad in old, faded clothes and regarding him with suspicion.

The more he looked around, the more disoriented he grew. How could an entire forest have just disappeared? His feet worked mechanically, one foot going forward after the other. Here and there small paths led into the green scrub on the right. After a while there appeared another cluster of mud-hut shops beside the road, with several changs before them where people were selling vegetables. The same hard, suspicious looks from the people, the men in faded green or blue wraparounds, equally faded shirts and rubber chappals, the women in their high orange-patterned wraparounds. There were a couple of flashy motorbikes before what seemed to be a hardware store, and around them stood a couple of well-built tribal youths laughing and chatting. They stared at him as he passed. One of them called out something in the rounded Bodo speech, and the others laughed. He walked on, a little quicker. A solitary tree stood near a high culvert on the road, and leaning on the cemented railings was a skinny young boy in jeans and a black unzipped hoodie which showed his bare chest. As Abhijit went ahead something made him turn and look, and he saw the young boy looking at him as he talked on his phone. The apprehension from the morning returned, and he was suddenly aware of how far behind he had left Kolamati gate.

To the left he saw more houses now, some amid bamboo groves, most of them larger and better built than the earlier ones, but they were further in. Beside the road were rectangular fields with raised edges, some with light-green paddy growing in them, others where the dark, muddy soil was being ploughed by cows, mud-splattered men and women moving slowly, guiding the wooden ploughs. He could see two or three large tree stumps protruding in the fields, and there was a covered wooden platform built on a solitary tree with its top chopped off. Between the road and fields was the makeshift wire fence, with plastic bottles tied to the wires in the middle. Abhijit stopped to look: it seemed to him like an old painting, maybe something by a Dutch master. How strange to think that once this had been a thick, shaded forest, dark even at midday, where elephants, tigers and deer had roamed!

Then he heard voices behind him, and he whirled around. The scrub on the right was high and thick and from a path leading into it emerged five or six children, a mixed group of boys and girls, the boys with catapults in their hands. One of the girls was clutching a dead bird. Their feet were bare and their clothes ragged. The boy who had spoken first now repeated his taunting remark in Bodo while the others laughed. Abhijit smiled hesitantly and moved back. The children stepped forward, emboldened now, and they started gesturing while repeating the remark: *jwngni mansia homgwn, jwngni mansia homgwn.* He turned and started walking, his ears suddenly red, fear and anger coursing through him. The children followed him, laughing and yelling.

Though he had read about the deforestation in the area, and people had told him about it (his uncle most recently), and he had seen how the satellite view in Google maps showed cropland and settlements in place of the reserve forest (the map view still showed those areas as green and untouched though), there was still a part of him which had believed there would be something left, somewhere he could find some peace. This wasn't it, being trailed by a bunch of rowdy children. They stopped following him after a while, but he kept walking, wishing to open up as much distance between them as possible. It was bright and sunny now, and the hills of Arunachal in the near distance were hazily visible. The idea came to him that he should walk till he reached them, and, wiping his face and neck with a handkerchief, he carried on. The road curved a little, and on the right, closer now, there were several tall trees.

To the left, there were a couple of homesteads not too far from the road, and the occasional large tree, ximolu or silk cotton he guessed, which had somehow escaped the axe. Between them, wide paths led into the interior. One place looked slightly more solid than the others, with tin roofs over the two large huts; in the bigger one, on the veranda facing the road, several people sat leisurely, talking.

They turned to look at him as he passed, and it struck him that they must see him as an intruder. His feet hurt and his breath grew ragged, but still he pushed on. It was somewhere on this road, near one of the wooden bridges now replaced by the culverts, that his father had met his end. He knew an FIR had been registered at the Missamari thana against 'unknown persons'. But what did one death matter in a place that had changed so completely, what did it matter whose finger had pulled the trigger?

A black mood descended on him then, and he found himself perversely wishing that he come across a couple of the insurgents—maybe he would be able to die there like his father. To his right the green wall of the forest was closer now, while to his left the few huts grew ragged in appearance, the area around them overgrown, as if the inhabitants didn't have the will to try and improve their condition. Who would have benefitted from clearing the forest, from chopping down those massive trees? It didn't appear to be the people he had just seen. The features of the near hills were clearer now; he could see a wide spur jutting down onto the plains, but even that appeared to be cleared of trees. The road took a turn to the right, and as he came closer, he saw an overgrown path that carried on straight from that point. He stopped there, trying not to focus on the heat and his weariness. Was this the old road that led to the mule camp and the Monpa village by the river? In that case where were the huts of the Nepali people? He hesitated, then turned to the right, deciding to get to the hills first.

It took him about half-an-hour to get there following the road, which turned and climbed ahead, a wide grassy path at one point to the right going off toward the trees. This stretch was forested on both sides of the rough road, not as dense as in the old days though. At one point along the final stretch, which ran straight to a bamboo-pole gate with a sandbagged guardhouse beside it, there was a pile of boulders, and a dirt track leading from it to the trees and undergrowth and which then seemed to dip down. Near the gate was an Arunachal Pradesh government signboard that said 'Kamengbari'.

The police constable at the guardhouse looked up from his phone and regarded the flushed, sweaty figure at the gate with curiosity. He asked Abhijit where he had come from and where he was going. Abhijit looked at the shabby Assam-type government quarters and offices with their netted verandas around a grassy expanse, the broken road going around the grass and up steeply into the hills above, and to the left beside the road a few towering trees followed by a couple of timber-planked houses with rusted tin roofs. He dimly recalled the uporor gau or upper village they used to talk about in the lower village by the river, and he remembered the name his uncle had mentioned, which he told the constable: Nyima. To his surprise the constable nodded and pointed him to the houses on the left. He walked around the gate and went ahead. The first house, he saw, had a mud-plastered dwelling beside it, with a wide opening and a door in front: it was a shop. A few steps went down between the two structures: he saw water drums and firewood down below. An elderly man in black shorts, an old polo tee and a woollen cap on his head came out of the house. The skin on his elbows and knees sagged a little, his long, smooth face was criss-crossed with lines, but his arms and legs were lean and muscular. Abhijit went up to him, told him whose son he was, and asked if Nyima was around.

'Arre, you are Saikia sir's son?' the elderly man said, taking hold of Abhijit by his shoulders, and talking excitedly in broken Assamese. 'Where have you appeared from? I'm Nana, do you remember me? Nyima is my son-in-law, he stays up in Rupa now. The old village by the river is gone. Your father would come there and sit with us.'

A wave of gratitude flooded through Abhijit. Someone still remembered his father! Nana was amazed that Abhijit had walked all the way from Kolamati gate, saying it wasn't a safe place any more.

'The forests are gone, all the old people are gone. Your father was a good man. I remember you came with him once to the village, you were a small boy then!'

He led Abhijit to the open veranda of his house and told his wife to get a jug of water and a glass. Abhijit sank gratefully onto the wooden bench, took off his sandals and placed his hot, swollen feet on the cool cemented floor. From where he sat, he could see the broken road going up into the green hills and then turning left around a bend, carrying on to the small settlement of Doimara.

The Beat Office Revisited

Abhijit spent some time at Nana's house in Kamengbari, where he declined the old man's offer of lunch and instead had tea with a packet of Good Day biscuits he bought from the family shop. Then he caught an auto that sometimes did the run from Missamari bazar to Kamengbari and back, if there were enough passengers. Nyima was up in Rupa, the old man told Abhijit, he came down in the winters to Doimara, about 12 km ahead on the road that climbed up into the hills, and where there had once been a saw mill.

Nyima's father-in-law told Abhijit that a few years after Pradip Deka's camp down below had been closed the army shifted the mule camp to Missamari, following which the Nepali basti moved as well. Their migratory village by the Belsiri river had weathered much malaria, and the river had moved westward once or twice, taking away some of the houses. The Bodos had taken over the Chariduar forest by then, and one of the insurgent groups served people in the village demand notices. After that the place was abandoned and the Monpas scattered, to Kamengbari, and up to Doimara and Rupa.

Nothing remained down by the river on this side, Nana

told him, just a few overgrown remnants of the camps that couldn't be taken away. On the other side were paddy fields and huts of the Bodos. Abhijit asked him about the forest, how it had disappeared. Nana shook his head, and said, 'They cut down everything and sold it, all the trees, in just four or five years. We used to hear it from up here at night, *dham dham dham*, the big trees falling down one by one.' The less valuable trees were set alight, rolled into pits, and covered with earth, to be turned into charcoal. Now all that was left was a small patch of Sonai Rupai sanctuary, which Abhijit saw in the distance to his left coming back in the auto to Missamari.

The long walk and what the old man Nana had told him put Abhijit in a sombre mood. The finality of the destruction was only starting to become apparent to him, as he sat squashed among several Arunachalis and some Bodos, and saw once again the huts and the ragged gardens and people ploughing the fields and the barefoot children. Something had kept him from asking the old man about his father; his intuition told him that Nyima, who used to drop by the forest beat office to meet his father, would be a better person to talk to. That would mean going up to Rupa in the Tenga valley. The old road from Kamengbari via Doimara and Khellong up to Rupa, through what was now the Eaglenest Sanctuary, was broken in several places and not fit for vehicles, Nana had told him: people took the Tawang road that went via Balipara and Bhalukpung to get to the Tenga valley and Rupa. Abhijit would later find out that the Rupa–Khellong–Doimara–Foothills stretch was the last leg during the Dalai Lama's escape from Lhasa to

Tezpur. The Dalai Lama and his companions had entered India at Chuthangmo near Tawang, instead of taking the-then regular route to India through the Chumbi valley.

Absorbed as he was in his own thoughts, Abhijit saw the Kolamati range office with the towering tree before it pass by, but made no attempt to get down. Further ahead the auto stopped in sight of the forest beat office, and this time he roused himself, paid the fare, and got down. How strange it felt to walk through the gates and toward the small office before him: a part of him felt as though his father would be sitting at the glass-topped table, a Charminar in one hand. To his left was a sort of barracks made from split-bamboo walls with tin roofing; before it was the tractor and trailer, the battered trailer filled with sand. His father used to burn the logs at night in the field behind the barracks. To his right was an open bamboo-and-tin shelter under which was parked an old white Gypsy, and beside it a wing of rooms from inside which he saw men looking out at him. He stepped up to the plinth of the office, knocked on the open doors to his left, pushed the green curtain aside and entered the room. For one dizzying moment he thought the stocky, brown-complexioned man in a dark brown department shirt sitting at the glass-topped, white-painted wooden table was his father, before realizing this person was younger, and had a more Mongoloid cast to his features.

The beat officer told him that his name was Gautam Pegu. Abhijit told Pegu who he was, that he was staying in Tezpur, and had walked all the way from Kolamati gate to Kamengbari. The beat officer was understandably surprised, not just at the long walk, but also at the mention of Khagen

Saikia's name. He had heard about him, Pegu said, and by the grace of bhogoban he was fortunate to be now sitting in the same chair where Saikia sir himself had sat many years ago. 'Your father was a very good man,' the beat officer said, 'very just'.

Abhijit looked down at his trembling hands and then around the room, overcome with emotion, trying to control himself. On the walls of the bare, whitewashed room were a colour chart with the different snake species of Assam, and an Indian Air Force calendar which showed, for that month, a Sukhoi taking off. The beat officer closed the open register before him and called a staff member to get tea. There was a door behind him and through a gap in the curtain Abhijit saw a single bed with a mosquito net above it, just like during his father's time. Pegu asked Abhjit what he was doing, to which Abhijit, to show that he wasn't a complete wastrel, said that he was a journalist and had come to do some research. The beat officer nodded, seemingly impressed. He himself was from a Mising village between Balipara and Bhalukpung, Pegu said, and he had served all over Sonitpur district. Abhijit then asked how his father had actually died. Pegu thrust his jaw forward, tilted his head back slightly, and narrowed his eyes.

'It was a very unfortunate incident. From what I heard, the insurgents came across him in the forest and shot him. No one knows what he was doing there though. The times weren't good then. A straightforward man like your father... they say if he had been around for a few months more, he would have been transferred to Nameri.'

Did Pegu recall a forest guard by the name of Rafiqul

Ali, known simply as Ali, a dark, bald man whom his father would like to take patrolling with him, Abhijit wanted to know. Ali would amuse the young Abhijit by imitating deer and bird calls. Where was he now?

'Ali? Ali retired several years ago. I wonder where he is now? He was from Tezpur, if I remember correctly.'

The office staff member brought in their tea in small cups, with some biscuits on a stainless steel quarter-plate and tamul pan and lime on another plate.

'Please don't mind,' Pegu said, 'we should have been able to organize something better for Saikia sir's son. If you ever come this side again...let me know. It's not safe wandering about those places nowadays, you could get kidnapped or even killed.'

Abhijit told Pegu that he didn't mind at all, he could live on tea and biscuits. He asked what had happened to the vast reserve forest, how and when it had disappeared.

'What can I say. The times weren't good, as I said. There came a time when we couldn't patrol the forest with our old .303 rifles. People came in on the railway line in the late 1990s, and they spread all over. Bodo people mostly.' Pegu shook his head. 'Most of Chariduar reserve forest, 460 square kilometres, is gone. The government carved the Sonai Rupai sanctuary out of it, 220 square kilometres, on the right side of the road, that's why a small portion of the reserve forest was saved, because it came under the Wildlife division. But even there, half of that is gone. There's only about 80 to 90 square kilometres of the sanctuary left.'

The green curtain at the door was pulled aside: Abhijit saw two well-built tribal youths standing there. Their stomachs strained against their t-shirts, and Abhijit noticed the ends of their jeans and their sneakers had dried mud on them. Pegu told them to wait outside: the curtain came down.

'The forest disappeared, just like your father feared it would,' Pegu continued, 'and what are the animals going to eat now, what are the elephant herds going to eat? They've started straying out of the forest looking for grain in the villages, tearing down people's houses and granaries. During the harvest season we hardly get to sleep, chasing the herds out of people's fields. Last night I had to go with two forest guards to chase out a male elephant from the army base. I had to fire twice with my rifle. A week back near Rangapara a herd from Sonai Rupai trampled a family of four to death. During your father's time there were hardly any elephants coming out of the forest.'

Here the beat officer took his phone and showed Abhijit a few photos: four bodies, two of them children, somehow covered with pieces of a torn blanket. The parts of the bodies sticking out were matted with mud from those huge feet, which were also responsible for the limbs bent at unnatural angles. Abhijit swallowed and looked away, and, to change the topic, commented on the shops he had seen along the Foothills road. Pegu said they were what was called a 'centre' in rural Assam, a small group of shops: the first one was Karki Centre, and the second, Gulai Centre.

They chatted for a while before Abhijit got up to leave. Pegu came out with him. The two boys were outside the wing of rooms talking to the forest guards inside. Seeing Pegu they turned toward him. Abhijit bid farewell to the beat officer and walked past the Bullet motorcycle on which the two boys had come; he saw dried mud on its wheels. He crossed the road, and when he turned, he saw Pegu and the two boys talking by the sand-filled tractor trailer. Presently they went into the office. Abhijit waited by the few small shops opposite the beat office till an auto headed for Missamari bazar came along.

It had been a long day and he was tired. From the shabby little bazar he caught another auto headed for Thelamara. As they crossed the tea garden and passed the paddy fields, with the sun sinking toward the bamboo groves and stands of trees in the distance, he felt a strange melancholy. All of this too might have been forest at some earlier period. Seen from that perspective, all men were settlers, and the herds of elephants and the deer and tiger and hornbills the original inhabitants. Abhijit had a momentary vision, like in a time-lapse video, of people spreading across this landscape, few at first, then in greater numbers, a mix of peoples, surviving however they could, the machinery of the government something very distant for them. He thought about his father, the time he had served at the beat office. Why would he have driven off into the forest on his own?

Abhijit was in the back of the auto, where he liked to sit, with three other people, and opposite to him was a young boy with a document folder and a book in his hands. In the close confines it was easy for Abhijit to read the book's title, something on geography, and he made a comment on it, to which the boy, who had a soft, babyish look, replied, and they got talking. His name was Saurav Saha, he was from Tezpur, he had recently graduated from Darrang College, and was now with an NGO for some 'work experience', as he put it. The NGO worked in the area of education, and he had been visiting villages around Missamari, revenue villages he pointed out, to complete a questionnaire. It was just for work experience, Saha repeated, after this he wanted to go to Kolkata or Delhi for 'higher studies'.

From the highway at Thelamara they caught a passing bus for Tezpur. It was dark by then and they had to squeeze in among the passengers, again a varied lot of people. Saha asked him what he was doing, and Abhijit repeated what he had told Pegu, that he was a journalist. The young man had opened up to him, and so Abhijit, not wishing to appear secretive, said that he was doing some research on the areas around Foothills, which was true in a way. Saha seemed interested in this, saying that some of those places were not safe now, and that he knew a local journalist called Padma Bora who had recently been threatened by some boys when he had gone that side, toward the Belsiri river; Padma Bora's father had been a friend of Saha's uncle, who ran an old hardware supply store in Tezpur town. They exchanged numbers, and Abhijit got down at Ketekibari, while Saha carried on to the town.

It had been a long day, and he was tired, yet sleep eluded Abhijit. He lay on the bed in the dark looking up at the white shroud of the mosquito net, while the fan pushed waves of warm air around the room. The morning coolness had faded; tomorrow would be a hot day. He hadn't been able to find out much, but contacts had been made: the old man at Kamengbari on the border, the beat officer with his thoughtful manner, even the young NGO worker who knew a journalist. In time they would be of help.

One scene from the day kept replaying itself in his mind, like the highlight of a tourist excursion: the Bodo men and women ploughing the dark-coloured earth with the help of their cows, an ancient human activity where once giant trees had stood, and of which only a few scattered stumps now remained. Under a blazing sun, man and beast were both splattered with mud as the plough turned over the rich soil that had been made fertile with the rotting remnants of the forest for hundreds of years. Near them, feet wide apart and sunk in mud, stout women bent from their waists and transplanted light-green rice seedlings, while further off were huts and bamboo groves (which would have been planted). It was hard for Abhijit to comprehend the disappearance of what he remembered from childhood as a forest so dense that even at midday it was dark and cold inside it. Sadness, anger, wonder—he had felt all of that, and something more: a feeling of awe at what he had seen, which was nothing less than the story of how man had spread upon the face of the earth. How had his father foreseen something like this though? That was another mystery.

The Forest Beneath the Mountains

Nyima, old man Nana's son-in-law, was a stocky youth from the migratory village by the Belsiri river. The Monpas would come down in the winters from Rupa and the Tenga valley up in Arunachal, and then go back in summer. Now though they preferred to be known as Sherdukpens. Nyima was an energetic individual, possessed of the trading spirit of his community, and he spoke in a rough, forceful manner, some remnant of the Tibetan influence from far above. Pradip Deka had got friendly with him after he had set up his camp near their village. He might have had to take permission from the elders, like Nana, and Nyima's father, whom Abhijit dimly recalled as an equally stocky figure, but whereas his son wore trousers and half-shirts the father like the other older men wore their heavy, homespun woolen garments in white or red, or a white eri tunic. Nyima's father would tell Pradip Deka's daughters and Abhijit about a sort of yeti found up in the mountains, bon manus, or forest person, he would tell them in his broken Assamese, or grephu as they called it in their language. The old man told them it used to move the boulders in the river looking for small crabs to eat. Within sight of the river with the green hills rising up behind it, and sitting in a smoky room adorned with animal skulls and pelts, it felt entirely believable to Abhijit.

Pradip Khura would sometimes take Nyima along when they went hunting at night in the Gypsy, with two searchlights attached by wires and clamps to the vehicle battery, and the soft top rolled up to allow people to stand behind. For someone of Abhijit's age, it was uncomfortable and tedious, but for all that there was a great thrill to it, and a feeling of being part of something illegal in the company of adults. As night fell at the camp, the kerosene lamps would be lit, followed by the fire outside (there was never a shortage of logs). Inside the rooms, by the flickering light of the lamps, the shotgun or rifle would be readied, the cartridges lined up on the table. It would be several hours later by the time the men actually set out, after dinner had been cooked and eaten, and one or more bottles had been finished, with a cassette of Richard Clayderman's piano tunes, which somehow was always in the glove compartment, playing in the Gypsy's cassette player. Abhijit would for some reason remember those scenes and hear that music again in his head many years later while watching Herzog's *Fitzcarraldo* in a friend's flat in Delhi on a burning summer's day.

He would listen to the men sitting around the fire talking about hunting in the old days: bringing a 'line bus' to the Foothills during an Assam bandh in the early 1980s, the owner muta Bhaiti or 'fat Bhaiti' driving the bus himself, a shotgun and a bottle of brandy to his right, a degchi of boiled eggs just behind him to the left, he would pick up an egg as he drove and crack it open on the steering wheel; Pradip Deka's shot from the bus window that knocked a deer off its feet; people going hunting for two to three days in the forest with only two shotgun cartridges, gunpowder, candles, ball bearings, and firing caps to 'pack' the spent cartridges; the forest department inspection bungalow at Sopai (to the west of Kamengbari) where they had strung up a deer, and Pradip Deka gave Lokhi a large glass of rum and he stripped down to his underpants to gut and skin the deer, the meat being fried later and the men eating it in the kilos. He would then feel something akin to what he felt looking at the old photo with the dead tiger at home: that he had somehow been born too late.

To be fair to the men, they had to wait till a certain time for the forest guards from the Kolamati gate to do a round of the Foothills approach road. Abhijit suspected there was a way of working out things, so that the Gypsy could set out on a round later. That was usually around midnight. Abhijit would go to sleep wearing his jacket, to be woken later by Pradip Khura shaking him by the shoulder.

'*Uth, jabo lage*,' he would say. 'Get up. We have to go.'

Abhijit would climb into the back of the Gypsy, still half-asleep. Pradip Khura's daughters, for all their enthusiasm, couldn't last till that late, and they were left sleeping inside in Biren's care, along with the ones who preferred a warm bed or more whisky by the fire outside to wandering around the forest at night, like Satish da the garage owner, Dhon the doctor, or Dulu da the contractor. As they drove off into the cold night Abhijit would look back at the flames licking up from the logs, and Lokhi's faithful worker Biren squatting by them. He would long for the warmth of the camp as they bumped along the dirt track, but that would be forgotten once they stopped at the village by the river to pick up Nyima, the moon sometimes shining on the rushing river, or when they stopped at the Nepali settlement to pick up a lanky man with a moustache called Kazi, or otherwise to roll up the soft top of the Gypsy at the back, one of the things Abhijit was allowed to help with. He would watch as the clamps on the wires running from the halogen lights were fixed to the battery and tested: the strong beams aimed up into the darkness and at the tall tree trunks ahead of them. The searchlights would be held by two people standing behind each of the Gypsy's two front seats, while the person with the gun, usually Pradip Khura, would be between them, the shotgun or rifle placed on the hood above the front seats.

Lokhi usually drove from there onwards, in first or second gear, a cigarette in one hand as the vehicle crawled along the narrow road flanked by the forest. Abhijit would be in the front seat, or in the back standing behind the spotters and the shooter (the rear seats were lifted up when the soft cover was rolled up). On either side the lights would probe the undergrowth between the trees, looking for the quarry, xogora pohu or barking deer that came out at night to feed. The damp, rotting, elemental smell of the forest mixed with cigarette smoke—it was like the smell of freedom for Abhijit. But there was boredom too, as the vehicle moved slowly in the darkness and they weren't supposed to speak. Sometimes he would start nodding off, coming awake with a start as one of the spotters tapped the hood and Lokhi braked. The searchlight would scour the shrubs for a sign of a deer, only to turn out to be a false alarm. Just after Kolamati gate there was a dirt track which went in left from the forest, toward a place called Gelgeli, and before turning in that way the engine and searchlights would be killed. The men would talk softly and wait, to see if the coast was clear. The hills of Arunachal would be dimly silhouetted against the night sky, and at times there was the trumpeting of elephant herds from within the forest. Sometimes, to his great thrill, Abhijit would be allowed to handle one of the searchlights.

At other times they would ford the Belsiri river by the Monpa village—the crunching of the tires over the rocky riverbed mixing with the sound of the rippling water—and climb some way into the hills on a dirt track. There was an inspection bungalow or IB of the forest department at a place called Sopai, on a hill overlooking a river, and Abhijit remembered Pradip Khura had taken a large group of them to stay there one bright moonlit night.

But death, when it came, would be quick. The searchlights angling forward and then moving back, over and over, then the tapping on the hood, followed by scratching, indicating that the driver should reverse, followed by more tapping, and there would be two or three deer some distance away in a clearing, their heads up and their ears flared, their eyes transfixed by the bright light, shining like black marbles.

Then the blast of the gunshot, one deer staggering while the others bolted, the acrid smell of gun smoke, and Kazi or Nana leaping down from the back of the vehicle and moving towards the animal, which would be crying out if not killed at once. If required they would deliver a coup de grace to the animal with a khukri or dao, and then it would be dragged back and hauled into the Gypsy, surprisingly heavy for such a delicate-looking creature. Then it would be a scramble to get back to the camp, in case the forest guards might have heard the shot and decided to come out: Abhijit always imagined bullets flying at them from out of the darkness, and Pradip Khura returning fire. He would prod the warm bulk of the deer with his feet and then with his fingers: flesh and gunpowder, blood and iron, life and death. As the body grew cold the ticks on it would start jumping off.

Back at the camp the deer would be gutted and hung up by its front legs at the side of the carpenters' shed to be skinned. Biren, the worker at the camp, was an expert at this, as was Kazi, and Abhijit remembered them in their underpants, their skinny, bloodstained bodies lit by the wavering firelight as they peeled the hide from the flesh with sharp knives. Pradip Khura would pour them extra-large helpings of army-issue rum into steel glasses as they worked. He would joke with Abhijit about not telling his father any of this (he would also give him some meat to take home to his mother). By then Abhijit would be sitting by the fire, dozing off. Those sleeping would have long been woken up by Pradip Khura or by Karuna with his booming voice.

The next morning there would be very little evidence of the night's ceremony—Biren would have swept the yard and buried the entrails somewhere far behind the camp—except for the various cuts of deer and piles of chopped-up meat inside the smoky kitchen by the storeroom, where Lokhi would be frying batches of deer meat cut into cubes (only years later would Abhijit associate the word venison with it) in a large iron kerahi on the wood-fired stove, mustard oil, jeera and tez patta along with some chillies the only other ingredients. Breakfast would be leftover rice with the fried venison and black tea, as they sat around the smouldering ashes of the fire in the morning sun. Nothing he had eaten since had tasted as good. There was so much meat their jaws would start to ache chewing on it. Ratan da, an elderly man from near Pradip Khura's place who supplied the searchlights, would take out a tweezer and a wad of cotton and proceed to plug the holes in his teeth—to allow him to chew better.

'When we would go for shikar in the old days, we would make a camp in the jungle and hunt for two or three days,' he would tell Abhijit. 'In the end there would be so much meat that we would have to bury some of it, even after setting aside several kilos to take home.'

Abhijit would try to imagine how it would have been in those days, with no roads and no cars to travel in. And in that smoky kitchen, he remembered Karuna asking him once, with what seemed like a sneer, '*Dekhiso*? *Paribi*?' as he watched Lokhi quartering a hind leg. 'Do you see that? Can you do it?' He clammed up then, but much later wondered how Karuna might have perceived him.

After breakfast, no one appeared to be in any hurry to head home. The carpenters who stayed nearby would turn up and start working on door and window frames without much urgency to their work. Dulu da would tell Pradip Deka that they had to meet the GE in Missamari on the way back, to which he would reply, 'We're going, we're going.' More often than not they would end up in the Monpa village, where Pradip Khura would distribute a few kilos of deer meat (usually the ribs and a leg) among the headman, Nana, and other people, then sit down to have some Golden Eagle beer. Abhijit and the two small girls would wander down to the riverside, and splash about in the cold, clear water that came down from the hills. They would leave only by late afternoon or early evening, Dulu da by now losing his temper with Pradip Deka, because if they didn't meet the GE their work would get stalled. Pradip Deka would wave away his objections and call out for more beer or whiskey. One day they would have driven out of the forest on that straight road with Abhijit not bothering to look back as they passed the Kolamati forest gate. The forest beneath the mountains and the river flowing through it—he would have expected them, the way a child does, to remain unchanged. But it would be more than twenty-five years before he returned to Foothills.

Abhijit once saw Nyima and Kazi in a 'line bus' (a vehicle with a tin-and-wood 'body' like the old blue-and-yellow painted Bedford city buses in Shillong) while he was standing outside Pradip Khura's place with a friend. The brown-and-white painted bus was headed in the direction of Tezpur town, and Nyima, who was standing on the footboard at the rear door, saw them and waved. Kazi was maybe in the seat before him, slightly stooped as he turned to look at Pradip Deka's place. Abhijit was too surprised to react, or maybe he managed a wave back. Did they stop by on their way back? They might have. But all Abhijit remembered was his surprise at seeing the two of them in Tezpur, those two men whom he associated with that separate life of Foothills. Nyima, who would have been in his late twenties then, would hire video cassettes from Tezpur and take them back to his seasonal village where he had installed a television and a video cassette player (bought with a loan from Pradip Deka) in a wood-plank room beside the few shops. That was the movie hall he ran for the people of the area. Maybe that trip to Tezpur had been to pick up new video cassettes. Years later, Abhijit would hear from someone that Nyima had bought a second-hand army Shaktiman truck which he hired out to carry loads.

Those line buses carried with them another memory for Abhijit, of winter picnics with a whole lot of people, where firewood, utensils, and supplies were arranged beforehand, and the bus would take them to a 'picnic spot' in places like Seijusa and Bhalukpung, or even Foothills, all approached through the forest and with the river nearby. Once they reached everything was unloaded, the chickens would be killed and plucked (his father was an expert at this), a fire would be kindled and red tea and boiled eggs made for everyone. Gradually these picnics came to an end, like Pradip Deka's hunting trips in Foothills: the Bodoland movement, and the activities of the 'organization', had spread and then the army was called out. The Assam Police, which should have been able to handle the situation better due to its superior local intelligence, had already been demoralised by political interference from the new lot of leaders in the state. In any case, by 1992 Khagen Saikia was no more and Pradip Deka's camp too was closed.

Later, while studying at a school in Shillong, Abhijit would know next to nothing of the larger world around him: the rest of the North East. He was taught mathematical formulas and made to memorize architectural features of temples in South India, he read cowboy adventures in his spare time and started listening to heavy metal music; the history behind those movements (and how they ended up being corrupted), the history of places like Foothills he would have to learn on his own own, just as he would learn about what had happened to his father.

Abhijit's initial research for a possible article on wild elephants—how they were being squeezed into ever-shrinking areas in Assam by the spread of human activity and the loss of forests—led him, through his uncle's enquiries, to an elderly lady in Tezpur who lived in the quiet old locality of Baroholia, near Darrang College (Darrang had been the older name of undivided Sonitpur district). She was a family friend, and had childhood memories of the hati mahals of the old days. After that story he had gone back to talk to her again, about the 1962 China war, and she had told Abhijit about the evacuation of people from Tezpur to the south bank by ferries after the fall of Tawang and Bomdila up in the Himalayas and the Chinese army advancing down toward the plains. She was among those who'd been evacuated (also Abhijit's father and uncles, who were children then) by ferry, while the English tea planters and the senior army and administration people were flown out.

It was hard to imagine, listening to the lady's matter-of-fact account, the chaos that would have come upon the small town, hundreds of people on bullock carts, jeeps and buses, thronging the steamer ghat (where Abhijit had stood that evening, and remembered the photo from 1835), waiting to get to the other side, the deputy commissioner and superintendent of police having flown out from the airport at Salonibari, and ordinary citizens (like Abhijit's late grandfather) deciding to stay back—they later provided the retreating Indian jawans with water. The night before they crossed over, she remembered the explosions they heard all the way from Missamari, where the army's ammunition stocks were being blown up.

Her memory was still sharp, and she told Abhijit how three years earlier her father, who then worked at the DC's office, had taken her in a jeep to Missamari to see the Tibetans who had come down. The DC had given orders for temporary bamboo and straw shelters to be built, and it became known as Lama Camp, on account of the Dalai Lama and his followers who had stayed there (they had apparently first gone to the Tarajuli tea garden across the Gabharu river, before being put up at Lama Camp). This would have been the beginning of the Tibetan diaspora, those who followed the Dalai Lama out of Tibet after the Chinese took over. The Dalai Lama had carried on to Tezpur (where her father had given him an orange to eat), and then by train to Mussoorie, where Nehru met him, and the occupants of Lama Camp followed him in stages to Himachal Pradesh. She still remembered the bamboo tubes in which the women churned atta and water, and their prayer beads.

There had been the Assam Rifles camp at Foothills then, at the start of the track that went up by Rupa to Tawang. Lama Camp became a part of Missamari army base, which during the Second World War had been a runway, one of the air bases in Bengal and Assam from where American Douglas DC-3s and C-47s had flown to Kunming in China's Yunnan province to supply Chiang Kai Shek's nationalist troops.

Missamari, Lama Camp, Foothills: such history! Yet nothing remained, except some scattered memories. All those times Abhijit had gone to the Foothills camp with Pradip Khura he didn't remember hearing anything about those momentous events. It was like the carved stone ruins from the ancient temple sites by the Brahmaputra river in Tezpur, Bamuni hills and Agnigarh, also the beautiful 5th or 6th century AD carved stone doorway at Da Parbatia (a Shiva temple had been built by the Ahoms over the site of the earlier temple), places he had visited long back with his parents, and which instead of real history seemed only to have myths attached to them, like the one about the Ban Roja or King and his beautiful daughter Usha and her suitor Aniruddha, Krishna's nephew, who had been imprisoned by the king. Krishna had come to free his nephew, and in the ensuing clashes rivers of blood had flown, or so it was said, which gave the name to Tezpur (tez meaning blood) and Sonitpur (sonit also meaning blood). Things had happened, and then been forgotten. People seemed to know very little of the past.

Monetising the Wild

About a week after meeting the old man Nana at Kamengbari, Abhijit met the reporter Padma Bora in Tezpur town. He thought it might help him with some background information about the Missamari area. Abhijit had spoken to Saurav Saha, the boy he had met in the auto coming back from Missamari, and Saha had said he could fix a meeting with the local reporter. By then Abhijit had settled into the routine of the house; all three people, his grandmother, his uncle, and the helper Julie, went about their own activities without bothering the others, and Abhijit easily adjusted to this system, doing his own reading and writing and taking the occasional walk into Tezpur town.

There was a fourth person, a middle-aged Bengali Muslim man called Ismail miya from the Gotlong area on the way to the Brahmaputra bridge. He would come over on his cycle whenever there was some heavier labour around the compound, cutting branches, cutting grass, doing a bit of plastering work, maybe even getting a gas cylinder from town. A lean, sinewy man, he would work at a steady pace, taking occasional breaks for a cup of black tea brought to him by the helper, or to prepare a plug of sada or tobacco with lime, which he kept in a green plastic container. He gave the impression of needing very little to get by, and seemed unaffected by the heat or rain, which Abhijit felt gave him a deep resilience.

To do his own bit in helping with the household, Abhijit took to going to the twice weekly haat or market at the nearby Mission Chariali. He would take two bazar bags with him and, before breakfast, walk to the haat, where the sellers would have taken up their positions since early morning. On the way he would take out money from the ATM at the hospital, folding and putting into his wallet the receipt, and mentally calculating how long his savings would last.

Slowly he got to know the topography of the market, which had expanded over the years. The autos and rickshaws crowding the road outside, the lane going in with the wine shop to the left, on haat days the man frying jalebis in a corner; the miya farmers (Muslims of Bengali descent) who came in groups in hired tempos had the main area, their fertilizer-enhanced vegetables spread out on plastic sheets before them, the fruit sellers and potato and onion sellers to one side, and at the back the individual local sellers with their home-grown vegetables and pigeons in bamboo coops and rounds of jaggery, the rice sellers and dry fish vendors and tea stalls under thatched roofs, more miya farmers under the large old ficus tree, then the fish and pork sellers right at the end, the salani or trucked fish taken out from ice-filled thermocol boxes, the pork chopped up by young Bodo boys with long daos and the meat smeared with blood.

When his father had been home from his job, he would sometimes bring Abhijit along with him to the haat, where he would stop to talk to friends of his, vendors he knew, including one rice seller with a bad leg. On his third or fourth trip to the haat, Abhijit spotted this man, limping about between sacks of different varieties of rice as he handed over change to a customer, the sacks including bora saul which turned sticky when cooked and the semi-cooked, pounded and flattened chira. On his next trip to the haat Abhijit went to the shop and bought two packets of koraiguri or roasted rice powder from the woman in the shop, possibly the man's wife, the man himself rubbing sada and lime as he gossiped with another customer. Abhijit looked at him, and then turned away. He had planned on approaching the man and asking him about his father, but something stopped him. There were one or two characters he recognized from the old days, boys he had ridden cycles with along the dusty village paths and played cricket with, and they would chat for a while, but too much time had passed and there was too much distance between them now.

He would return home, his arms aching from holding the heavy bags, and turn out their contents in the kitchen, the vegetables and the greens and the fish, and his uncle would come and help sort the produce, telling Julie what would be cooked for lunch, a tenga with the fish, the greens fried, some colocasia leaves from the garden for the mati mah or dal. Abhijit would take a bath and eat his breakfast, and then settle down to some reading, with a feeling of well-being brought on by the physical labour. His uncle in his quiet way seemed content to let Abhijit handle the shopping from the haat, and even other things from the main town market. Slowly there were people Abhijit grew friendly with at the haat: the Nepali man who sold potatoes and onions, the miya man who sold both salani and local fish, the Assamese man from Bihaguri who would come with a small haul of his own vegetables. The political divisions seen on the television news and on social media (which he hardly used himself) seemed far away and distant in the markets, Abhijit noted, or even anywhere else.

About a week after his long walk to Kamengbari, he went to town one day to buy some curd and cream from a dairy near the old chowk bazar. His uncle had asked him to get the items for his grandmother, who liked from time to time to have a bit of curd with jaggery, or sticky rice with cream and sugar. Abhijit had also called Saurav Saha, the youth from the NGO, and they met at a sports goods shop just ahead of the then-closed Anwar Hall, where Saha was sitting behind the counter with the elderly shopkeeper, everywhere in the small shop heaps of different sporting items—jerseys, football boots, cricket pads—wrapped in dusty plastic. The owner got three cups of tea from a tea stall around the corner and they talked; it appeared the shop owner knew Abhijit's father, and both his uncles.

'Tezpur was a small place back then,' he said, 'everyone knew everyone else.'

And once again Abhijit was left with the question: why did my father kill himself?

From the sports shop they walked a short distance ahead past the old Parijat Hotel and the new MVI office to the office of the journalists' association, a modest tin-roofed structure by the footpath, inside which a couple of people were sitting in a rough circle of chairs and chatting. One of them got up and came to the door when he saw them. Padma Bora wanted to have a smoke, so they walked back to a pan shop, Abhijit walking behind the two of them. The day's heat still lingered, and as he walked he shifted the plastic packet with the pot of curd and the container of cream from one hand to the other.

The journalist lit a cigarette. He was middle aged, with a moustache and a paunch. Saurav Saha introduced both of them. Bora studied Abhijit, looked down at the packet in his hand, and said, feigning amusement, 'You didn't get curd and cream in Delhi I suppose?'

Abhijit ignored the jibe, and replied in an even tone that yes, there was good curd and cream available in Delhi.

'And butter,' the journalist continued, 'they add butter everywhere, even in the dal! I went there some years ago with the CM's media team.' He pretended to shudder. 'I don't want to go back there again.'

Abhijit asked him who he worked for, and Bora named two newspapers and a magazine he contributed to, all of them from Guwahati. There was a prickliness to the man, a need to maybe to show this boy, who'd grown up in Shillong and worked in Delhi, his true place. He asked Bora about Foothills, the incident by the Belsiri river. Saurav chipped in to mention Abhijit's walk to Kamengbari, but the journalist didn't pay any heed to that, just smoked his cigarette down to the butt as he squinted across the road at the boundary wall of the Sadar thana, and told them what had happened.

'A friend of mine who was doing a government contract told me this story,' Bora said. 'He's from the outskirts of Tezpur and owns a dumper. On the advice of someone he knew, he sent the dumper with a driver, a handyman and four labourers to the Dhankhana crossing or "centre" near Ramnathpur forest village, ahead of Missamari, where there was a contact. Money was supposed to be handed over, following which the truck would be allowed to go through a Bodo village to the Belsiri river and fill up sand from the river bank. The sand there is fine and of good quality, coming down with the river from the Arunachal hills, and cheap as well.

'What my friend hadn't known was that the vehicles which collected the sand, and stones from the river this way, usually tractors with trailers attached to them from the nearby villages, and which then sold on the loads to contractors inside the Missamari army base or outside at other building sites, these vehicles paid an annual tax to the boys from the faction of the Bodo insurgent group operating in the area, as *they* claimed the Belsiri river and its surrounding areas fell within the Bodoland they were demanding. The truck was detained, and my friend had to go and make a payment over and above the payment for the sand to release the truck and his men.

'When the contact at Dhankhana centre was approached by my friend he claimed to have assumed that the dumper had been cleared by the forest beat officer who apparently handed out the permission in an unofficial way. So then my friend went to meet the beat officer to apply for 'permission' to lift sand from the river, but the beat officer made excuses and declined. Probably because my friend wasn't from around the Missamari area, and was also a bit of a loudmouth. So that was that, and when I heard the story I decided to go and do some "investigation" into the matter.'

'So I set off for Missamari on my motorcycle, and first visited the Gabharu beat office.'

Abhijit commented here that the beat officer in question must have been Gautam Pegu, to which Bora ponderously replied that he couldn't reveal the person's name.

'I met the beat officer,' Bora went on, 'and asked him about what had happened with my friend's dumper, and the allegations about permission being granted to people to lift sand and stones from the fringes of what was still on government maps a reserve forest. The beat officer denied all knowledge of what was happening, and said that he couldn't be responsible for what was essentially a law-and-order problem, the boys from the faction of the insurgent group operating in the area.

'From the beat office I went to Dhankhana centre, taking a left from Kolamati gate. I passed Nepali and then Adivasi houses on the way, many of which had old tractor trailers parked before them. The contact was a Nepali youth, and he met me in a tea shop at the nondescript centre. I told him I was there on behalf of a contractor at the army base who wanted sand and stones. The youth was a bit suspicious, but he still told me about the annual vehicle tax and the rates per tractor trailer for sand and stones. There were two locations on the river: one near Ramnathpur forest village, and the other near a Bodo village. I said I would like to see both locations. At first he was hesitant. It was only after I said that I was interested in large quantities that he got on my bike and guided me along a muddy track that passed huts and bamboo groves to the riverside. There I saw a group of men shovelling sand into a tractor trailer. I asked them some questions, discreetly took some photos with my phone and then returned to the centre. Here the youth got down, saying he wouldn't accompany me to the second village.

'So I took directions from the youth,' Bora told them, 'and drove on, coming to the Bodo village up ahead and driving through it to the riverside, where there were two tractor trailers being filled, one with sand from the banks, the other with stones from the riverbed, the trailer backed halfway into the river at a shallow point. Some distance ahead a railway bridge forded the river, part of the line between Missamari and Belsiri stations. I stopped my bike and got down and went toward the second tractor and was taking a few photos when I heard someone calling out. I turned around to see a couple of youths sitting inside an open bamboo structure with a thatched roof, like those at the haat. It was near the river, but hidden by a thick bamboo grove from where I had stopped my bike on the dirt track by the riverbank. There was a Bullet motorcycle near the open hut. Three of them then came marching up to me. They were muscular youths with short haircuts, and asked me what I wanted even as they started pushing me around. One of them even snatched my phone and deleted the photos of the tractors. I told them I had come on business, to buy sand and stones, and wanted to talk about rates, but they told me to get lost and never return, one of them putting his hand behind his back as if to draw out a knife or gun. So then I left, coming out of the village and then getting to the Thelamara road through Garubandha.'

You should have gone to the beat officer last, Abhijit thought, but didn't say anything. And then he remembered: the Bullet motorcycle. It was Saha who asked the question: had someone informed the boys sitting there keeping an eye on the tractor trailers?

'What do you think?' Bora asked them.

'Was it the beat officer?' Abhijit asked.

Bora just smiled wryly. Abhijit asked the journalist if he had done a story on it. He told them he had written something, but 'who wants to read about corruption in the forest department and boys in insurgent groups, it's nothing new.' He had told the reporter of an Assamese news channel about the matter, but the person had been scared to go there lest he get kidnapped. And then he told Abhijit that he was telling him all of this as a family friend of Saha's, and that he shouldn't go roaming around those places, they were dangerous. Abhijit thanked him for his time, and they parted ways.

Dulu da, the contractor who had sometimes come along to Pradip Deka's camp, was still in Tezpur. Abhijit got his number from his uncle, called him, and met him one day in town, in a hardware store beside the old pond in front of the Sadar thana. The enterprise belonged to an elderly Bengali gentleman, and Pradip Deka would pick up his supplies from here. Dulu da had aged, and spoke to Abhijit with warmth. 'I still remember your father whenever I go to Missamari,' he said. 'The beat office, Pradip's camp, the Monpa village. Where did those days go?'

He now did some small contract works for the MES at the army base. He invited Abhijit to come along with him, and so a few days later they set off early one morning in Dulu da's old but well-maintained Maruti 800. They turned right from the highway at Thelamara, going past villages and green paddy fields, the morning sun rising. Dulu da made it clear that he was not going beyond the army base.

'From Kolamati gate onward you travel at your own risk,' he said. 'There are people who'll make a call as soon as they see you passing by, and later the insurgents will pick you up from Gulai Centre on the Foothills road or from Dhankhana on the way to Ramnathpur. Those people have a good network.'

He asked Dulu da about Ramnathpur; wasn't it one of the old forest villages?

It was one of the fourteen original forest villages in Sonitpur district, Dulu da said, set up on the outskirts of the reserve forests. Ramnathpur had come up on the border of Chariduar RF, on land granted by the late forest minister Ramnath Das, who had a connection to Shillong. Scheduled caste people from around Bihaguri had been settled there, and they had started growing sugarcane. At the mention of sugarcane, Abhijit found himself remembering a visit to the village with his father: the atmosphere of poverty, and being given sugarcane to eat by the headman, whose house they had visited. The man, with the surname Das, had told them, while his wife pounded dhan or paddy with a foot-operated dheki and his mother fed his handicapped son on the veranda of the house, about seeing deer when they went to collect firewood, and tigers carrying their cows away. As a child he had found the skeletal heads of rhinos while ploughing the sugarcane fields. When he mentioned this Dulu da chuckled.

'That's how it was in those days,' he said, adding that if you told children about all that now it would sound like xadhukotha: fairy tales.

Abhijit had said nothing about his long walk to Kamengbari, and now he thought it was best not to mention it. Dulu da had always been a safe and cautious person, and maybe that was why Pradip Deka, an outspoken, impetuous character, had liked his company. In appearance he was small and neat, and drove with his hands on the lower part of the wheel, his elbows on his stomach. There were dangers in those areas, he said, groups of boys from a splinter faction of an insurgent group who roamed the foothill areas with their guns, collecting tax from the Bodo villagers for timber felling, which still went on across the border in Arunachal, and from people supplying sand and stones from the rivers. The Foothills and Belsiri area had a 'platoon commander', Dulu da told Abhijit, a Bodo youth named Rankhw (the w pronounced as u/y). There had been kidnappings on the Foothills road itself.

Possibly guessing Abhijit's line of thought, he said, 'Those days when we used to go hunting in Foothills are long gone, the forests are all gone.'

Abhijit asked him how it had happened, and his answer contained more than a little of the common Assamese attitude toward tribals: 'There isn't a more destructive group than the Bodos, I'll tell you that. They cut and burn and kill everything they can. Look at what happened to the Manas sanctuary.'

As they drove past the tea bushes of the Kolakuchi garden, Abhijit brought up his father's death.

'I've always wondered what really happened,' he said, inviting Dulu da to speak.

But the elderly man's view of it was similar to that of Abhijit's uncle.

'What happened? They found him alone and shot him. As good as animals they are.'

They entered the army base, passing by the replica of the Red Fort's ramparts, with the semi-permanent camps of some contractors at the end of what would be a golf course. The base, which Abhijit remembered as having just a few structures scattered about before, now seemed vast, spreading anonymously with its buildings and barracks. A deserted roundabout, and then the offices of the GE and BSO, which Abhijit had visited years ago with his father, low and painted red-and-white, with undergrowth and trees beyond the high fencing at the back. They drove past the GE or garrison engineer's office to that of the BSO: the buildings and store officer.

The BSO was from UP, a smug, self-satisfied man taking the sun outside, well dressed and groomed, his life in order. He called an old carpenter with a white beard who was painting some almirahs outside the main store, and they got into the car and drove over to the BSO's quarter nearby, where Dulu da and the carpenter inspected a swing that had been built for the BSO's wife and son. The wife brought them tea and snacks while the BSO spoke about his habits (no fridge water, running in the afternoon), how his son never ate chocolates or chips (but he was very plump, maybe from being fed ghee), about the rice that came from back home, and how he was a very desi type of person. His concerns seemed put on (with Dulu da sympathising mechanically as he checked his phone), his manners seemed a copy of someone else's, and Abhijit had a feeling his own life might have been a source of wonder to himself.

The carpenter was squatting nearby with his cup of tea, and when Dulu da asked why he hadn't cut his beard, he said he had been busy repairing the family house. He was from the Bahbari area across the Gabharu river, and he told Abhijit he had worked for several contractors, including Pradip Deka. They dropped the mistry and BSO back to the office, and Dulu da told Abhijit he had paid the BSO 6 lakh rupees in two years, and there were three more contractors like him under the BSO. There was also money to be made from supply work. The BSO would comfortably clear about 50 lakh rupees from a three-year posting, over and above his salary. The worst corruption was in the army, Dulu da said, and in the AR and BRO. His own bills had been held up because he hadn't paid up.

They drove on past walls and buildings under construction and came to a large, dusty camp, half-constructed buildings in the distance, iron rods and sand piled up, and a rough, whitewashed row of rooms. Three men were sitting in chairs out in the sun near their cars. Some distance away were the green-painted hangars of the

Army Aviation Corps. Dulu da introduced them to Abhijit: one was a former shikari from the Orang sanctuary also with the title Saikia; a tall, loud north Indian contractor called Jagat Kumar; and a JE or junior engineer, a fair, plump Punjabi man in a blue shirt. The shikari told them about a poacher in Nameri they called tera or 'crooked', on account of his bent big toe, and how he was shot in the jungle. Jagat Kumar, whom Dulu da knew from before, talked with the JE about the CBI looking for some contractor. The JE mentioned a Bengali investigator who kept taking photographs of the construction sites with a camera. '*Uska memory full ho gaya*,' he said, and they all laughed.

The talk moved on to a programme they had to arrange for some army higher-ups coming for an inspection. Jagat Kumar told the JE, 'The army officers love it when you line up stones and put chuna on them and raise the jhanda. So we'll whitewash the stones beside the track and lift the tricolour. Jai Hind!' Abhijit felt he had been given a glimpse into a different sort of existence altogether. Dulu da then moved with his chair nearer to Jagat Kumar to discuss some business, and a while later everyone got up to leave, Jagat Kumar in his large SUV, Saikia in his Gypsy.

Dulu da told Abhijit that Jagat Kumar had been given power-of-attorney by a Delhi-based company which handled large infrastructure works. 'Another ten years and this place will become like Chandigarh,' he said. A large mountain division strike corps was supposed to come up in Missamari. They came back through the old bazar, past the storage depots and the famous dosa restaurant and old, discoloured army quarters and then took a crumbling road that passed through Khelmati and Bahbari, going up and down wooden bridges which reminded Abhijit of the old Foothills road, coming out on the highway not too far from Mission Chariali. It was an old precaution of Dulu da's, going by one road and returning by the other.

On the way back, Abhijit happened to mention that he had met the Gabharu beat officer Pegu. Dulu da said Pegu was a friend of Jagat Kumar's, and both men met regularly to discuss the sand and stone supplies from the Belsiri river required for the projects at the army base.

'He's a smart fellow,' Dulu da said about Pegu, 'always thinks before he replies. He's made lakhs of rupees from the sand and stone business. He and Rankhw's group share the money.'

Remnants of the Reserve Forest

As Abhijit did his research for his story on the man–elephant conflict in the north bank region of Assam, specifically in Sonitpur district, he found that there was a connection to the group that had fought for a separate state, and the group still fighting for a separate country, for the Bodos. The statehood group had signed an accord and captured power. They had their stronghold to the west of the BTAD, or the four districts which made up the Bodoland Territorial Area Districts, while the independence group (of which there were two factions by then) was stronger toward the east of the BTAD. And intricately linked with both these issues was the condition of the forests along the Himalayan foothills, most of which had been cleared by settlers. Chariduar reserve forest, which Abhijit had seen as a child, had with an area of 460 sq km been one of the largest patches of forest in the whole of Asia. It had decreased in area to less than 100 sq km, and what remained—as the Sonai Rupai wildlife sanctuary—was only because it now fell under the forest department's Wildlife (and not Territorial) division, which had stricter rules.

The beat officer Gautam Pegu mentioned those figures to Abhijit, and it was with Pegu that he went one day into the Sonai Rupai sanctuary (named from two small rivers flowing down from Arunachal). Abhijit had stopped by at the Gabharu beat office one morning, thinking he would have a talk with Pegu and then head out to Kamengbari again, but the beat officer said he would take him and show him what remained of the old reserve forest.

Pegu had been at Kolamati gate office and the Gabharu beat office (one Wildlife, the other Territorial) during 1994–99. He had seen the encroachment taking place in Chariduar RF with his own eyes. While Abhijit waited for him outside the beat office, the morning already turning hot, a tired-looking elderly forest guard told Abhijit that he and a few other guards had been patrolling early that morning trying to catch people stealing sand using tractor trailers from the Gabharu river to sell to the Missamari contractors. Abhijit wondered how the expansion of the army base would affect the surrounding ecology. As they drove toward Kolamati in the department Gypsy, Pegu, who was wearing jeans and a grey t-shirt, told Abhijit about the encroachment in Chariduar RF. There were Adivasis and Assamese too among the settlers, but the majority were Bodos, and they were the ones who logged and hunted the most.

'People came from all over the state in the late 1990s,' Pegu said, 'poor Bodo families from Jonai, Lakhimpur, Baksa, Kokrajhar. They were told by some of their leaders that the Chariduar RF was a tribal belt which would be included in Bodoland, so they should occupy the place. First they would make "lines" by clearing the undergrowth at night and burning it a few days later, then they would fell or burn the trees. Plastic-sheet covered dwellings would appear, and they would scatter mustard seeds in the new soil. You should have seen the size of those mustard! Later they would plant paddy in the level areas. We tried evicting them many times. They would surround us, threaten us with their daos.' In Batasipur, to the west of Foothills, a major eviction drive was called off the night before, after bulldozers and the police had assembled.

At Kolamati gate Pegu talked to the Wildlife ranger, a mild-mannered Dimasa man; he left for Tezpur a while later, and along with a young guard Pegu took the kutcha track going in beside the office, the soil soft and clayey, the forest rising up around them, with the occasional enormous tree. How strange it was, Abhijit thought, to be driving down this track in daylight, the same track Pradip Khura's Gypsy would have taken in the dead of night with him on board more than twenty-five years ago, the searchlights looking for deer. Then the troubles started, and people were afraid of entering certain places.

A large makhana or tuskless male elephant suddenly appeared before them. The guard got down with his rifle, but when he shouted the elephant moved away. As for other animals, there were barking deer, jungle pigs (who loved to dig up the earth to get at roots), and jungle fowl: they saw a glossy, multi-coloured male strutting ahead of them. There were a few tigers and leopards in this forest, estimated with camera traps and the old plaster-of-paris method. They crossed Kherbari, where the grass or kher was burnt in winter to make new growth appear, and then they came to the Gelgeli forest camp, a bare double-storeyed building of grey concrete in a clearing, chickens scratching around in the dirt and a bogori or jujube tree in front.

There were three forest guards there, two Bodo boys (one from Udalguri), and a short old Bengali man from Karimganj. They walked along a sandy path to the Gelgeli river which came down from the mountains. A bortokula or stork rose up from behind some trees, beating its wings. Pegu was talking about the Orang sanctuary, where he had spent three years. He had joined during the dry khorali season, and you could walk around everywhere then, but it got very difficult once the rainy barixa season started. In Orang he learnt how to ride an elephant, and about beehives—the smaller end has honey, while the larger end has the larvae and eggs. They had camps there 2 kilometres apart, and at night they would shout out to each other: hey, eaten your rice? The Gelgeli river was clean and pristine, flowing through white sand and pebbles. There were trees on the other side and in the distance a hazy view of the mountains of Arunachal, white patches of landslips visible against the pale green.

Pegu said the track was rough across the river. You could go up into the mountains but it was a tiring trek. He had shown the trails to the police and CRPF who went to look for insurgent camps, but all they found were abandoned sang ghor or tree houses, mostly belonging to illegal loggers. During his posting during the 1990s they found a camp deep inside the forest from the Foothills road, a U-shaped structure made with "off size" or crooked tree planks left behind by loggers, arranged into a proper camp for at least a hundred people. It had belonged to the eastern group who were fighting for independence for the Bodos. He said the cadres wore football spikes to get a good grip while walking through the forest. The guard, a young boy from Kawoimari near Bihaguri, said they had recently caught some people up in the hills with chainsaws. Pegu asked him if those logs went through the tea gardens and reached Rangapara, and the guard said yes. 'There are no good trees left in Assam,' Pegu said, shaking his head, 'all cut and finished, and now the hills of Arunachal are slowly turning bald as well.'

They came back to the camp, and the other guards took them through the forest behind the camp to a wetland called guxani beel or the godesses' wetland. Just where the forest began were the brick remnants of a small temple, where apparently the Nepalis still came every year to do puja. It was about 4 km through the forest, following the trail, dead trees lying across the track, rotten or felled during storms or by some other means, tree roots, creepers, lantana and dead leaves underfoot. The guard from Kolamati stopped once saying he heard a sound, and they all stood still, straining their ears. Abhijit had a new sense of the forest with its towering trees and unseen animals, of the wild, which teaches people both fear and humility, connecting them to something deep within themselves going back in time.

They walked through the uneven terrain, rays of sunshine coming through high trees, going down and then up across small streams, their shoes muddy. Abhijit saw a chattering squirrel up on a tree, and heard the motor-like hum of hundreds of bees as they scouted a tree top for a new hive. They were among the few things elephants were scared of. There were trees with marks on their trunks where elephants had rubbed their tusks and bodies. There were towering bhelu and dhuna amari trees whose resin was burnt, tall straight kali trees, young cane plants like betel-nut, the overhanging roots of an immense banyan tree. They came to the beel in the middle of the forest, with tora pat and nol grass in it. Pegu said the elephants uprooted the grass, beat it to remove the earth from the roots, and ate it. Nearby were fresh, steaming lumps of brown elephant dung, flies buzzing over them.

On the way back the guards from the camp felled a couple of outenga, or elephant apple, for their midday meal, and the old man from Karimganj picked up a log, telling Abhijit: 'we need logs to cook our rice.' They came out in the grassy area, having covered a large circle. It was hot by then. They drove back from the Gelgeli camp. The guard who was with them said they were supposed to go on patrol a minimum of once a day, sometimes twice, and reports had to be written for the higher-ups. They ate rice twice a day, with dal and vegetables in the morning, fish or meat at night. They got their pay regularly, he said. He was a simple young man from a humble background. Abhijit felt that someone like him with a bit of anger could have joined some of the outfits. Pegu dropped him at Kolamati and drove toward Kamengbari on the straight road.

The western side of the forest had disappeared, and according to Pegu the settlers had even gone across the road—blacktopped by the GREF about ten years ago—but had been pushed back from there as Sonai Rupai had by then been declared a wildlife park.

'All the staff fled during the troubles,' Pegu told Abhijit.

'Some were killed in the jungle. The forest inspection bungalow at Sopai was torn down, the one at Hugrajuli burnt down. Before, the forests above Dhekiajuli were so thick the sunlight wouldn't penetrate inside and it would be damp, you had to leave by 2 pm else it would get dark inside there and you would lose your sense of direction. And if you go there now? It's just like what you see here.' They passed the huts with paddy and straw stacked outside, the wire fence before them, children and their mothers by the roadside, the stumps of trees still visible in the paddy fields after two or three decades. A few houses had even been cemented.

Pegu pointed out the wires strung across poles on the left side of the road, beyond which was a vast emptiness where the forest had once stood.

'Jhatka fencing for elephants,' he said, 'running on 12-volt direct current from solar panels. They turn it on in the evening. If a person gets a jhatka he's as good as dead.'

Pegu chuckled, and pointed to the solar panels on the tin and thatch roofs of the huts. Abhijit looked again, transfixed, upon the whole scene. The narrow road from his childhood with thick forest on either side of it running to the Arunachal border was now open; on his left were scattered huts amid cropland, only a few tree stumps here and there, on his right a few tall simul trees with Germany bon and lantana growing everywhere, the forest in the distance. Near the Kolamati gate there were a mix of communities, Pegu said, but here the villagers were mostly all Bodo, and they were ploughing up the dark, rich soil and planting rice. Pegu said the people got 25 to 30 mun (a measure of nearly

40 kg) of paddy per bigha, whereas usually people got 10 to 15 mun from their fields. They also grew chillies, colocasia and some jute. Near the hills was the bhabar belt with stony soil where crops wouldn't grow.

'The forest department had plantations here,' Pegu said as the huts by the road started reducing in number, and a few silk cotton trees appeared. 'Udal, azar trees, a whole salbari of sal trees. These people cut them all down.'

'What did they do with the trees?' he asked.

'What would they do? They sold if off cheap, just 100 to 150 rupees per cubic foot. Titasopa, bonsum, sal, segun, mekuridima: such fine wood. The insurgents took about 20 to 25 rupees a CFT as their cut. Gulai Centre was the main place for all of this. Gulai means the circumference of a tree trunk. They would take the logs down to the train line at Belsiri or Batasipur on cycles or bullock carts and load the logs on the train to send them down to the sawmills at Tangla and Goreswar in lower Assam, even up to Kishengunj in Bihar.'

The Kamengbari checkpost came into view now. They crossed a pile of boulders being loaded onto a truck by three labourers, with two tough-looking men standing nearby keeping an eye on them. Pegu stopped the car and got down to talk to them. They drove on once he finished his conversation, and the policeman at the checkpost raised the pole seeing Pegu inside. They drove up to a point above Kamengbari where they had a hazy view of the remaining forest to the left, the AR camp and the Belsiri river below, paddy fields and huts beyond the river. They were startled by a *whup whup* sound of large wings: two pairs of great hornbill flew overhead and disappeared in the trees nearby, one pair making a *kok-kok* call. Pegu explained that permission had been taken by someone from Arunachal for lifting 1,000 cubic metres of boulders from the Belsiri river in the Arunachal section, and transporting it through Assam to another contractor at Missamari. An ex-insurgent from Rangapara town was involved too. They had two trucks, as one couldn't bring a full load of boulders up from the river.

'In the old days,' Pegu said to him, 'the Assam government border pillar was on a hill further ahead, on the way to Doimara. The forest department would come and clean the area around it and paint it once a year. Then the troubles started, and the pillar was forgotten. Someone knocked it down. Now the Arunachal government with the help of the Monpas has fixed the border at Kamengbari.'

'Did they always come down to the village by the Belsiri river?' Abhijit asked.

'Their migratory village was originally at Doimara,' Pegu said. 'Then they made their way down to the plains by the Belsiri river. They're very greedy for land, these people.'

On their way back, Pegu stopped on the road for Abhijit to take a few photos on his phone of the cattle ploughing the wet, dark soil, the stout women transplanting the saplings, the makeshift elephant fencing by the road. Pegu showed no interest in going into the settlements—from what he said Abhijit gathered he had entered those places years ago, and didn't have any particular desire to return.

'The forest department carried out eviction drives at the beginning,' Pegu told him as they drove back to the beat office. 'We confiscated grain, burnt the huts, arrested people. But they would return within fifteen days. Once there was firing in the field near Kolamati gate, as scores of Bodos were moving toward the range office. The Garubandha thana OC ordered his men to open fire. Three settlers were shot, one by the OC with his own revolver, and twenty people were arrested. The whole place was reeking of raw blood after that. I tied up several men with ropes. If I go inside those places I might meet the same people again,' he said with a laugh.

Abhijit fell silent, thinking how people, after a time, with no other avenues open to them, would try and make money out of the resources of the wild. Perhaps guessing his line of thought, Pegu started telling him about the difficulties in apprehending loggers and poachers and bringing them out, even when they were found with cycles, axes and guns inside the forest. The settlers would gather round and get violent.

'The ranger doesn't like shooting,' Pegu said, 'but I say you should just shoot them!'

When they reached the Gabharu beat office Pegu asked Abhijit to have tea at one of the small shops opposite. It was hot and humid, and Abhijit was glad to rest awhile before starting back for Tezpur. Pegu talked about his two sons, who were both of marriageable age. A lean woman in a green sari, her body whittled away by hard labour, gave them tea while her husband kneaded dough for frying singaras. Pegu then told Abhijit a story.

One year on 14 August they caught four Bodo men inside Sonai Rupai sheltering in a sang ghor with axes and pipe guns. They were cutting trees, and looking to kill animals if they could. Pegu and the guards took the four men to the beat office, and the next day he and the ranger set off for Tezpur with the four men in an Ambassador to produce them in a court. On the way at Missamari the army caught them, with the pipe guns, and wanted the four men to be handed over to them, possibly so that they could pass them off as insurgents. But the two forest department men refused, and a stand-off ensued. Then Pegu saw a Nepali circle officer from Dhekiajuli whom he knew, who had come to get fuel, and he spoke to him. The circle officer spoke to an army officer and arranged for them to be released. It was late afternoon by then, and they had to lock the four men up at Garubandha thana for the night, before taking them to Tezpur the next day, to present them before a magistrate.

More than a year later the trial was called at Tezpur, and the lawyer of the four men charged Pegu with having picked them up from the roadside. Pegu lost his temper then, and told them he hadn't been bitten by a mad dog to go and pick up people from the roadside. With the judge looking on, he told the lawyer that people like *him* were ruining the country. Pegu had written down the names of the men's fathers on his hand, and when he glanced down the lawyer objected, to which Pegu retorted: if you stop looking at your paper (the chargesheet) I'll stop looking at my hand. 'I told them,' he said to Abhijit, and to the couple running the tea shop, 'I told them, that if I had so much matha (brains) that I could remember those Bodo men's names after more than a year, I wouldn't have been in the forest department. I would have been a scientist in America by now!' The four men were fined a few hundred rupees and were in jail for a couple of months, after which they were out again. Pegu laughed and said, 'The youngest of the four later joined the insurgents, I heard.'

What Abhijit didn't ask the beat officer about was the sand and stone business going on at the Belsiri river side. Dulu da the contractor had told him that Pegu was running a racket supplying sand and stones from the river to the contractors at the Missamari army base, and that the insurgent group active in the area was getting a cut as well—this would mean Rankhw's group—with the money being collected by linkmen. On government maps, the Belsiri was still flowing through the reserve forest when it entered Assam, and thus commercial activities couldn't be allowed on it. However with as large a construction site as the Missamari army base just a few kilometres away, the lure of free sand and stones from the river was just too much. And the more sand and stones were removed from the river, the less flood protection there was in the downstream areas during the monsoons.

A Night in the Village

Abhijit soon returned to Kamengbari. This time he waited in Missamari bazar for an auto headed that way, and reached Kamengbari at noon. At Gulai Centre the auto stopped to drop off some passengers, and Abhijit saw the boys standing around the bikes, just like the previous time. When they got to Kamengbari a column of Assam Rifles jawans were coming down the road, returning to camp from a patrol. The young men looked tired and sweaty with their guns and backpacks, and Abhijit watched as they silently filed through the green-painted sheets surrounding the camp. He went to the old man Nana's house, where Nana's wife made tea and Abhijit again insisted on buying a packet of biscuits from the shop. They sat on the wooden bench outside on the porch, and Nana recited a litany of the area's woes: remote, lack of facilities, the insurgents going up into the jungles. The main problem, according to him, was that the police and forest departments from both the Assam and Arunachal side didn't undertake regular patrolling along the border.

Abhijit took down the son-in-law Nyima's number from the old man. Nyima was doing some contract work at a large dam project on the Kameng river, somewhere off the Bhalukpung–Tawang road. He asked the old man about their earlier migrations. Nana told him how, when they used to come walking down from Rupa with their mithuns to the village by the river, it would take them three to four days. A labourer in an orange t-shirt appeared, asking for something from the shop. As Nana went to fetch the item from the shop Abhijit spoke to him: he was a Bodo, and said had come there with his family from Chirang district in 1996, when he was a child.

A while later Abhijit took Nana's leave: he wanted to go up into the hills. The old man told him to be careful, and reminded him that the auto went back to Missamari at 3.30 pm. He followed the broken, crumbling road which zig-zagged up the hillside. Only a few large trees were standing here, one of which had three huge beehives hanging from a stout branch. There had been an army firing range somewhere above Kamengbari, he remembered his father saying. Where could it have been? It didn't take him long to come to a vantage point at a bend in the road from where he had a good view: of the remaining forest down to the left, curving with the horizon at the far distance in a green haze, the AR camp and the tin-roofed huts below, and to the right, beyond the Belsiri river flowing along the rocky river bed, were the paddy fields and huts of the settlers, smoke curling up here and there from huts nestled within bamboo groves. Years ago, when he had been a child, he imagined it would have been green in all directions as far as the eye could see, but already this new view seemed like something settled to him, a landscape altered by human hands. From the bend a path led through the undergrowth and trees along the hillside, and Abhijit followed it for a short distance till he came to a small clearing from where he could see the river and the paddy fields, and the wide near bank of the river, choked with green undergrowth, no sign remaining at all of the two camps or the Nepali basti or the old village.

He came back to the road and walked ahead, toward the green-cloaked hills under a burning midday sun. At one point he could see on his left, above the channel of the river, the spur of a hill which had been cleared of its trees. Soon he came to a sort of pass, from where the road gently wound down, more of a kutcha track now, while up ahead the hills of the Kameng area opened up. Here and there were white patches on the hills from landslips. Suddenly there was a *whup whup* sound above him, and a pair of great hornbills flew overhead in a flash of white and orange, one of them calling out hoarsely. The green hills still covered in jungle and the sight of the birds awoke in him something like exhilaration. Was this what his father had felt too, when he had patrolled the forests down below?

He walked some distance ahead, then stopped under the shade of a tree and had a drink of water from the bottle he had bought back at the shop. The old man Nana had told him that the small settlement of Doimara with its now abandoned saw mill was 12 km from Kamengbari, sitting above the Belsiri river's path. Abhijit decided to return again some other day, to try and make it to Doimara. He could feel the heat and his tiredness as he walked back. Approaching the point from where the road had descended between a cleft in the hill, he saw a few young boys coming down towards him. As they crossed him, talking and laughing, he caught the whiff of bidi smoke, and saw that one of them was clad in an unzipped black hoodie—the same youth he had seen lounging by the high culvert near Gulai Centre. He quickened his pace, feeling isolated and vulnerable all of a sudden.

When he got back to Kamengbari he found that the auto had already left, even though it wasn't yet 3.30 pm. Nana told him that the auto driver had heard something about a police operation on the phone about half an hour earlier, and had left in a hurry with just a few passengers. It would be impossible to go now, he said. Abhijit could stay at his place and wait for the morning auto, which would reach from Missamari at around 10 am. Abhijit should have used his common sense and listened to Nana's advice. But that familiar black mood had descended upon him as he had made his way back down to Kamengbari, set off by the heat, by the sight of those youths, by the cleared forests—he couldn't really say. Even the old man, who was being hospitable, irritated him—why couldn't he have made the auto driver wait a while longer?

Paying no heed to the old man's pleas, he started walking down the road and was soon in the semi-forested area before the huts started. The harsh light of midday had already mellowed, and as he walked he looked at the trees to his left—the tall simul and sal trees he could now identify. Soon the scrubland started, and as he made his solitary way along the road he thought how it would be if he were the only person left upon the face of the earth, with the human race soon to be extinct. On the road were large lumps of elephant dung, some dry, others more recent. Then came the first sight of the homesteads to the right, and very soon there were people, in twos and threes, standing outside their huts or by the road, talking and looking at Abhijit as he passed. He remembered what Nana had said the auto driver had told him, about a police operation, and slowed down and then quickened his steps. If there were police, he would tell them who he was.

He had walked a few kilometres, but he ignored the tiredness, and soon he was crossing the high culvert and approaching the huddle of shops at Gulai Centre. People were standing about, talking and moving this way and that to get a better view down the road, where a white Gypsy and a run-down Sumo stood by the road, police commandos milling about. Nobody appeared to take notice of him, and he asked an elderly man with a meagre spread of vegetables on his chang as to what had happened. The old man said, the police had just shot a boy. When his eyes adjusted better to the scene, he could see through the legs of the policemen the dead body lying on the road. A feeling of panic came upon him, and he controlled an urge to start running back toward Kamengbari and Nana's house.

As he stood there he became aware of a group of youths to his right, the boys he had seen around the motorcycles, though today the bikes weren't around. One of them nudged another one and jerked his head toward Abhijit and said something. He was now feeling increasingly nervous. The police commandos started moving toward the shops, the ones in front shouting and gesturing with their guns that the people should move away. Where was he to go? He looked around and entered what seemed like the only tea shop there, a hut really, with an open door and a lengthwise opening for a window, dark and smoky inside with benches and long tables at three ends, a few people sitting there, and at the far end an elderly Bodo woman squatting at the hearth and frying something in a pan. He looked around and went and sat at a table near a young man wearing a light blue half-shirt with side-parted hair, a small glass of tea before him, someone who stood out in these surroundings. He had a small stack of exercise copies at his elbow, the sort used in schools (but without any brown-paper covering). Abhijit nodded at him, but the young man just looked at him, his face weathered and chiselled, a rural hardness to his body.

The elderly woman now rose, having taken out whatever she had been frying onto a plate, and handed these items, something like a pitha or malpua Abhijit saw, to some of the customers. He asked her for tea, and she poured him a glass from a kettle. When she brought it to him, she asked something in Bodo. He might have replied in Assamese, maybe saying that he didn't know the language, but the youth said to him, in Assamese, that the woman was asking him where he had come from. Kamengbari, he replied. This seemed to satisfy her, but the youth kept looking at him. Did he stay there? the youth asked, to which Abhijit replied that he had gone visiting.

As he drank the sweet hot tea, he noticed that it was already dusk. A police commando poked his head through the door, looked around, said something roughly in Bodo, and withdrew. The people inside sat quietly, talking in soft voices. A mother with her young daughter, dressed in faded old clothes, looked at him furtively from the bench opposite. What was he to do now? He tried making some conversation with the youth. What had happened? An operation, a boy had been shot dead, some others with him escaped, the police commandos had gone after them. Abhijit came to know that the youth beside him, whose name was Dilip Basumatary, worked as a teacher in the school in nearby Jiabari village. He told Dilip that he was a freelance journalist. The teacher appeared to be impressed by this, but suspicious at the same time, as he asked Abhijit why he had gone to Kamengbari. Abhijit quickly said he had gone looking for a friend of his father's, which was true in a way.

The answer appeared to satisfy the teacher, and they drank their tea and then came out of the shop. The light was fading now, the sky losing its colour even as it turned a pale orange to the west, far beyond the shabby line of shops. Up ahead the police Gypsy was now absent, only the Sumo stood by the side of the road, with a few commandos lounging on it. The dead body of the youth was gone. Abhijit looked this way and that, trying to figure out what to do, and the teacher must have noticed this, for he quietly said that the situation wasn't good at the moment. Abhijit could come to his house, which was nearby, if he wanted to. Relief washed over him, and soon they were walking along a kutcha track between paddy fields. He looked back once: under the darkening sky the shops at the centre and the solitary vehicle appeared tiny, lost in the vast openness.

The teacher walked quickly, while Abhijit, stumbling in

the gloom on the uneven track, trailed a few steps behind, stepping into a muddy puddle or two. They passed bamboo groves and scattered huts; he could smell wood smoke from the evening meal being cooked. Some of the huts had small, dim lights outside, charged by solar panels, he guessed. They came to a short, low bridge laid with bamboo poles and wood planks, and as they walked across the loose planks lifted and fell, and for a moment Abhijit was back with his father in the jeep at night, crossing the wooden bridges on the Foothills road with their clattering planks. Up ahead the teacher took a right onto a smaller path along which they crossed huts in spacious individual plots, before finally turning into one such plot. There were three huts in a rough U-shape, and the teacher took him around the hut in the front to a courtyard with another hut to the right, and a more roughly constructed one opposite the first hut, all lit by the dim light from a single bulb hanging above the narrow veranda of the first hut, in the corner of which was a wooden loom.

The teacher stepped up to the veranda and from behind the loom drew out a stool for Abhijit. Sit here, he told him in Assamese, and then went past the curtain into the hut, from within which came the sound of voices. Abhijit sat on the low stool. Through the open doorway of the second, smaller hut he saw the glow of a fire and a figure before it. It was dark now, and completely silent, apart from the voices inside and the occasional clatter of utensils from the kitchen. The third hut, without any light, was probably for storing grain. He looked up into the sky, where there were a few stars, trying to comprehend where he was. Dilip

Basumatary came out, having changed into a woven green wraparound and a vest, and hung his trousers and shirt on the clothesline. He asked Abhijit if he wanted to wash his hands and face, and pointed to where the domkol was, some distance from the third hut, and handed him a towel. Abhijit went and worked the handle of the hand pump and washed up. There was a grunting sound near him, and as his eyes adjusted to the darkness he saw two dark, bulky shapes moving about: pigs tied by ropes to wooden posts.

He went back to the veranda and hung up the towel on the clothesline, and the teacher came out of the kitchen with two cups of black tea. This is how we live, he told Abhijit, handing him a cup, there's nothing else I can give you, but you are welcome to have rice with us and spend the night here. The teacher drew out a stool for himself and sat near Abhijit. The teacher's lack of artifice touched his heart. It was like catching a glimpse of an older, earthier type of human being. They drank their tea (with salt in it, not sugar) and talked, and he came to understand something of this household in the middle of the dark emptiness.

Their family were Baptist Christians from Baksa, to the west, the teacher said, and his parents and two elder brothers had come here in 1995, to clear the jungle. Dilip and another brother stayed behind with their father's brother, and after Dilip passed his matric ten years later, the uncle brought him here, to Amlaibari, after which he was offered a job at a venture school in nearby Jiabari. So now he taught at the school, which took children till class 5, and which ran on people's contributions. They had 120 students at present. Books and materials were provided by the state government. Even though they voted in the state assembly and national elections, they didn't have a panchayat system, a big grouse for them, due to which there were no government schools, hospitals, roads, police stations. For electricity they depended on portable solar panels to charge inverter batteries, which were also used to electrify the makeshift elephant fencing by the road after dark.

It was a hard life, Dilip told Abhijit, there were no jobs, and all they could do for a living was grow mustard to sell in the market, grow rice, keep pigs, or go into the forest to cut trees, even as they faced the upodroh or depredations of wild elephants. One thing though, the notun mati or new earth was rich and didn't need any fertilizers.

The electric fences ran on direct current, and the previous year a girl slipped in the mud and fell on the fence at night and was killed. The boys from the insurgent group troubled them with demands for food and taxes. But those boys were all outsiders, the teacher quickly added, no one from this area.

To study ahead of class 5 the children had to go to Missamari. Some parents had now started sending their children there, but they were few in number. For medical treatment they had to go to Missamari or Tezpur. Some boys went out, not for government jobs, but to work in 'companies'—Abhijit took this to mean security guard, delivery boy, that sort of thing. Besides the insurgents, the police and army would come visiting sometimes, threatening them to reveal where the insurgents were hidden. So, this is how we live, he said again. Abhijit felt strangely humbled—

the disappearance of the forests seemed a trivial issue compared to how these people existed. And yet, hadn't they come willingly, searching for 'new earth'?

Just then there were noises, people shouting from the direction of the Foothills road, and the teacher turned his head and listened. Abhijit asked him if the operation was still going on, but Dilip shook his head. Those were wild elephants coming out of the forest. He remembered the lumps of dung he had noticed on the road. The loud, hoarse trumpeting of what sounded like a male elephant rang through the night, and a shiver went through him. Dilip though appeared to be unconcerned, and turned back to Abhijit and began asking him about where he was from, where he had worked, what he was doing now. Abhijit told him that his father had been in the forest department and had served in the area, but left it at that. He briefly talked about his career and added that he was doing some research on the Foothills area. Dilip nodded and said they needed help, everyone saw them as encroachers and blamed them, something which could be righted only if they received government pattas for their land.

As Abhijit was considering this statement, he saw a beam of light moving over the pigs, followed by voices. Two figures came around the hut, a man and a girl. As they came closer he saw the man wore a similar woven wraparound like Dilip's, and even looked like him, just that he had a slight paunch under his shirt and a receding hairline. The girl wore a red dress, the sort of frock worn by young girls, and as the light fell on her, he realized with something of a shock that she was a teenager, with small breasts and smooth, bronzed legs and arms. The man, whom Abhijit had identified as one of the two elder brothers, now spoke to Dilip in their rounded Bodo tongue, about some problem it seemed. As he spoke his eyes kept flicking at Abhijit, who felt Dilip was explaining who he was, hearing the words 'Tezpur' and 'journalist'. The man went toward the kitchen, and the girl stepped up to the veranda where she spoke in a bantering tone with Dilip, even as she looked at Abhijit. Her hair was tied back in a ponytail, and the red dress, through use, had faded into ordinariness. Her face was fair, as if she used skin lightening cream, and her oval eyes seemed set apart slightly more than usual, which gave her face a pleasing asymmetry. Abhijit looked at her, and then looked away, suddenly uneasy.

When she had gone inside, Dilip told Abhijit that his brother Binod had returned from a nearby house where a four-year-old boy was very ill; it had happened suddenly, and his brother was asking his wife to prepare a herbal remedy—she was known for that in their village. They suspected malaria; it was prevalent in the area. Later, Abhijit would find out that the incidence of malaria in the Chariduar reserve forest area had risen as more and more settlers had come in and the trees were cut down.

It was soon time for dinner. Dilip told him that they usually ate early and went to bed, as there was nothing else to do. 'What to do, the place is backward,' he said. Abhijit told him he didn't have any problems with that. Before they ate, his host took Abhijit inside to meet his parents. The rooms were sparsely furnished and dimly lit. The first room had a cane settee, a mat, a wooden chair, a wooden table with a few tattered books on it, an alna with a few clothes hung on it, and a single bed. A curtain hung over the door leading to the second room; in the third room were the parents, part of the original settlers, with the father, who looked old and ill, lying on the bed, while his wife, in a traditional dokhona, sat on it, bent over what looked like a shirt, sewing, her granddaughter in the red dress beside her, her face lit up by the glow from a mobile phone. Dilip introduced him, and as they spoke he could feel the girl's eyes upon him, a sort of raw curiosity in them. She didn't speak to him though. Dilip said her name was Laimwn, and that she wasn't studying at the moment.

He was taken to the second hut, the kitchen, where an emergency light had been switched on in the smoky interior, unevenly lighting the utensils and hearth and rough shelves. Binod sat silently on the ground, while his wife, a stout woman with a beady eye, kept an eye on Abhijit as she ground two or three types of leaf on a mortar stone. Her face was fair like her daughter's, but with a sharper nose, and she was wrapped in a faded dokhona. Dilip's parents and his niece followed, and they all sat on the earthen floor while Dilip and his mother served the food: steaming rice, vegetables, some sort of watery dry fish chutney, a thick, grey curry with leaves in it, and small fish boiled with salt. Dilip told him the chutney was known as napham, while the curry, made of pithaguri or rice flour and xak, was onla. Knowing the names didn't help him though, as the food was too earthy and pungent for him, and he had to force himself to eat it. Binod's wife finished grinding the medicine, and she scooped it into a plastic container which she gave to her husband to deliver to the sick child's family. Abhijit was the first to finish, and excused himself from another helping of rice and went outside, taking the stainless-steel plate with him despite Dilip's protests.

In the dark, with the faint light from the huts, he washed his hands and the plate with a scrap of soap he'd found on top of the hand pump. That earlier sense of relief had given way to a feeling of claustrophobia: it was almost as if the darkness was pressing down on him and he couldn't breathe. The dim lights, the wet ground beneath his feet, the poor household, the sick child nearby being treated with herbs, the way the girl had been looking at him with her wide-set eyes as they ate, even the pigs near him—he felt as though he was in a place he had no means of comprehending.

Afterwards he sat with the teacher in the front room, while Binod's wife and daughter cleaned up in the kitchen, and then left for the sick child's house. He checked his phone: there was no signal here. Sickness and death were common, Dilip told him. Their father had never fully recovered from a fever that had come upon him two years ago. One of his two brothers had died soon after they had come to clear the jungle, with no treatment available. Then Binod had lost a son too. Now there was only Laimwn left, and they were worried about how she was growing up. But when Abhijit tried to find out more about that, Dilip started talking about something else, then got busy arranging the bed and lighting a piece of mosquito coil. Despite Abhijit's protests, Dilip lay down on the mat on the floor with a thin bedsheet, leaving the bed for the guest.

Once the lights were off, Abhijit wrapped his sheet around himself—it wasn't too hot by then. Sometime in the night he heard the other three members of the house returning and entering their room.

In the early morning he was woken by voices outside the hut. For a moment he didn't know where he was. Then he saw Dilip was missing from the mat, and the door open. In the half-darkness of the hut, the smell of human beings and clothes lay heavy on the warm air. Yawning, he got down from the bed and drew the curtain aside and stepped out. The father was seated on the veranda, while both sons were standing before him, their arms crossed. Looking at them, he knew something was wrong. Dilip told him: the boy had died during the night after his fever had gone up. His mother, his brother's wife, and Laimwn had gone to be with the family, and the three of them would be leaving in a while. The child would be buried soon. Abhijit sat down on the veranda, shocked. In the early morning light the huts and the scrub around them (in which a hen and its chicks were pecking about) only served to remind him of those giant trees which had stood here once, a boy and his father driving through them in a jeep.

The teacher said that he would make some tea, and if Abhijit would wash up he would go and drop him to Gulai Centre, from where some transport might be available. Twenty minutes later they set out from the house after Abhijit had bid farewell to Binod and the father: both men merely nodded in return. As they turned onto the wider kutcha track on which the wood-plank bridge lay, Abhijit saw many people, families, who were headed to the church for the burial. Just before they got to the bridge Dilip stopped a passing motorcycle: it was a youth he knew, and he was headed toward Missamari, to pick up someone and a couple of items for the funeral. Dilip asked him to take Abhijit along and drop him off at Missamari bazar. They shook hands and then they were off, the youth steering the motorcycle along the bumps in the road. At Gulai Centre a few shops were open. Abhijit got down at Missamari bazar, from where a while later he got an auto going to Thelamara. He was back at his grandmother's house by mid-morning, and after a bath and a little rice to eat he went to his room and lay down on the bed, but it was a long time before he fell asleep.

Lessons in History

He had gone missing for a night, but Abhijit's uncle didn't seem unduly worried, hadn't even tried to call him. The only thing he asked Abhijit was where he had been, to which he replied that he'd stayed the night with a friend from Delhi who was originally from Tezpur. His uncle nodded, looked as if he would say something, but seemed to think the better of it. It was as though he knew, or suspected, where his nephew had really been. As for Abhijit, the events of that day, which he later made notes of, took on an unreal dimension for him: the dead body of the young insurgent lying on the road, the small boy dying of malaria in the middle of the night, the pretty girl stuck in the darkness of that village. Had his father foreseen all of this, somehow? And what would happen to the girl, what sort of a life would she have? He felt an itch to return to Kamengbari, and to make the journey ahead to Doimara, below which the Belsiri river flowed on its way down to those now disappeared forests. His grandmother smiled sadly at him when he sat near her the next morning, having his tea, and told him a story about her grandfather bringing back home a deer he had shot in the forest, along with its calf that had refused to desert its mother. She raised it for a few months, taking it around on a rope tied to its neck, but the calf turned so unruly that her grandfather took it and left it in the forest, and then she had cried for days.

Pradip Deka and his friends were all gone, mostly done in by the bottle and their wild ways, but one character from that group who was still around was Karuna, he of the bloodshot eyes, bristly moustache and booming voice. Karuna meant compassion, a quality Abhijit couldn't easily associate with the man's rough-hewn exterior. Abhijit's uncle suggested he go meet him for his research on the elephant story, and so he went out to Dipota on the outskirts of Tezpur one cool overcast summer morning to look for the place. It was down a gravelled path that branched left off the highway just before the old Dipota post office, and there were two houses in the midst of a lawn with bamboo groves and trees around them. One was an old house from the British times, while the other house was a more recent Assam-type dwelling from around the 1980s. A black Ambassador under an open garage with a tin roof completed the picture of old-world sleepiness similar to Abhijit's grandmother's house. Karuna lived in the old house, and when he came out and saw Abhijit sitting on one of the two cemented benches on either side of the porch he didn't recognize his visitor till Abhijit introduced himself.

Addressing Abhijit as 'baba', Karuna asked what he was doing now and how his uncles were. A quarter of a century on, Karuna appeared haggard, which made his features of old more intimidating, but there was none of the sneering tone Abhijit seemed to remember—had he just been misled by the man's gruff manner back then? Karuna led Abhijit into the sitting room with its simple old wooden furniture and cupboards, switched on the ceiling fan, and went inside to put on a shirt—he had been in his trousers and vest when Abhijit had arrived, the skin on his arms sagging a little, but the muscles still there underneath. A worker appeared, someone who would have been with the family for years, and Karuna roared at him to get tea and some pithas, and telling him that Abhijit was the late Khagen Saikia's son. They talked there in the darkened sitting room, and it struck Abhijit how he was talking confidently to this fearsome figure from his childhood. Karuna had grown old, he had grown up, and things had changed.

'You want to know about elephants?' Karuna asked in his sandpapered voice. 'Then you should talk to that old Muslim phandi Dilwar Saikia. He caught a lot of elephants when the hati mahal system was still there in Assam. The South Africa government called him to help them with elephants some years back. They kept him for five years with five-star facilities, now he's back in his mud-plastered hut running a shop out in the front. People with talent are never appreciated in this country, that's what I always say.'

He wrote down directions to the phandi or elephant catcher's place, somewhere off the highway headed back into Tezpur town. The old roughness was still there in Karuna's voice: he was one of a disappearing breed. The hati mahal system had lasted till about the early 1980s. The elephants caught and tamed in this way were mostly used for hauling timber in the forests. By the mid 1980s though a new wave of deforestation had begun, one that would almost wipe the state's forests clean in the next two decades, especially in the foothills of the mountains all along the north bank region.

Karuna helped himself to some pan tamul from the brass xorai after he had his tea, and lit a small, foul-smelling cigarette. His parents had passed away many years back, his elder brother stayed in the other house with his family, and there were two sisters, married elsewhere. Karuna had never married, and stayed alone in the old house. He had a share in a new tea factory near Balipara, where he helped out with the operations, saying it helped keep him busy. Abhijit just had to mention the Foothills camp, and he started to reminisce about the old days. 'Pradip da was the one who taught us,' he said, 'to buy photika, the local liquor, in 5-litre jerry cans when we went hunting. And Dilwar phandi was the one who would supply me with shotgun cartridges that had been re-packed after firing. He would wrap them in carbon paper and put them inside the rods of his cycle frame—the army jawans could never detect them.'

A few days later, Abhijit accompanied Karuna to the tea factory, which had been built on a filled-up former brick quarry in the middle of paddy fields a few kilometres before Balipara, to the east of Tezpur. Abhijit had seen the interiors of a tea factory as a child, so he knew things like the large withering beds and fans, the CTC (or crush-tear-curl) rollers with their sharpened teeth, the googi or drum that produced the granules associated with CTC tea, the fermenter and dryer and sorting beds (this last bit of machinery in the new factory was made by an old Chinese-run firm in Makum in upper Assam), and though they were a vast improvement on the old factories in the tea gardens, the process was essentially the same. Abhijit felt there was a fundamental simplicity to the entire chain: the tea plants, the factory, the finished product.

A pick-up truck with a load of green leaf pulled into the unloading area between the withering beds and the factory proper, and as it was being weighed by the workers Karuna told him that they, being a 'bought leaf' factory (as opposed to a tea-garden factory) had to be careful of what they bought, as people tried to inflate the leaf weight with stalks and stems from the plant. They would randomly test 100 grams: ideally at least 50 grams had to be leaf, but there were factories nowadays that accepted 40 or even 30 grams, putting the rest of the plant into the tea. The present price of leaf was 16 rupees a kg, and could go as high as 27 or 28 rupees a kg; an average of around 20 rupees was good, he said. They purchased the leaf from small tea growers along the northern areas of the district, from places like Tupia, 18 Mile, Bhalukpung, Rangapara, where forest areas had been cleared, logs turned into charcoal and sold, and tea gardens established. What the British had started, the local people were now taking forward.

Karuna wanted to meet a tea grower on the way to Bhalukpung, and asked Abhijit to accompany him. 'You'll see what has happened to the Balipara reserve forest,' he said.

It was a hot, sunny day with clear skies, and from the highway with its speeding buses and slow autos they could see the eastern Himalayas rising up in the distance. Karuna stopped his car at the crossroads at Balipara as he wanted to pick up some beer: 'Last night I had a lot of drinks,' he explained. There were more shops at Balipara than before, and several workshops for Sumo taxis and buses on the road that headed toward Chariduar, where there was the abandoned two-storey wooden bungalow for the APO or assistant political officer from the NEFA days, then the forest gate and an Assam Rifles camp, and the usual 'centre', which Karuna said was an adda and collection point for the insurgents.

They passed villages and paddy fields in what had been dense forest till two decades ago, the mountains towering up in the blue sky, then crossed a GREF worksite with whitewashed tin walls at Dharikati: the same Dharikati where Abhijit's uncle had seen elephants being driven into an enclosure decades ago. They drove through a remaining stand of forest, with a pair of army men every half-a-kilometre or so keeping watch beside the road, and Karuna drank his beer and talked about the official (and unofficial) mahals for sand, gravel, and stones which came under the forest department. 'Forest, police, insurgents... they're all in the same place, they're all linked,' he said in his rasping voice. 'It's all number two money...people become ministers just to make money.'

There was a Garo village on the way—their ancestors had apparently been brought there by the British to set up rubber plantations—with low hills to the left of the road, and the land sloping down to paddy fields and huts on the right (beyond which was the Nameri wildlife sanctuary, with the Bhoroli river flowing through it, the only significant patch of forest left in the north bank region, along with the

Sonai Rupai sanctuary in the Foothills area). A rough track to the left went down and under a concrete railway bridge, then disappeared into the undergrowth and trees. Further on the train line rose against a hill (a train driver had once been kidnapped somewhere here), even as the road rose up gently to the right on a deserted, shaded hillock, before turning left and and running straight through the green paddy fields, the Bhoroli river to the right, the towering mountains even closer.

Karuna told Abhijit about the recent kidnapping of an engineer with a hydropower company when he had been on his way back from Tawang to Guwahati; he was passing through this stretch in the evening, and his vehicle had been stopped by two bikes at the hillock they had just crossed. The man was put on a bike (the driver was left behind), and the bikes went down the rough track under the railway bridge. The track continued for some distance before petering out in the hills and he was handed over to another group. Karuna said the engineer had been released after money had been negotiated and paid.

They drove to the '12 Mile' Centre, where a weekly market was held on Mondays, to look for a boy called Dhananjoy (the place where the engineer had been lifted was '10 Mile'). Pan shops, two butchers selling pork, people selling clothes and shawls, Bodo people mostly, bikes and pick-up trucks and Sumo taxis by the road. Dhananjoy's sister-in-law, a young woman with a baby, asked a youth called Swgwmsar to go along with them. They went off the highway on a muddy road through the paddy fields. A girl and a boy returning from school stepped aside, the girl in a white sari, the boy pushing a cycle. They passed dense bamboo groves, jackfruit trees, huts and stacked hay, pigs, dogs and children: a peaceful village existence. The place names were all Bodo: Maidangsri, Daifanjuri, Kunthaibari. Where they stopped, opposite Dhananjoy's house, was a plot planted with tea, five to six years old now, with tamul shade trees, and in the distance through the bamboo groves the hills of Arunachal. A well had been dug for water. There was no way one would realize, unless one already knew about it, that here had been another vast reserve forest, the Balipara Reserve Forest, from more than a century ago. The youth who had come with them said Dhananjoy's family members helped out with the tea garden. Swgwmsar was a friendly boy, recovering from the pox, which had left marks all over his face and legs and arms. He had worked in cement quarries in the Nongtalang area of Jaintia Hills. He said, when Karuna asked, that they were mostly Hindu Bodos, and that the insurgents didn't come to their areas.

Beside Dhananjoy's house was a Swargiary family; one of the boys was Mahesh, and he was Swgwmsar's friend. There was a path with shrubs and flowers, three mud-and-bamboo huts with earthen floors and rusted tin roofs, one of which had a veranda with a bench where Karuna, Abhijit, Swgwmsar and Mahesh sat as two old ladies, Mahesh's mother and his aunt, sat on the ground and cut tamul for them while they bantered with Karuna. Around them, their fields were cleared for cultivation (they had 12 bighas in all—a significant measurement, as Abhijit would come to learn), with vegetables, sugarcane, tamul trees, and young tea plants, a year or two old at the most. Further behind a group of young boys was readying black plastic packets with soil for the tea cuttings. Beyond that was another tea patch, then scrubland, the train line, and a low, long forested hill, beyond which there were people cultivating vegetables, Swgwmsar said. Dogs and chickens wandered about, chunks of pork were being dried on a dola on the roof of a hut. Mahesh Swargiary's elderly father said, when Abhijit asked, that he was originally from Goalpara in lower Assam, had moved up to Lakhimpur with his father, and had then come to the present location in 1995. 'Forest-*or mati dokhol koribo ahisilu*,' he said: 'we had come to lay claim to Forest Department land.' It was only much later that the enormity of that simple sentence would sink in.

Mahesh told them that Dhananjoy was out, so they went past Dhananjoy's compound, with its timber and mud huts, stacks of hay outside in the sun, a woman hanging out wet clothes, and entered Swgwmsar's place: a pathway, huts around a courtyard, and land for cultivation behind. He wanted to grow tea but didn't have money; Karuna said he would help him out with the cuttings and saplings, but that Swgwmsar had to make up his mind. The youth got a bottle of laopani or rice beer from one of the huts (his mother and aunts made it), a thick, white liquid in a Royal Stag bottle, a strong, tasty brew. They each got a glass-and-a-half from it, and Abhijit paid him 30 rupees. They got back in the car and dropped Swgwmsar back at the 12 Mile Centre, where he said he had some work. 'Centre-*ot bohi leksar mari thakile nohobo*,' Karuna bellowed at him as he got down: 'It won't do to sit in the Centre and while away your time talking.' And to Abhijit as they headed back along the highway: 'Of course they pay the insurgents, house tax, and tax on the tea gardens too.'

On the way back, along the forested stretch, they turned left and drove through the trees to an old forest village, Rihajuli, where Karuna said he had to meet someone. That person was one Jiten Das. His household had solar-powered jhatka fencing strung on bamboo poles on the outer perimeter to stop elephants from entering. The elephants trampled the paddy fields, along with deer and wild pigs. Just outside his place were two large pits excavated by JCBs for road construction, and where he now reared fish. There were two mud-plaster and tin-roofed houses, and paddy fields beyond the large vegetable garden beside the house (a separate bari for xak), where elephants and wild pigs appeared at harvest time.

They sat on the veranda. Abhijit could smell wood smoke, old clothes and blankets. Jiten Das's youngest son occasionally worked as a boatman at the nearby Nameri Eco-camp, and he used a short dao to cut some tamul pan for them. There were runny-nosed children around and Jiten Das's wife, as sinewy and weathered as her husband, held a plump six-month-old boy who looked at Abhijit with a fixed stare. He had lost his mother, the youngest son's wife, after she was afflicted with some coughing sickness (she had been taken to Tezpur, it had been twenty-one days since she had died). Karuna berated them for not letting him know about her illness. But life went on for them. They served a lunch in the smoky kitchen of sticky rice, dal, fish head with vegetables, and carp straight from the pond, fried, the flesh white and sweet. Jiten Das told he had caught 55 kgs from the smaller pond in front of their house at the time of his daughter-in-law's shraddh ceremony; he had released fish pona or hatchlings there earlier.

They had been there for more than forty years in the government-established forest village on the outskirts of the Balipara reserve forest. Abhijit saw a tall, wizened old man and woman inside the first house, most likely Das's parents. Nearby there was overgrown scrubland and scattered trees. People had cut down the trees much earlier and started cultivating mustard; now that wasn't allowed, and the army's Eco Task Force was planting trees. They followed a narrow trail through the 'Germany bon' infested forest (Karuna said the British had brought it from Germany during the war for camouflage as it spread easily), the trail going up and down, the branches of shrubs whipping the car body, till they stopped at one point and walked to where the Bhoroli river or rather a xuti or channel of the river flowed, beautifully blue and serene, the sun setting on the other side: pebble-strewn bank with green grass rising up to the forest line. In the distance were the dark peaks of Arunachal with clouds at their peaks, white gashes from landslides or earth cutting. On the high, sandy bank were three or four straw-encrusted dung piles of an elephant. Das later said they could have met the wild elephants in that area. Abhijit heard the cry of a jungli murgi. Das climbed up a wood apple tree and plucked some for them. Karuna had taken along Das's licensed single barrel shotgun, worn with age and handling, with woven cane locks, along with some refilled KF cartridges, but didn't see anything worth shooting.

They turned back, and at a turning on the path near the village where some children were playing, Karuna stopped the car and sent Abhijit walking ahead with Das to see a canal or garh ali, a sort of channel with raised sides that was supposedly dug during the Ban Roja's time. It was covered with vegetation now, a relic of a bygone era. The shape of the canal was discernable, and it seemed to come down from the mountains towards the Jia Bhoroli river: a watercourse, or a sort of moat, or a road, who knew what it was? Or could it have been from the time of the British, for floating logs from the forest down to the Bhoroli, and hence on to the Brahmaputra? As with the remains of the stone temples in nearby Tezpur, there were only myths here, no facts.

They drove down the path, turned the car (and almost got stuck in the mud), and came up to a rough hut. Karuna yelled from the car and a lean muscled boy in an old brown vest and rolled-up trousers came over from across the path where he was working on a patch of cleared land. Karuna told Abhijit he was an ex-member of the xongothon or 'organization' from Gohpur who was hiding out in Rihajuli with his Nepali wife from Arunachal, and that he might be with the Maoists now. Abhijit caught a glimpse of the wife inside the hut: she looked older than him, and was wearing a blue salwar. The boy, dark-complexioned with slightly crooked eyes, told Karuna he was working at cultivating now, and had harvested a crop of kosu from that patch.

They sat at a table in a covered area beside the hut and for Karuna the boy poured out 9 Star whisky from the Frontier Distillery in Tippi. Abhijit took in the mud-plastered hut, the dark kitchen with smoke trickling out of it, the damp pile of bricks and shrubs, the elephant jhatka line outside, the dry gram on a square of newspaper to chew along with the cheap whisky, the unseen older woman inside the hut. Poverty and a hard life. Karuna told them it was better to eat less, in order to keep lean and live longer. In the car, going back to Tezpur, he told Abhijit, 'That fellow was in the xongothon. Look at him now, breaking the land like a bhija mekuri (wet cat).'

It was dusk by the time they neared Tezpur. Karuna asked Abhijit to come along with him for some 'drinks', as he put it. It was a 'dhaba-cum-bar' in a field on the outskirts of Tezpur, a cemented building with an air-conditioner that didn't work and grimy curtains, but you could buy bottles at the wine shop rate. Insects flew in from the darkness outside. Though he had been drinking throughout the day, Karuna was still steady on his feet and in his speech. He started telling Abhijit how the ULFA had spread in the areas around Tezpur, how men had come from upper Assam towards the late 1980s and gone around holding meetings in villages, how the boys (especially the unemployed) had been swept up in a revolutionary fervour to achieve independence—till the army started their operations.

More interesting for Abhijit were his stories of going hunting in Pradip Deka's old jeep, and one of those places were the forests above Diring tea estate near Pabhoi, to the east of Balipara. There was a Karbi village there, and Pradip Khura would buy local liquor from a certain Karbi man who had a Bodo wife. The couple had two sons, one of whom was now a known insurgent leader by the name of Ringkhang in the camps in Myanmar. '*Moi janu nohoi, xeibur ki,*' Karuna said, his eyes red, his face dark and lined above the bristly white moustache: 'I know what they are.'

He was a sole surviving bard of those old days. They had once gone hunting beyond the Kolamati forest gate, and there they ran into the Kacharis or Bodos in the forest. They hid their guns and said they were there for a picnic. The Kacharis had moved into that area, and wanted to know what they were doing there.

Abhijit wasn't drinking, and, as Karuna tossed back one drink after another from a half bottle of cheap whisky, he finally worked up the courage to ask about his father. Did Karuna remember him? How had he died? Could it have been a case of suicide?

'I remember him very well,' Karuna said. 'We were all a bit scared of Khagen da. They killed him, those Bodos. Why would he commit suicide, and leave you and your mother behind? Everyone liked him.' He looked into his glass, and then said, almost to himself, 'There was that case up in Dirang, but nothing came of that.'

'What happened in Dirang?' Abhijit asked, but Karuna then shook his head, and changed the topic.

Abhijit later felt that by asking Karuna questions about the old days, especially while drinking, he might be making the man dredge up memories he couldn't handle.

The Catcher of Elephants

Abhijit went looking for Dilwar Saikia, the phandi or elephant catcher Karuna had mentioned. He lived in a village off the highway going west from Tezpur, before Dipota; there was a GREF stockyard near the village. The people were mostly Assamese Muslims, and the village had an old reputation for the fierceness of its inhabitants. With Abhijit was the mouzadar, or revenue collector, of the area known as Bahbari, which stretched from behind Bihaguri to Rangapara. He was young for a mouzadar, in his early thirties, and lamented that the position didn't have the prestige, or money, associated with it earlier. Karuna had sent him along with Abhijit.

The mouzadar showed Abhijit a rough video on his camera of a herd of some sixty to seventy elephants moving through a sapori, a low-lying area by the river, near Dipota called Arimora. Elephant herds came down in the winters from the hills of Arunachal Pradesh to feed on ripe paddy and sugarcane and moved back up into the hills as the Bhoroli river rose. 'The elephant is an eating machine,' he said, 'eating from one side and excreting from the other.' Now their habitats were shrinking, making them enter human habitation for food more frequently.

The young mouzadar told Abhijit about the huge tusker that had been at their place during his grandfather's time, how it would take his father and the other children for a ride, how it would come when his grandmother called it and gave it some rice to eat. Once when it was bitten by a cobra it shook off its mahout and went and showed its leg to his grandmother, looking for solace. He told Abhijit about the Sootea MLA's huge male elephant Ramu, a Forest Department favourite which had recently gone in alone and chased away a wild herd with three tuskers from a village.

They finally found the place in a side lane, an ordinary mud-plastered hut with a tin roof, a small shop at the front selling cold drinks, chips, eggs, potatoes. Dilwar came out to meet them, in a lungi and a white vest. He was close to eighty, with a trimmed white beard, and a direct gaze, one of the few remaining phandis in Assam. Physically he was vigorous, and seemed like a man two decades younger, something to do with alertness and the life he had spent in the wild, Abhijit felt. They went inside: it was a small place, but with some furniture and a fridge and television. He had caught elephants by both the garh and kheda methods, he said, for training in the hati mahals. Abhijit asked him about rhinos in the Foothills area, for he had read about it somewhere. Dilwar said there were rhinos there earlier, but the last one had been shot in 1975. Rhinos always went to one particular place to excrete, which was their weak point, for that was where poachers would lie in wait. No doubt Dilwar had shot rhinos as well.

He admitted to shooting tigers and other animals. 'I'll go to jail if I talk about it,' he said, laughing. There had been hati mahals in those days at Charduar and Bhalukpung and Sootea. The sorkar would reward you with money if you shot tigers; now you would go to jail. He was in South Africa for five years, training three elephants from Assam for a zoo, and was kept 'like a minister', with an apartment and a car with a driver. Now he mostly stayed at home, making fishing nets which were sold for 2500 to 3000 rupees each, and going to the nearby masjid for namaz, twice or thrice a day. The first meeting was a short one, and Abhijit said he would come to talk again (Dilwar was even ready to come to Abhijit's place in Tezpur, to tell his story). He was one of the few remaining links to the old days, to a vanished wilderness, of which Abhijit had seen glimpses during the trips to Foothills.

Abhijit went to meet him a second time to get more information about the elephant story he had to write for the newspaper. He also wanted to find out more about Dilwar. The former phandi was sitting in the tiny shop in front of the house, dressed in his lungi and a vest, looking out. Abhijit sat with him. His guru as a phandi had been one Xondhiram, he said, a borphandi from Bengbari near Harisinga, to the west of Tezpur, and now in Udalguri district; the man died at ninety-eight and had once caught twenty-nine elephants in thirty days. Dilwar had started his apprenticeship under him as a mahout in Bengbari around 1962: he recalled hearing artillery fire during the China war toward the end of that year, and tying the elephants and taking them to another camp. He talked about the Monpas who had fled from the hills, bartering their gold for rice, and bathing en masse in the river, men and women together.

They had fed them at the elephant camp, as they did the fleeing Indian soldiers once the orders came from above.

His family had owned elephants earlier. He had shot a tiger from atop an elephant while a teenager still in school; instead of the cash reward he asked for a gun licence, which he later got on the day the present DC office opened, from the 'gun clerk'. He talked about rhinos appearing in the sapori or riverbank areas till the mid 1970s, and people killing deer in the Foothills area and bringing them out after paying 45 rupees at the forest gate. Killing of rhinos and elephants was prohibited from earlier, but deer and other animals were allowed to be shot, then from 1966 it started getting a bit strict, and from 1971 it wasn't allowed at all, though it still went on quietly. There was a ranger who had taken Dilwar's elephant for a month and shot more than fifty deer (and whose staff later seized his gun for killing a deer, but he was set free and given compensation). The barking or xogora and spotted deer were tastiest, but those killed in the month of phagun (February–March) were sour because of the sour things the deer ate then.

There was a Kachari boy from Udalguri, the son of a man he knew, who was with the 'extremists'. His name was Krishna Brahma, and he had once taken Dilwar to a gun-making camp up the Mansiri river (east of the Belsiri river) and above some pungs or salt licks in the Arunachal foothills where pipe guns and bombs were being made. The boy then joined the insurgent group fighting for an independent Bodoland, and Dilwar never went back there again: 'if there was an operation they would have said I had told the security forces,' he said.

They would catch loggers sometime in the forest and let them go after fining them, or chase them off, as they had some authority working in the government mahals, and once he and a Mising mahout caught two Nepalis and an Assamese man for poisoning a few hundred fish at a place inside the Nameri sanctuary (maybe with bleaching powder, or with poisonous herbs) and then smoking them on a big log chang. The places in the foothills with trees, boulders and streams, places like Dopdopi above Rangapara, were treacherous: even the army thought twice before undertaking operations there.

He had caught about eighty-five elephants in all from 1962 till the mahal system was stopped in 1980. Some catches he still remembered vividly, like the young tusker or datal he had caught with a fifteen-year-old female elephant near Dipota. The night before, the phandis had done a puja, both Hindus and Muslims. After that they drank quite a bit in order to keep their courage up. It was a moonlit night and people were fishing on the Dipota river. The tusker was grazing nearby in a torani. It was in the water feeding on the plants when Dilwar went and lassoed him with a jute rope (which the phandis made themselves), choked him and brought him down, his elephant bracing herself against a tree. Then he loosened the lasso a bit and allowed the tusker to rise up, before bringing it home, much to the amazement of the villagers. That male was almost 8 feet at the shoulder, while the female elephant he was on was 7.2 feet—shorter than the required 7.5 feet.

Grown elephants caught this way were sandwiched between two tame or kunki elephants, and tied to one, with the other elephants gradually moving away as the newcomer got tamer. He had mostly caught elephants by the older method of kheda shikar. Dilwar said older elephants were easier to train as they understood beatings. These were delivered with canes, on the face near the ears. They were abused with the filthiest swear words—that was part of getting the psychological edge over the elephant. He was full of information about the mammals: there were four types of male elephants, and three type of female elephants. When in arousal the male would accompany and guard the female, even attack her. The period of gestation was between eighteen to twenty-three months, depending on whether it was a female or male. If an elephant ate too much salt followed by paddy and earth, he said, there would be internal swelling and blockage and it would die (as they don't have separate stomach components the way ruminating animals such as cows, goats and buffalos do).

Then there was the old mahal system, which his uncle and Karuna had told Abhijit about. Dilwar gave him details about how it had been organized. Each stakeholder in the mahal usually had two elephants, one a worker and the other for shikar, and eight people, with one mahout and one phandi for shikar, and three people each (including ghasis for cutting grass) to take care of each elephant. There were thirty-two mahals where an average of thirty elephants were caught, usually from November 1 to March 15; then there was shikar in the rainy season too—so that would be about a thousand elephants caught each season, but all that ended from 1979–80.

Abhijit hadn't mentioned Pradip Deka and Karuna till

then, but when he did, Dilwar's face lit up, and he described how Deka would get a carton of whisky bottles from an army colonel with just a word. Talking about those two old characters led him to comment on how there were no original forests left in Assam, only a few patches up in Arunachal Pradesh. Dilwar said the things he had seen and done in his life were from *puroni kal*, the old days, and *puroni kal aru nai*, or, the old days were no more. He said no one from today's age would be as 'fulfil' as he had been. A life in the wild, with wild animals; it would have made for a different kind of man, something still evident in his physique and bearing and direct gaze. Later, coming back to Tezpur, Abhijit would feel that the past was close enough to be touched: but it was all gone.

One of Dilwar's sons came and sat in the shop, and Dilwar walked Abhijit to their original house nearby, to show him some horns. He had left that house after his wife, who was an Adivasi woman, had been ill treated by his family members. But the wild buffalo horns he had promised to show had been put away, one of his sisters said, because people kept coming to see them (or maybe they had been sold); the elephant tusks had been sold long back with the permission of the forest department and the deer horns distributed to the forest department. 'Look at the pucca houses of my relatives, and my own bamboo and tin shack,' he said as they walked back to his shop. 'But wherever I go people like me, because I'm a straightforward person.'

As Abhijit left there were a couple of boys playing carrom by the roadside in the bright sunlight. Dilwar's stories filled his thoughts on the way back. Such knowledge simply allowed to go to waste! He had talked about the Nyishi hunters from Arunachal who would have poison (possibly aconite) inside their bamboo arrow holders, they would dip an arrow in the poison and then let it fly. All that was needed was a scratch, and the hunter would track the animal down as it died fifteen to thirty minutes later. Then there was the type of bamboo whose one sunga or cylinder between joints would hold up to 16 litres of water. They would cook rice, curries, and tea in *opoita bahor sunga* while in the jungle, for convenience and for the taste it imparted.

When he had made his 'fulfil' comment, he also said it was during the prime of his youth, and it had all been a great adventure, like the time they went looking for a lost elephant in the jungles (there was even one which was taken away by the insurgents) and happened to stray into Bhutan where they were detained by the Bhutanese forest guards. Later two deer were shot down in Assam and brought up to a camp near a rum factory by a river and they had a party with drinks and deer meat. Then they were given Bhutanese currency and let off. Dilwar said they gave the money to the forest ranger and that was the last they heard of it.

That evening Abhijit ended up having a solitary dinner at a gaudy new hotel that had a feel of spurious authenticity, like the doorman in his dhoti and gamusa, while the diners, people trying to climb up from their rural roots, were already obese and opinionated about modern life. Or it may have been that Dilwar's elegy for a vanished world was playing in Abhijit's mind.

The young mouzadar was to later tell him: 'Dilwar is a good man, but after he drinks no one can stand to be around him on account of his filthy abuses.' Abhijit found that surprising to hear, but then again, not really so. Being in the wild would give a man a different sense of his self: was this why Dilwar had chosen to marry outside his community? Had it been the drinking that had caused him to leave his old house? And were the abuses the same he had once used on the elephants he had tamed?

In the course of his research for the elephant story Abhijit also met a forest officer at his official residence in Tezpur, an old house on top of a hill overlooking the Brahmaputra river. The place had a rundown air about it exacerbated by the monsoon dampness. Abhijit found the officer at his desk in his study, writing a speech for the chief minister for some wildlife-related event. He read out a bit of the piece, with its flowery abstraction of formal Assamese speech. He had grown up in Gohpur on a tea estate bordering the now disappeared reserve forest, and as a botany student in Tezpur's Darrang College he recalled trips to Bhalukpung on the Assam–Arunachal border and going along *lunglungia bat* or shaded paths to collect specimens no longer present there. He had joined the Forest Department in 1986. He drew for Abhijit a diagram to explain how encroachment took place in the Biswanath reserve forest in 1995, a planned strategy that saw thousands of settlers claiming the land: the undergrowth was cleared at night, then plastic sheets would be raised for shelter. The trees from the interior parts were felled first. His account of how the people had settled matched what Abhijit had been told by the beat officer Pegu.

But he also pointed out how before that, boys from the

'organization' who had surrendered to the army or police, and then started bossing people around, were the ones who had started cutting trees all over the state and trucking them to towns and cities and to train stations. The officer mentioned the lack of forest staff, and the diversion of their duties toward policing. He had a childhood memory of a khura—a younger brother of his father—coming back from hunting on an elephant with deer, and dropping the carcass on the ground with a thump. 'It was a sokh,' he said, using the Assamese pronunciation of a Hindi word: shauk. A recent wild elephant census in Assam had put their numbers at around 5500, the officer said, adding that those figures seemed highly inflated to him.

Leaving his office, Abhijit remembered Dilwar phandi telling him about the place called Hatipilkhana (where Abhijit's father would later get the department jeep fixed at a garage), where elephants were earlier kept when Tezpur was a small settlement, and where his family had land which was sold at 18 rupees a bigha. He went down to the Ganesh ghat after meeting the forest officer. The river was a sullen brown under a grey sky, clumps of vegetation floating past, mud and rocks on the bank, the hills and the bridge faint on the horizon, a terrifying vastness. Abhijit tried to imagine how it would have been two or three centuries ago: a boat approaching, forests on the banks (no roads then), the wilderness, the heat, wild animals. And immense herds of elephants, stomping through the forests.

People feel nostalgia for what they have known, for their memories of what they have known. Abhijit's nostalgia would be different from say what Karuna, or Dilwar Saikia, with their memories, would feel: if they chose to feel that way. And what of the elephants? Were there any among those long-lived creatures that remembered the forests of yesteryear? Did they somehow communicate that with the younger members of their herds, the way the phandi had told Abhijit of the old days?

One of Dilwar's comments, about there being no original forests left in Assam, Abhijit understood fully only later, after talking with his uncle about it. Elephants are large animals which require vast areas to wander—this allows areas they feed in to regenerate. However, when herds are confined to smaller patches of forest, regeneration isn't complete, and over time the nature of the forest itself changes, and not for the better.

Dilwar Saikia had given Abhijit good background material for his article on elephants, and something even more valuable. 'Go to Udalguri and find Krishna Brahma,' the old phandi said, mentioning the insurgent's name when Abhijit had asked Dilwar about his father's death. 'Talk to him. He would have been moving around the Foothills area when your father was at the Gabharu beat office.'

An Excursion Gone Wrong

A week later he was back in an auto spluttering along the Foothills road on a clear morning. He saw the kutcha road down which he had gone with the teacher Dilip Basumatary, and felt a pang of nostalgia for the night he had spent in the village. At Kamengbari he was in luck, for one of old man Nana's relatives had come from Rupa—via the longer Bhalukpung–Tezpur route, as the shorter road via Khelong to Doimara through the Eaglenest Sanctuary had been broken in places by landslips—the previous day and was about to leave for Doimara, and Abhijit was able to hitch a ride with him. It was just a 12 km stretch, but these were the hills and there were only patches of crumbling road present. The small Maruti car moved cautiously through the mud and the gravel, the high, green mountains of the Kameng region suddenly opening up ahead of them at turnings.

As they came down an incline, the tyres crunching on the gravel, Abhijit saw to his left a small valley, with a scattering of houses, some seemingly abandoned, which the person driving told him had belonged to a saw mill, now closed down following the Supreme Court's ruling in 1996 on logging in the North East. Doimara was just a few dusty wood-plank houses, a half-built culvert before the turn off to the scruffy little settlement, where there was one small shop and two cemented structures. A company of Arunachal police was there playing cards in the shade, and further ahead the old inspection bungalow, now apparently occupied by a Sherdukpen 'nobleman'. Abhijit sat on a bench outside the shop with the man he'd taken a lift from. The shop owner's son told Abhijit it was a 'remote area', that was why there was nothing there.

But Abhijit liked it. It felt like some deserted town in a cowboy Western (there were cans of strong beer and quarter bottles of a cheap whisky on a shelf in the shop). His father would no doubt have visited it when the saw mill was operational. But these people didn't know anything about Khagen Saikia. They spoke to Abhijit as someone who knew old man Nana and Nyima. The shop owner's son and the man who had given Abhijit a lift told him how they had recently caught a lot of fish in the nearby river after damning it with stones and running a current into the water from a diesel generator. In the end, feeling restless, Abhijit decided to go for a walk along the road. There was apparently an old bridge about 2 km ahead over the river. The men told him it was safe as long as he went to the bridge and came back, but to be watchful, as sometime there were boys from the insurgent group wandering about the hills.

He set off along the straight, narrow road beside which the scrub rose up high, the gravel crunching under his shoes. The sun beat down on him, but the sight of the hills rising up around him lifted his heart. The drone of insects filled the air. Today he had come prepared: on his shoulder was a backpack with a bottle of water, a towel, soap, a packet of biscuits and a book. They had told him to be careful, but this was up in the hills, and after the night in the Bodo village he found a new confidence in himself. The road curved slightly around a hill, and then turned left toward the bridge.

Here and there through a break in the vegetation he could see down below to his left the Belsiri river flowing along its stony bed. The bridge was an old, rusted iron structure with half-rotted timbers, some of which had been ripped out, and under it was a large pool of water from the river which came rushing down through huge boulders. A dirt track went down beside the bridge and then climbed up, and Abhijit saw that vehicles went that way instead of taking the bridge; a rough dam of large stones reduced the water at the crossing point, and it was behind this that the pool had formed, under the bridge. He drank some water, topped up the bottle from the pool, and sat on a rock under the shade of the bridge. Nearby, on a patch of damp sand, were several butterflies in varied colours. Below the weathered cement support of the bridge was evidence of a picnic: the blackened remnants of a fire, used paper plates and crushed plastic glasses, empty packets of meat masala, and the shards from a liquor bottle that had been smashed on the rocks: someone's idea of fun.

The sight of the broken bottle disturbed him—it reminded him of the children he had met on the Foothills road; solitude seemed impossible to find. He decided to look for a more deserted spot, and started walking over the boulders beside the river. It wasn't easy work, as at some places the bank of the river shrunk and the edges rose up so that he had to climb over the boulders, the lower edges of some of them slippery with moss. About twenty minutes later, however, he caught sight of the river opening up ahead; a few more minutes, and he found himself on a sandy strip beside a clear pool. Around him the mountains rose up, bamboo and wild banana trees blanketing their sides. The road above couldn't be seen from there.

He took off his clothes and waded into the shallow end in his underpants; as the water rose, he gasped in shock at how cold it was. Standing in chest-deep water, with the sound of that water flowing through the rocks, he felt within him a quiet elation, a feeling of having arrived. Watching the water sluicing down a large rock ahead of him and making a pool by another rock and then foaming down toward him, Abhijit was reminded of looking into the flames or embers of a wood fire, eternal movement, hypnotic. He stood in the sun with his eyes closed, then went back to where he had placed the soap and towel on a rock and proceeded to have a bath. Later, after draping his wet underpants on a boulder to dry, his shoes and socks beside it, he ate a few biscuits and drank some water, then sat down on the sand, leaning against a warm rock as he read his book. The exploits of the lonely British colonial officer in the Lushai Hills soon made him drowsy, and he put the book aside and closed his eyes.

He must have slept for a while, for when he opened his eyes the sun had slanted to the west and the pool was in the shadows. The mirrored surface of the pool, the sound of the running water: how peaceful it was. He thought of his father at the camp that night, singing, firelight on his face. The camp was gone, but the Belsiri—of which this channel was the main tributary—still flowed. He felt an itch, and when he sat up and checked, saw small red bites below his pants on his ankles and bare feet. It was the dim dam fly, which nested in human or animal excreta, and caused terrible itching with its bites. He had forgotten his insect repellent.

That was when he saw them. Two boys sitting on the rocks on the other side, under the overgrown ledge. One of them raised a hand. He froze, for though they were dressed ordinarily enough in pants and dark t-shirts, he saw they had guns on their laps. They had the dusky tribal features of rural Bodo boys. The other boy yelled out something, and Abhijit raised a hand in reply. Then the two of them stood up. They looked muscular and fit. One went up the river and the other went down, and Abhijit was confused for a moment, till he saw them jumping across the rocks where the river narrowed. They were coming for him.

Apart from the initial shock, he was surprised to find himself calm and breathing regularly. They were young, he saw, when they reached him from either side, barely out of their teens, their hair was shaggy and they had broad flat noses, carrying what looked like AK rifles casually in one hand. They looked him up and down. One of them asked, in rough Assamese, what have you come here to do? He understood their puzzlement, for who in their right mind would come there alone? He even saw the humour in it. '*Phuribo ahisu*,' he said, I've come visiting. The other boy frowned, and Abhijit realized they wouldn't share his sense of irony.

They looked into his backpack, and leafed through the book, then told him he was to come with them. He nodded. Was this what he had come looking for? He asked if he could put on his underpants and shoes. They told him to hurry up and they turned around. As he got dressed, he wondered what would happen if he made a run for it: if he tried to scramble over the earth and stones of the near ledge and run into the jungle. They would probably shoot him even before he hauled himself over the ledge, or, even if he got away, the two of them would catch up with him and shoot him. Still, it was not so much the fear of death as the thought of what lay on the other side—the auto ride back to Missamari, his grandmother's old house, the life he had abandoned in Delhi—that prompted him to go along.

They went up along the river, one boy ahead and one boy behind him, and crossed the river at a point where it narrowed. When he lost his balance stepping down from a boulder and almost fell into the water, the boy behind him leapt forward and held him with one strong hand. They crossed and went straight up into the jungle. The boy in front, the one who'd spoken to him first, slung the AK rifle on his shoulder and unsheathed the dao hanging at his waist to chop and slash at the creepers and vegetation that rose up around the trees. Uphill they went, and by the time they reached the deserted kutcha road, Abhijit was sweating and gasping for breath. They quickly crossed the road and kept going up the steep hill through the jungle, Abhijit's shoes kept slipping on the damp loose soil, till they reached the high crest of the hill. They stopped and rested under the trees, a gentle breeze blowing through them, and the humps of the other hills, green and unpopulated, could be seen, gradually descending down into the hazy plains. Abhijit took off his backpack and drank some water from his bottle. The two boys refused the water when he offered it to them; they didn't look tired at all.

They waited there for a few hours, sitting on the damp ground till it grew dark. When Abhijit took out his phone, one of the boys took it from him, switched it off, and put it in his own pocket. He removed a leech from inside his socks; the insect bites were itching now but he forced himself to ignore them. The boys sat quietly, watchful, getting up from time to time to look down either side of the mountain. He asked them where they were taking him but there was no response. When it was dark, they started moving down the other side of the hill. They went slowly at first, and then at a steadier pace as some sort of narrow path seemed to open up in the jungle. He remembered the police commandos he had seen at Gulai Centre, and a sudden thought struck him: was there an operation on, and were these two trying to get away? In the darkness, stumbling over tree roots and stones, he willed himself to keep calm.

For some time there had been the sound of flowing water, then the trail suddenly ended and they were out into the open: in the starlight Abhijit could see the churning white of a river flowing along its rocky bed and the dark bulk of the mountains beyond it. They were moving toward the west, that much he could make out. The boys whispered among themselves for a while, then holding him by each hand they walked him to the water's edge, their AK rifles in their other hand with the barrels up. They splashed into the water and he could feel the cold water getting into his socks and up his pants even as his feet tried to get a grip on the slippery rocks. The water quickly rose up to their hips, then receded, and they were across. The boys drank from the river and washed their faces, and Abhijit did the same. Now they walked up the river, along its banks, and it was back to the same balancing and climbing on rocks and boulders, this time in the dim starlight with pants that were soaked. He felt a grudging admiration for the boys' toughness; within himself he felt a great weariness, though mixed with something like happiness.

At one point the boy in the lead, the first one to have spoken to Abhijit, stopped. He unsheathed his dao and looked around, then climbed up onto the narrow ledge and entered a rough path in the jungle, Abhijit and the second boy following him. The path, if it could be called that, was choked with undergrowth in parts, and the boy hacked furiously with his machete. They went roughly parallel to the river for some distance, before turning away from it and going up a steep slope. Here the earth was muddy, and as his shoes sunk into the muck, he felt, for the first time, irritation at their continuous march.

They crested the hill and then started going down. Abhijit slipped and fell twice, and the boys must have felt his annoyance as well, for they told him they were nearly there. After a while the boy in front stopped near a large, towering tree, plucked a leaf from a shrub, and raised it to his lips to make a call of sorts, which was answered seemingly from somewhere above. As they crossed the tree Abhijit looked up. He thought he saw something shifting in its lower branches. Presently they came to a small clearing in the jungle where amid the tree trunks were three tent-like shapes in the dark, and a couple of figures sitting around a smoking fire. He was made to sit on a fallen log, and as he listened to the two boys talking softly to the others, from time to time a small flicker of flame lifted from the smoking embers, and he could see the other tanned, slant-eyed faces regarding him impassively, like actors in some ancient drama. There was a tall youth sitting in the middle; he seemed to be the one with authority there. At last he asked Abhijit his name, in surprisingly good Assamese, and then said, 'You'll have to stay with us here for some time. We'll talk tomorrow. You must be tired, eat some rice and go to sleep.'

Abhijit was too exhausted to even think. He washed up from a bucket of water, ate some cold rice and tough meat given to him on a stainless steel plate, took off his shoes, and crawled into the corner of one of the 'tents'—rough wood planks raised up on stout tree branches, with a tarpaulin sheet draped on bamboo poles—where after tossing and turning for a while (he used his backpack as a pillow) he fell asleep. He slept deeply. When he woke, the shelter was lit with the soft glow of the sun coming in through the blue tarpaulin sheet. For the first time he felt worried, a deep, hollow, sick feeling, and he closed his eyes and thought with regret of the bed in the musty-smelling room in his grandmother's house.

At last he forced himself to open his eyes and sit up. There were canvas backpacks and dirty blankets tied into bundles strewn about on the planks. From outside came the soft murmur of voices. His whole body was stiff. He made his way out of the shelter and stood barefoot before it and looked around. The clearing, which had three tents or shelters, and a place to sit around the small fire, was covered from above by the tree tops. On one side a hillock rose up, and there, high up on two separate rocks, sat two guards with automatic rifles in hand, sentries on lookout over the camp. There were boys moving about here and there, their rifles slung on their shoulders, dressed in a motley assortment of clothes. Near the fire sat the youth whom Abhijit thought of as the leader; he beckoned, and Abhijit went over. The fire burnt low, the youth was boiling water in a small pot on it. Abhijit sat on the same log as the previous night.

'Our boys were doing some patrolling yesterday,' the leader said to him. 'What were you doing there beside the river?'

He repeated what he had told the boys: he had come there visiting. The leader frowned, and said very few people came there, especially alone. What was his business? Abhijit thought for a moment, and then, as briefly as he could, told him about his father, and how he had died in the reserve forest, and how he himself had returned home. The leader listened without interrupting, just asking him for his father's name at the end. When Abhijit told him, he thought he saw a flicker of recognition in the other man's eyes. He told Abhijit that he was Rankhw, the commander of the unit. Then he shouted out to one of the boys, who had been chopping wood with an axe but who dropped it and came running. It turned out to be the first boy who'd spoken to Abhijit the previous day. The commander told him, in Assamese, that he was to take Abhijit to a nearby stream for him to wash up.

Rankhw stood up, and said with a smile, 'Come back and have some tea.'

He was good looking and relaxed, with short cropped hair, and Abhijit found himself trusting the commander. The two boys from the previous day took him down the slope from behind the camp, and soon they came upon a small mountain stream where he managed to have a bath—the boys gave him his towel and even a pair of shorts and an old t-shirt, so he could wash his trousers and shirt in the stream. When they returned, the two boys—the taller one, who had led the previous day, was Borai, the other, short with a round face, was Phanjit—showed him where to hang his clothes to dry, on a rope strung up between two trees. He noticed three solar panels charging phones outside the shelters.

Rankhw called him for tea—black tea without milk or sugar in steel glasses—and as Abhijit drank the commander looked at his legs pockmarked with red weals and asked if they were caused by leeches and dim dam flies. When Abhijit said yes, Rankhw nodded, and said he would give him something for the bites. Strangely, Abhijit felt relaxed and not threatened in any way, even as Rankhw explained again that he would have to be with them for a couple of days. That was before the second-in-command walked up, a stocky youth dressed in black, with a fleshy face, his hair tied into a ponytail.

Laughing, he put the barrel of his AK on Abhijit's forehead and made a firing sound, to the amusement of some of them. Rankhw didn't laugh though, Abhijit noticed. His name was Thulunga, Abhijit would later find out, and he made it clear that he considered their captive to be a 'spy' and an 'Indian agent', and that it was better to execute him straight away. Rankhw shook his head and barked something in reply. Thulunga backed off, muttering to himself. A while later, Rankhw handed Abhijit a small bottle of citronella oil, and asked him to apply it on his arms and legs. Then he said, 'As long as you are here, no one will harm you. You are our guest. But if you try to escape, you'll be shot straight away, because we're watching you. Understood?'

Abhijit didn't say a word, just nodded.

Among the Insurgents

They kept Abhijit for six nights before letting him go. He estimated there were in all twelve members in the camp, including Rankhw and Thulunga, the top two, and Borai and Phanjit, the two who had picked him up. There were others who would show up at the camp in twos or threes, sentries he imagined, as well as a few who left and only turned up two or three days later. But the four boys whose names he picked up first were the ones he was to grow the most familiar with.

Borai and Phanjit, the lanky one and the round-faced one as he came to think of them, were always near him, even sleeping in the same shelter as him. Phanjit expressed incredulity at how Abhijit had landed up with them. '*Ki manuh re toi?*' he would ask shaking his head, 'What sort of a person are you?' And Abhijit would look down at the ground and smile: it seemed to him a very apt question. That attitude, and the general relaxed atmosphere of the camp, gave his captivity a surreal feel. He was treated well (except of course by Thulunga), and sometimes he could almost imagine it being a camping trip in the jungle.

His two immediate captors were, similar to the rest of the boys, from a rural background: they both came from farming families in the foothills above the town of Biswanath Chariali, to the east of Tezpur. Like Amlaibari, the village Abhijit had spent the night in, it was cut off from the outside world, and he had the feeling that part of why they had joined the group was because there was nothing to do at home, no other avenues for them. They had a hard life, they told him, and he understood how *this* life, even with the chance of sudden death, could look inviting to them. Borai was steady and measured in everything he did, but round-faced Phanjit, whom Abhijit had found surly on that first day, was mercurial, and sang from time to time: Hindi film songs, Bodo love songs. 'When all this is over,' he told Abhijit one afternoon, as they sat near the stream, 'I'll have money with me, and I'll produce a Bodo video film. This fellow can be the hero,' he said, pointing at Borai, who grinned and threw a stick at him.

Abhijit asked him what the story would be, and Phanjit said it would be something out of their lives—living in the jungles, being chased by the army and police, while back in the village a girl waited faithfully for her love, and in the end everything would work out well. It was touching, and for some reason Abhijit suddenly felt very afraid for these young boys.

A large part of his good treatment, he understood, was because of Rankhw. That first day at the camp, after a lunch of rice and cold fried deer meat, Abhijit had sat against a tree, reading his book on early British administrators in the North East, when the commander had sat down before him, and gestured for the book. Abhijit watched as he looked at the cover, read the back-cover text, and leafed through the book. Finally he had said, much to Abhijit's surprise, 'If the British had stayed on, maybe we Bodo people would have been in a better condition.' The commander was, compared to the rest of the boys, an educated man. He told Abhijit that he had graduated in political science from a Shillong college before joining the 'movement', by which he meant the one for an independent or sovereign Bodoland.

Rankhw kept a sharp eye on the running of the camp, what supplies were being used, who went out on sentry duty. The deer meat, Abhijit found out, came from a barking deer shot lower down in the jungle one night by one of the boys who was a good hunter; the meat would last them for days. On the second or third day, in the evening, two young boys appeared at the camp carrying rucksacks: Abhijit saw some boys helping them unload packets of rice and dal, biscuits, potatoes and soap from the packs. One of them kept looking at Abhijit, and it was only later at night, sitting around the smoking fire (the flames weren't allowed to go high), that he remembered who the boy was: one of the group of five or six he had seen while walking up from Kamengbari for the first time. How long ago that seemed now!

It was the same day Abhijit had asked Rankhw what they planned to do with him. He didn't have any money, he said, in case they were planning to ask for ransom, and there was only his grandmother and an old uncle in Tezpur. The commander smiled, and said they had to check out his story. Over the next two days they talked frequently. The commander seemed to welcome it, maybe seeing it as a chance to put forth his views. He told Abhijit that he was one of the earlier cadres, trained in the foothills of Bhutan above Udalguri, and that their chief, Ringkhang, had been trained before that in Bangladesh. He was now in the camps in northern Myanmar.

'Why do you want independence?' Abhijit asked him at one point. 'Is it even possible?'

'See, the thing is like this,' Rankhw replied, 'I don't hate the Assamese, or Bengalis, or Muslims. I had friends from those communities while growing up in Kokrajhar. But without full control over our own land, which Delhi and Guwahati don't want to allow, we will continue to be marginalised. Besides, we are the original inhabitants of the land, the sons of the soil. Possible or not we must fight, we must struggle.'

It was only when Abhijit asked him about the western group that had fought for statehood, and then settled for a governing council within Assam, that Rankhw showed a flash of anger. The other group had compromised, he said, out of weakness, out of a lust for power, and they couldn't help the Bodo people.

Pushing his luck, he asked Rankhw if they with their limited numbers could really fight the army and the police. He had expected Rankhw to get angry, but the commander with a far-away look in his eyes only said, 'I can't turn back on this road I'm walking. I will probably meet my end somewhere in these jungles.' There seemed a deep sadness in him then, and Abhijit was at a loss for words. He told Rankhw about his father, how he had died, how Abhijit had visited him before the incident and the night-time trip to the Foothills camp. The commander listened intently.

'They said the insurgents found him in the forest that day and shot him,' Abhijit said. 'Is it true?'

'I can't say,' Rankhw replied, 'You're talking about a long time ago, when I was just a child.'

Abhijit remembered something then, and asked if the Forest IB or inspection bungalow at Sopai was still there. Rankhw appeared surprised that he knew about the place: it was in ruins now, he said, the old IB to the west of Kamengbari, and the other IB further west of that one, at Jhingabil, a two-storied wooden structure from the days of the British, had been burnt down following an attempt by the forest department to evict the new settlers, maybe some fifteen years ago. Later that day he saw Rankhw looking thoughtful and writing on a piece of paper.

Abhijit also asked him how most of the vast reserve forest down below had disappeared, the forest he had seen as a boy with his father. Here the commander turned philosophical, and said that trees could be grown again, but what was more important for their cause was that the Bodo people controlled their own land themselves, directly. It was their land, he said, which the British had declared as reserve forests without asking them, and cleared the forest in other areas to set up their tea gardens. 'This Belsiri river is named after a Bodo queen from long ago,' he told Abhijit, 'and further west the Dhansiri river, that is named after one of our queens too.'

If Rankhw was thoughtful and polite, his second-in-command Thulunga was the exact opposite. He would look at Abhijit with a fixed stare, and then mutter a few words, at which his hangers-on would laugh. 'Oi, you dog that doesn't get to eat,' he said once, in rough Assamese, 'once that deer meat is finished I'll do halal on you and cut you up and cook you.' One of the boys found this very funny, while for the rest of the day Abhijit buried his head in his book behind a tree or in the shelter, unable to read though with the fear and anger coursing through him. On the morning of the day before they had to flee the camp, Thulunga picked up an axe and put its edge under Abhijit's chin, turned his head up and said something vicious in their language. Rankhw had hinted that they would release him soon, however with Thulunga around it felt like nothing could be taken for granted.

The sun was out every day, but under the shade of the trees it wasn't too hot. Abhijit settled into a kind of rhythm: sleeping, reading, going to the stream, eating. There was just rice, boiled dal and potatoes, with the dried or fried deer meat, and black tea with biscuits, but he had never been a big eater so he was able to get by. In spite of Thulunga, he started to feel a sympathy for these simple boys, and as he sat near Borai and Phanjit and they cleaned their AKs one at a time, he felt something of a bond with them. They even started teaching him a few Bodo words.

He asked Borai what '*jwngni mansia homgwn*' meant, the words the children had taunted him with on the Foothills road, and the cadre solemnly informed him that the phrase meant 'our people will catch you.'

On the fifth day it started raining from early in the morning. He sheltered under the plastic sheet strung up from the tree branches, but it was crowded with the other boys, and Thulunga was there too, looking at him and passing comments, and in the end he crawled back into the shelter with his book. The inside of the shelter was stuffy and smelt of sweat, and one of his black moods descended on him then, brought on by the rain, by Thulunga, by his dirty clothes, by the wood planks on which he lay. He had been abandoned by his father, then his mother, and he would most probably die here in the jungle and be buried in some unmarked hole. Self pity washed over him. In a while he fell asleep.

He was woken by someone tugging his feet, and when he opened his eyes he saw Phanjit's round face inside the shelter: 'Get your bag and come out! We have to move!'

Abhijit stumbled out with his backpack into the rain and put on his shoes. Around him the boys were rushing about, stuffing things into backpacks and air bags, rolling up the tarpaulin sheets. Rankhw and Thulunga were talking to an animated sentry, and he heard a low, steady *tat-tat-tat* from somewhere. Then he understood, and suddenly his legs felt weak: the security forces were coming! Things were a blur after that. They left the camp in a single file, himself between Borai and Phanjit, who had their AKs in their hands and cocked.

The group went uphill, then downhill, along a stream, and then uphill again. They trekked the whole day, with the occasional water break. All sense of direction deserted Abhijit as he slipped, stumbled and fell on the rough, slippery tracks. There was very little conversation, and he could sense the fear among the boys too. At dusk they halted on a high ridge. His limbs were sore and he was terribly hungry. Dinner was a handful of uncooked rice and some cold meat. He chewed on the hard grains like the others and washed it down with a little water. Rankhw was deep in conversation with the sentries, and when Abhijit approached him, he ignored him. Feeling hurt, he went and sat alone. Just before it got dark Thulunga and a few others, who were part of the second group, arrived. Spotting Abhijit he walked up to him, started abusing him, and then swung the butt of his rifle at Abhijit's face, striking him on the cheekbone. He slumped to the ground, anticipating more blows, but Thulunga walked off and sat with Rankhw and the others. When he sat up, he saw Thulunga talking to Rankhw, with the latter looking at him.

Borai made a small shelter for the three of them with branches and a plastic sheet, and gave him another plastic sheet which he managed to wrap around himself as he lay on the ground. The rain had stopped, and insects chirped in the night. He was too tired to worry about leeches or snakes and fell asleep. In the middle of the night he was woken by a noise, and poking his head out from the sheet he heard a crashing, trampling sound come closer through the jungle. For one confused moment he thought it might be an armoured vehicle rolling up the slope, till he heard an elephant cry out. It was a herd passing close by, and he held his breath till they had passed. Phanjit, who was near him, said, 'Sleep, they won't bother us. They can smell our guns, and they stay away from us.'

So he went back to sleep, only to be woken, from a strange dream of British military officers cooking breakfast in the jungle, by someone shaking him. He lifted his head out of the sheet, and in the damp, dark early morning saw Rankhw squatting beside him, a finger to his lips. The commander asked him to get ready quickly and quietly. Five minutes later Abhijit, Rankhw, Borai, Phanjit, and another boy were going down the hillside, following the tracks of the elephant herd. The rest of the boys, apart from two sentries, were asleep. It was early, but already humid, and sweat soon ran down Abhijit's grimy skin. Where were they headed? About thirty minutes later they stopped on a narrow ledge above a stream, and Rankhw told him the boy would take Abhijit down to the plains and on to the Foothills road by a sideways route. Saying so, he handed back Abhijit's phone and wallet.

He was overcome with emotion then, and somehow managed to thank Rankhw for saving his life. The commander smiled and led him away from the others. Then he said, 'We might have killed you. Thulunga wanted to finish you off yesterday, he said you were a spy. I had your story checked. It seems okay. But I'm letting you go because of your father. One of our boys told me a story about him. Khagen Saikia, beat officer at Gabharu. He was from a village near Amlaibari, close to Kolamati gate. The boy's parents were from near Gohpur and had come in the late 1990s. But a few relatives had come before that to clear the jungle in the late 1980s. His aunt had come, with her husband and two children. The husband would drink and get violent. One night he attacked her with a dao and cut her arm, and she took her two small boys and walked all the way to Kolamati gate beat office. Your father was there, and he told his staff to take care of them. The next morning he took them to Tezpur civil hospital himself in his jeep. The boy told us this story about his aunt and then said, not all Assamese people are bad, some are like our brothers.'

Abhijit looked away from Rankhw, his eyes falling on but not really seeing the stream and the forest. The commander then showed him a folded envelope in a small plastic bag. 'You need to do something for me,' he said, 'There is a tea shop at Gulai Centre run by an old lady. Give her this letter. Do you know the Centre?' Abhijit said he did, and that he knew the tea shop too. He asked the commander how he could get in touch if needed, to which Rankhw replied that Abhijit was to come to the Dhankhana Centre and ask for a boy named Jaikhlong, an overground worker. He asked Abhijit to memorise a number, but on no account was he to reveal the name or number to anyone, especially the police or army.

Then it was time to leave, and they hurriedly said their goodbyes. The boy, who had handed over his weapon to Rankhw, led him across the stream. He looked back once as they entered the trees: the commander was standing at the edge of the forest, and he waved at Abhijit, who waved back. As he tried to keep up with the boy's swift pace uphill, he remembered waving at his father, years and years ago, the last time he had seen him alive. Though the going was tough, and Rankhw had told him to look out for army or AR patrols, he was free now, and a great exhilaration filled him as he thought about his father. Khagen Saikia still lived on, in people's memories and in stories, even in the rivers and the forest which remained.

It was almost midday when they came down from the hills. They had waded across the tributary of the Belsiri at one point, going west, then doubled back going south-east. They walked over uneven grassy land under a burning sun till they came to the rice fields, and a path and then another took them to a larger path running past huts and bamboo groves. The boy entered a house where they were given water to drink by a woman, her children and several others staring at Abhijit. Then a motorcycle turned up and he was asked to get on by the boy and sent on his way. The rider drove fast, and Abhijit had to hold on tight to avoid getting thrown off at the bumps. Before he realized it, they were rattling across the wood-plank bridge he had crossed with the teacher Dilip Basumatary, and then the shops at Gulai Centre came into view.

The rider, a young boy similar to the one who had brought him out of the forest, told him an auto would be coming from Kamengbari soon, and sped off, seemingly in a hurry. But Abhijit wasn't bothered, even by the handful of youth standing around their motorcycles before the hardware store. He had survived captivity, and Thulunga—he wasn't scared any more. He went into the dark, smoky interior of the tea shop, where the elderly lady was making tea. A few patrons sat quietly and patiently on the benches. Abhjit asked for tea and something to eat. A while later she gave him a glass of red tea, and a fried pitha on a piece of newspaper. He ate hungrily, and asked for another tea and one more pitha. The lady served him, and went out through the side door with some dishes. Abhijit followed her outside, handed her the envelope, telling her it was from Rankhw. She nodded and slipped it into the folds of her dokhona, like it was something she had done before.

He went back inside, and sat at the table, eating his sweet pitha and drinking his tea, thinking about Rankhw, his splendid bearing, and how he had remembered that good deed done by Abhijit's father. The auto would be along in a while, and he would be back home by early evening. There was no charge in his phone and he couldn't switch it on. The tea-shop lady had finished washing the dishes and come back inside. A girl slipped in through the side door. Abhijit looked at the slim figure in a blue skirt and white t-shirt, and realized it was Laimwn, the teacher Dilip Basumatary's niece. What was she doing here?

The girl chatted easily with the elderly lady, who then reached into her dokhona and took out the letter. She handed it over to the girl, and as they talked, she indicated with her chin toward Abhijit. Laimwn turned, and saw him for the first time, and froze. He looked into those wide-set eyes, and, as had been the case the first time, felt an agitation within himself. Then she turned, and slipped out through the side door. He drank the last of his tea and considered following her out. That first day he hadn't even spoken to her. Just then the auto from Kamengbari stopped on the road outside, and several people in the tea shop stood up. Abhijit paid the elderly lady and hurried out, managing to get a seat at the back.

He could look out from where he sat, and as the auto sputtered along the road which took a slight curve, he looked back. He could see behind the tea shop the slim figure of the girl silhouetted against the fields, her head bent over the letter which had been sent to her by Rankhw. Abhijit sat back and watched the huts and paddy fields and men on cycles recede, a strange storm building within his heart.

Hunters of Men

When he got back to his grandmother's house, Abhijit could see that his uncle had been very worried. Hiren Khura put his arms around him, and when he took them away Abhijit saw that he was shaking.

'I went to the SP's office. They said you had walked into the jungle above Doimara. Why had you gone there? I thought you had been killed by those people!'

So he sat down and told his uncle everything, about going up the river, being taken to the camp by the two boys, fleeing from the camp, being set free early in the morning, and how Rankhw had told him about his father before they had parted. His uncle listened and seemed to calm down. He told Abhijit that he was not to return to those places. It was hard for him to explain to his uncle why he was drawn to the area in the first place, as he couldn't locate the exact source of motivation within himself. Maybe he was just someone who preferred to live in the past than in the present.

'I hope people don't start taking an interest in you now,' his uncle said.

Abhijit shaved, had a bath, changed into clean clothes, ate, and then slept for more than a day, getting up from the bed two mornings after he had been set free. In that time, whenever he had woken a sort of panic gripped him, as images from those days flashed before his eyes: the two boys sitting on the other side of the river, Thulunga lifting up his chin with the cold axe blade, the chatter of the guns as the security forces advanced. Fear seeped into him, and he realized it would be within him for some time now, and change him as a person. It was a relief to sit with his grandmother, who knew nothing of what had happened, and listen to her tell him stories from the past: of how her father had taken the whole family on a bullock cart to watch *Joymoti*, the first Assamese film, made by Jyoti Prasad Agarwala, at Jonaki cinema hall in Tezpur town (the hall had been built by Agarwala too), how during the great earthquake of 1950 the ground had cracked open and shook for days with the distant roar of mountains crashing down into the rivers.

As Abhijit rested at home and tried to put the memory of the kidnapping behind him, he had time to think about the past, and his life till then. For the first time, he understood clearly how a deep nostalgia had been seeded in him by the disappearance of his father, and the disappearance of the wilderness he had known along with the disappearance of people like Pradip Deka, even the disappearance of a certain kind of Shillong from the old days, leading to an appreciation or an idea of loss, of things having passed, of effort being ultimately futile, even the feeling of having been lost in a city such as Delhi.

Some of the neighbours who knew about the incident asked him what had happened when they saw him outside the house. A few days after he had returned his uncle came and told Abhijit that there were two people looking for him. It was a bright hot day, and he had to shade his eyes as he went out to the veranda. They turned out to be Saurav Saha, the boy from the education NGO, and Padma Bora, the journalist. He didn't particularly care to meet the journalist then, but today Bora was polite. Abhijit invited them inside. They asked him about his ordeal, with Bora trying to ferret out details, and Abhijit recalled what his uncle had said, about people getting interested in him, so he kept things vague: he had been taken, mostly kept inside a makeshift tent, and then released. Maybe they had mistaken him for someone else, he told them. They left after a while, and as he saw them off till the gate, Saha told him that the NGO was expanding the scope of its operations and was looking for more people.

That evening there was a call from Gautam Pegu, the beat officer at the Gabharu office. He had heard about the incident from some people in the area, and asked how Abhijit was faring, then asked him to come over one day, preferably in the afternoon, as there was some work for which he needed Abhijit's help. Plus, he was Saikia sir's son after all, and the Gabharu staff would like to show their appreciation of Saikia sir by having his son over for a meal, in memory of his father. 'Our staff would be very happy,' he told Abhijit. 'So you'll *have* to come.'

The next morning Hiren Khura showed him Padma Bora's story in the Assamese newspaper about Abhijit's kidnapping, embellished with details which Abhijit had never mentioned. He was angry and a little scared at first, till it gradually came to him that there wasn't any real information in the story which someone like Rankhw might object to. In fact, the story portrayed the whole group as grim-faced, hardened insurgents.

His uncle had informed the SP's office about his return, and that day there was a call from the office asking him to come over for a while. So his uncle took Abhijit on the old scooter to the SP's office in the afternoon. The traffic had lessened at that hour on the road headed into town, and his uncle dropped him at the gate and drove off. The SP's office hadn't been renovated, and was still the old Assam-type structure it had always been, apart from the refurbished SP's room. Abhijit was taken there first where he was met by the SP Santanu Bora, a short man with a sprinkling of white in his close-cropped hair. The actual questioning took place in an ASP's room, and Abhijit took in the file-stuffed cupboards and glass-topped desk and realized it was like any other government office, only perhaps neater.

The ASP was a young Assamese Muslim youth, and he put Abhijit at ease with his gentle manner. He couldn't be vague as he had been with the journalist, so Abhijit told the officer everything, reasoning that whatever he said would only be in their files: as for operations, those were already going on in that area. In any case, the ASP was interested in names, and numbers: how many men, how many guns, what time did they sleep and wake? There were two police commandos in the room too, listening, one a young-looking tribal boy, the other a drier, older Assamese. The only thing Abhijit couldn't explain properly was why he had gone there in the first place. The ASP didn't make too much of it though, and cautioned him about entering those forests again. When they were done, he sent Abhijit back to the SP; the young tribal police commando accompanied him.

The SP went over some of the questions the ASP had asked, but then started to talk to him about his life, what he was doing. The police commando sat nearby listening quietly. Santanu Bora seemed like a gentle and friendly man, and Abhijit found himself telling the SP about his father and about his recent walk to Kamengbari. The SP listened, hardly interrupting except to question him on some detail, and at the end he didn't speak but just looked at Abhijit with a gentle smile.

Then he asked, 'Are you religious minded?'

'No, not really,' Abhijit said.

'Ok. There's something...ascetic about you...I feel. Anyway, this here is Haphang.'

The SP introduced him to the police commando, a Bodo boy, and told Abhijit to take his number and keep in touch with him.

'Any problem, if those people call you again, just inform Haphang, okay? He's heading our operations against the insurgents in the Foothills area.'

Abhijit said he would.

'You saw people hunting in those areas, when the forests were still standing,' the SP said. 'And now we have to hunt people there.'

Then it was over. Abhijit walked out, his shirt wet with perspiration and sticking uncomfortably to him. The one thing he hadn't told anyone was the letter he had delivered. As he walked in the midday heat past the Church field toward the bus depot to look for an auto, he thought about how the SP's last line reminded him of what his father had said on that last night over a quarter of a century ago: 'These forests will also be gone one day.'

That evening he tried to write about what he had been through, the kidnapping, meeting the policemen. Very soon though he could feel the inadequacy of words to capture the true essence of things. He understood how clichés were the only thing to fall back on, the complex situation of the different insurgent groups among the Bodos (and the linked deforestation and plight of the elephants) would, for example, in a Delhi newspaper be reduced to mere words. He gave up, and thought about the Bodo police commando: surely he would have experiences worth listening to?

Abhijit called him. He sounded open and friendly on the phone, and said they could meet when he was home from operations (his wife and children were in Tezpur). Abhijit went to his residence in the police reserve area of Tezpur one morning. There was a gate, a paved courtyard, an open garage covered with tin sheets, a medium-sized house with metal grilles on the ground-floor veranda, a ceiling made on the first floor. They sat on plastic chairs in the open garage. Abhijit noticed a black motorcycle nearby without numberplates: only later would he realize why. There were shoes and sandals on the outer steps of the house, and Haphang's young son came out looking for him. The police commando was in his early thirties (he had been in the police force ten years, he said), and was wearing jeans and a dark shirt. His hair was cut short, and there was faint stubble and a few pimples on his boyish-looking face. He was from Gohpur, to the east (and so was his wife), where his father had relocated to from Barpeta in lower Assam in the 1960s.

Haphang (actually a nickname, which meant "round face" in Bodo) had returned that morning from their camp north of Laudangi, in the foothills, and slightly to the west of Kamengbari. Abhijit asked him about the ASP who had been killed near Laudangi earlier that year while returning from an operation; Haphang said 'ASP sir' had made a mistake by returning by the same route, the road which went up from Dhekiajuli past Batasipur and Laudangi, a landscape like the Foothills area where the reserve forest had been replaced by settlements and paddy fields. There were three or four cadres, who after getting information about the police party told the nearby people to vacate the area (there was a school there). As the vehicles had slowed down at a depression on the dirt road, they had opened fire from inside a bamboo thicket at very close range. The ASP was survived by his wife, a four-year-old daughter and a son who had been born just ten days before the ambush.

He himself had returned from an operation just a few days back, Haphang said, as his wife came out and served them tea. The daughter, a few years older than the son, looked at them from the veranda. It was near Dhekiajuli, two boys who were part of a group of six recently returned from Myanmar and were starting to extort money from people (the other four were near Rangapara). The usual routes to Myanmar were via Tinsukia and Ledo or Dimapur and Mon. Arms were brought later by others, sometimes in hired cars. Haphang and two others had gone along with a source, a surrendered cadre who knew the two insurgents. They were in the same batch earlier. The policemen had gone dressed as labourers, with cycles and bags (to carry their AKs, everyone had a pistol tucked into their waist), one of them in shorts.

In a semi-jungle area ('where is the jungle left in those areas?' Haphang asked) when the two saw the source they got up and starting running. Haphang fired a burst through the paddy and the boys stopped. He yelled at them to surrender. Then he called the SP to ask what should be done with them (the earlier SP would apparently say, kill them). But this SP asked if they were locals (one was a local, the other from Chirang, where a lot of cadres came from), and said it would be better to let them live. The two were taken to the SP office and interrogated, and were now in jail. But most got out on bail within three months. They became surenderees, or rejoined the insurgent group: it was impossible to lead a normal life after that.

There were around fifty to sixty cadres in the Karki Centre and Gulai Centre areas, he said, even venturing till Garubandha and Dhankhana, and kidnappings took place right from the road. He was operating from the Missamari thana in Garubandha. Operations based on specific information didn't take them long, otherwise they had to spend long periods in the jungle. They had informers among the people. They also used the 'surrender' boys to guide them. Sometimes they went up into the Arunachal hills on operations, and come across wild elephant herds, but they stayed away, possibly from the smell of the guns. He said, 'we wear "civil dress" and go around like the ugroponthi (extremists) themselves.'

They worked with the help of sources, local people who told them of cadres' movements and visits to people's houses in villages. Without the sources they wouldn't be able to function. During the present operation, sources were getting 1 to 1.5 lakh rupees for information that led to a kill. People had faced harassment from the army and police during operations, but over time, the use of sources had given more focussed results. They also worked with cadres from the surrendered or overground group in identifying people and places. Haphang admitted the police effort in killing the cadres of the eastern group in Sonitpur had been done under him.

He usually picked a team of four or five with him, Bodos and Karbis. He showed Abhijit pictures on his phone, he and his fellow commandos, showing off a little: in camouflage gear with black scarves, holding aloft AKs, by the Sopai river, in Bhalukpung by the river. In the jungle they would sometimes lie in wait for two to three days, carrying bread, roti, bananas, and water, waiting for the cadres to go past. He had sources, and once word came in they moved at once, he didn't need any authorisation. If they were moving through villages at night they would sleep inside haystacks, he said, and in the villages they wouldn't pay for rice, only if they wanted a chicken or some pork for dinner.

What he told Abhijit marked him out as a killer, someone who hunted the cadres of the insurgent group. But his manner never hinted at that; he seemed a normal, well-groomed tribal youth on a bike, attending to his own business, playing with his son. Abhijit would later be reminded of what Graham Greene had written about the Gurkhas after going on patrol with them in Malaya in the 1950s: 'The Gurkha is a mercenary. His vocation is to kill his official enemy, and perhaps because he has a genuine vocation he is extremely tractable.'

There were still a few cadres in the camps around Taga in upper Myanmar, Haphang told Abhijit, about 250 male cadres and 50 to 60 female cadres. A female cadre had recently been caught in Dimapur with an AK-81, she was close to the military commander of the group, believed to be hiding out in south Bhutan. Weapons were brought from Dimapur in private and government vehicles. The group was having trouble sending funds to the camps in Myanmar now with increased pressure from the SFs or security forces. Their weapons coordinator, who had come overground with 7 AKs, was now in Guwahati jail.

The police had their AK rifles and pistols, so did the boys on the other side, and they had Chinese grenades as well, which were a worry for the police. Haphang mentioned an incident where he was chasing a cadre inside the forest close to the Arunachal border, when the boy stopped and turned around and took out the pin from a grenade. Haphang shouted at him to throw it away, saying he would get him surrendered. When the boy threw it away, Haphang crouched and then shot the boy a few times as the grenade exploded.

He said it was a job, he did what he had to do, but at the same time, he did sometimes feel sad at having to kill his fellow Bodos. After all, he was under threat as well, and it was because he had a good network among the Bodo people spread out along the foothills in Sonitpur district that he could perform. Abhijit asked Haphang about the kidnapping of the hydropower company's manager on the Bhalukpung–Balipara route. It turned out that Haphang had been part of the rescue operation.

The information about the vehicle and passenger had been given by an Arunachali person in Tawang, and the boys (from a faction of the eastern group) were waiting on motorcycles, headphones from their phones in their ears, listening as spotters told them the vehicle had crossed Bhalukpung and then the 12 Mile Centre, before they stopped the vehicle and took the manager away on their bikes along the dirt track running under the railway bridge and up the Maldang pahar where the rest were camped: eight cadres in all with seven AKs among them. Haphang managed to get in touch with one of them through a surrenderee, said he had arms to sell, and called the boy to Balipara, where he showed him a pistol and gave it to him without taking any money, as an opener. Abhijit interrupted to ask Haphang what the going rates were, and the police commando said 4 lakh for an AK, 1.2 to 1.8 lakh for a German 9mm pistol, and 80,000 for a 7.65 or 7.62mm pistol.

Haphang continued with his story. He called the boy again, saying he had grenades and ammunition with him, and this time they caught them (there were two of them, they weren't arrested) and brought straight to the northern range DIG in Tezpur. The parents of the two boys were brought from Udalguri and Rowta, and Rs 3 lakh was given to each set of parents to make the boys surrender. The two then went to Balipara, when the commander called them.

They took two cases of beer with them, and meat, which they feasted on in the camp, while Haphang and his men followed the trail and stayed near the camp, climbing up a hillock. The camp was on another hillock about 40 to 50 metres away just after a trough, and they could see what the kidnappers were doing.

He had sent along a letter to the manager, telling him they were coming, and asking him to tear up the letter. The two men on sentry duty took over at 8 pm, and one of them kept pinching the captive to keep him awake. By then the ASP, a SI and even the SP had arrived at the rear. Finally around 9.30 pm the captive walked away to take a piss, by which time Haphang had crawled near the camp, and grabbed the man saying he was from the police and dragged him along. Someone must have heard something then, because a voice shouted out, *hoi, kun hoi*? Who is it? Haphang moved faster, and firing broke out, the police on the hillock retaliating. A grenade was flung by the insurgents, and it exploded near the SI, tearing out parts of his calf and buttock. *Gutei tej sobote*, Haphang said: there was blood everywhere. The insurgents got away, running away into the hills.

Karuna had mentioned to Abhijit about a Bollywood actor turning up with 20 crore rupees in bags, because he said a politician family's money was invested in the hydropower firm, but Haphang said it was because the actor was related to the manager. Whatever the reason, most of the money was saved, with only about a crore being spent here and there. The police team must have got a reward of some sort too. Abhijit now understood why there were rumours that no encounter had taken place, and that the manager had been released on payment. But the injured SI had spent a few weeks in hospital, and Haphang had received a gallantry award.

Haphang said the cadres had been in touch with the 'mastermind' in Myanmar. Later, they were picked off one by one by the security forces, with the last one being killed in an encounter just recently. He said the eastern group had split after the 2008 bomb blasts in Guwahati, and then further after the gunning down of an independent tea planter at Tezalpatty near Seijusa. Those cadres had all been eliminated too—the security forces had known who had killed the planter.

Return to Foothills

On a drowsy afternoon as he lay in bed, Abhijit thought about the stories Haphang had told him. He remembered Rankhw waving to him at the end, the serious teacher, his niece with her wide-set eyes, and he realized something inside of him needed to get back to that landscape. So he called Saurav Saha, and that evening went back to the town, where he met the NGO worker at the old tea shop which was known for its rosogollas. Over tea and kachoris Saha explained what sort of surveys his group carried out. They wanted to start covering the villages that had come up in what had earlier been reserve forest land, non-revenue villages that didn't have any panchayat rights, and he sensed Abhijit's interest. Abhijit told him he could make a trip to the Foothills area and talk to some people—he thought specifically of the teacher Dilip Basumatary—and take things forward from there. Saha said that would be good, and asked wasn't he scared to return to that area? To which Abhijit replied that the people there knew him now, so he would be safe.

He set out the next morning, telling his uncle that he was only going as far as Missamari to meet the beat officer. However, he caught one of the Kamengbari autos from the Missamari bazar, after having made a call to Dilip Basumatary, and when he got down at Gulai Centre around midday the teacher was waiting for him. There were a couple of boys standing around their bikes outside the hardware store, but the sight of them didn't make him anxious any more. They went into the tea stall and sat on one of the benches and asked the woman for tea. Abhijit told the teacher about the NGO's activities and what he wanted to do, for which he would need Basumatary's assistance. Basumatary seemed interested, especially when he learnt that they paid well, but there was a measure of hesitation too. Abhijit had the sense that Basumatary suspected there might be something connected to issues of encroachment and eviction. So Abhijit brought this up, and said that the programme was just what it said it was. They agreed to go ahead with it, and Dilip said he would try and get hold of a motorcycle for them to tour the area. It was only then that the teacher brought up Abhijit's kidnapping, asking him about his time in the jungle, but on the whole he didn't seem to want to know more about the episode. He said they, the people of the area, just wanted to stay in peace.

They drank their tea, and Abhijit mentioned that he had seen Laimwn on the day he'd been released (but he still didn't say anything about the letter). He asked the teacher about her, but not too much as to make him suspect something. Basumatary said that her parents were thinking of sending her to Baksa to study. 'Her life is just getting wasted over here,' he said. 'Most of the time she's not at home nowadays.' On the way back, in the auto, Abhijit wondered if she went up toward the forested hills to meet

Rankhw. Once the programme started, maybe he would get to see more of her. The Kolamati range office passed by; that gigantic tree standing before it he now knew was a bhelu, a reminder of what once was.

He got down at the Gabharu beat office. It was afternoon, and overhead the rain clouds were gathering, the humidity increasing. Gautam Pegu was in his office, and stood up and shook Abhijit's hand when he entered the sparsely furnished room.

'You've come. Good, good. I was just about to call you and find out where you were. What an experience you had, isn't it? But I told you on that day itself, didn't I? That those places weren't safe? It's a miracle you survived! Sit, sit. How hot it is, isn't it?'

This sudden voluble behaviour from the beat officer was puzzling. Pegu shouted out to one of his men for tea, then sat down and wiped his face and neck with a hand towel. Next he picked up his ancient mobile phone and made a call, speaking in Hindi. Pegu appeared jittery: about fifteen minutes later Abhijit heard a car door slam shut followed by brisk footsteps on the cemented floor outside. The green curtain was moved aside and a tall, lean man in an army uniform entered. He was north Indian in appearance, with a prominent nose, thinning hair and a dark shadow on his cheeks. Pegu stood up again, shook hands with him, and introduced him to Abhijit as Major Dev. He stood too, and shook the major's hand. Now he understood. They sat down, and the major turned to Abhijit.

'So you were picked up by Rankhw's gang,' he said, 'and then they set you free?'

His manner was pleasant, but there were things hinted at which Abhijit didn't like.

'One of them wanted to kill me. I was lucky to have been released.'

'Who wanted to kill you? What was his name?'

What good would it do to try and hide things, he thought, and said, 'Thulunga.'

A faint smile appeared on the major's face, then he turned to Pegu and said, in Hindi, 'Pegu sa'ab, can I take him for a round?'

Pegu shifted in his chair, his hands clamped together. 'Abhijit, he would like to ask you something. Will you go with him? Just for a little while.'

He followed the tall major out to a white Sumo with tinted windows and no numberplates. The major opened the front door for him, then got in behind. Abhijit turned to look as the driver started the vehicle: in the back were two jawans, their AK rifles held straight between their legs, and the major was behind him. The car smelt of sweat and oil. The driver, also in army uniform, with a crew cut, drove fast. In no time they had crossed Kolamati Gate and were on the straight Foothills road. Where were they taking him? Abhijit tried to empty his mind of thoughts to remain calm. The major told the driver to slow down a little, and leaned forward and said to Abhijit, 'Listen, I need your help. We have reports some of these people are helping Rankhw's gang. I want you to look out and tell me if you spot anyone you saw at the camp, ok? Anyone who was there, or who turned up there. Even to deliver things. Keep your eyes open and let me know. All right?'

Abhijit nodded, and looked out through the darkened glass at the scattered huts and people moving about, a feeling of nausea rising up within him. He had come looking for something, and he had got himself mixed up in something else. They crossed the first centre, Karki, and Abhijit dutifully scanned the shops: the Bodo woman selling pork on the chang was gone, he noticed. Then the straight road through the familiar denuded landscape, the sun beating down, the clouds towering over the nearby hills. He looked at the few people walking or cycling past, the shops at Gulai Centre, the usual gaggle of boys around the bikes, and then a familiar face stepping out of the old woman's tea shop. Abhijit stiffened, tried to control his breathing. They went on, crossing a group of people, mostly women and children, who stopped and stared at the vehicle.

'If I see someone, what will you do?' Abhijit finally managed to ask.

'Why? Who did you see? Was it one of those women?'

'No. I was just wondering.'

'Don't worry. We'll just talk to them. Like how I'm talking to you.'

The Sumo went all the way to the rough checkpost at the inter-state border, where it halted, and the major got down and walked over to the AR camp, from which he emerged about fifteen minutes later. The three men in the car kept quiet and ignored him. Abhijit could see old man Nana standing outside his place with a couple of other men. He held himself rigid, afraid that he might somehow reveal who it was he had seen coming out of the tea shop: one of the boys who had come to the camp with supplies.

On the way back the clouds broke, and rain lashed across the road. People were taking shelter in the shops at both the centres. When they got back to the beat office the three men got down and went over to the tea shop across the road, while Major Dev, still sitting in the back, asked him a few questions. They were similar to what the ASP had asked him, only the major was more interested in why he had gone up there, and also what he thought of Pegu. If anything, Major Dev was more polite than the ASP, but Abhijit felt a fear and wariness he hadn't at the police station, maybe on account of the army officer's sharp eyes.

'So, you were wandering around this place trying to find out something about your father's death?' he asked.

'Yes. That's why I came back from Delhi.'

The major nodded and looked out through the dark glass. 'We all have different motivations, don't we? Tell me, what do you think of Gautam Pegu?'

'He knows about this area. He knows what happened to the forests.'

'I see. Anyway, let's exchange numbers. In case anything comes up. Ok?'

The rain had lessened by the time he stood at the office gates and watched the white Sumo speed away toward Missamari. Pegu came out of his room as Abhijit walked back in.

'You weren't inconvenienced, I hope? The major told me he wanted to talk to you, how could I refuse? Anyway, come in, come in, I've asked for tea and biscuits.'

Abhijit sat in the office and drank the tea from a small cup and half-listened to Pegu chattering on about having sent his staff to get pork from a nearby village. The rain had stopped, and the afternoon was lengthening into evening. He had expected himself to feel angry at having been used in this way, but now he just felt a tired resignation. The question occurred to him as to whether he had been looking at the world the wrong way all this time.

'All right, you've finished your tea, come on now. I have something for you.'

Abhijit followed Pegu, who was in his department trousers and a half-sleeved shirt hanging loose, around the office and across the patch of grass behind it to two old rooms, which when Khagen Saikia had been here were used to house mahouts and other such guests. One of the rooms, with a rough fireplace at the back, had been opened. It was lit by a bulb hanging from the dirty ceiling. A staff member in vest and shorts was sitting on a low stool peeling potatoes, while on a rickety wooden table stood a bottle of whisky.

'You drink, don't you?' the beat officer said. 'I got some good whisky for you.'

Abhijit said yes, he sometimes did. The truth was he hardly drank, and didn't smoke—his mother had been dead against any of that.

'Good, good. My staff will be back soon with the pork. Deuri here'—he indicated the man peeling potatoes—'is an excellent cook. We'll have a good dinner tonight, in Saikia sir's honour! You can stay here if it gets late, okay, Abhijit?'

Abhijit nodded, and sat down. He was tired of saying yes, tired of being put into situations not of his own making. So he didn't protest when Pegu poured him a glass of whisky. He gagged at the bitter taste but forced himself to swallow the brew: maybe this would bring him closer to his father after all. Pegu went off after that, saying he had a few things to finish. Abhijit drank his whisky, and checked his phone. There was a new message: KEEP IN TOUCH and below that, MAJOR DEV. He put the phone away.

It was dark by then. Two staff members came in and squatted near Deuri; they looked up at Abhijit from time to time and smiled. Then the pair who had gone to buy the pork returned: one of them started washing and chopping the meat outside, on the narrow veranda, while the other lit a fire in the fireplace. Everyone was busy, and Abhijit started feeling better. He asked if he could help with anything, but the men told him to sit and relax: he was after all Saikia sir's son. Pegu returned with a few packets of bhujia he had bought from the tea shop across the road. He poured out whisky in plastic glasses for his men, and the party started in earnest.

Pegu poured him a second peg, and after that he was unsure of what happened. There was plenty of laughter, as Pegu told stories about how scared people had been of Saikia sir, his temper, and Abhijit joined in it too. His father hadn't been forgotten: that made him feel good. Pegu leaned over to him and said something about Major Dev, about how one had to be careful with him, and it occurred to Abhijit that maybe he actually feared the army officer. Some coarsely chopped salad and fried pork were served on small plates to accompany the bhujia. As the night wore on Abhijit felt his head spinning. His phone rang once: it was his uncle, and Abhijit decided not to pick it up.

At one point, feeling increasingly dizzy, he staggered

outside and held on to one of the corner posts of the veranda. He could hear shouts and laughter from inside. Pegu came out and asked him how he was feeling. Abhijit groaned in reply, sank to his knees, and threw up the whisky mixed with the snacks. They gave him water to wash up and drink, and Pegu asked two of the staff to take him across to the office and make him lie down on the bed. He remembered how he had spent the last night here with his father so many years ago. A great sorrow gripped him, and he fell asleep. A roar of laughter made him come awake with a start, and he sat up in the dark in panic before remembering where he was.

Using the torch on his phone he went to the toilet in the adjoining room, then opened the doors of the room and stepped out. Everything was dark, as if the lights had gone off. He made his way around the office and across the grass towards where the men were. The lights *were* gone: there was only the low flickering light from the fire inside the room. As he came closer he could hear Pegu's voice, loud, and slurring a little, 'Everyone says it, even I say it, that he was a good officer. But the man had some faults. That's why he went into the jungle and shot himself!'

Abhijit stopped, and moved slowly toward the corner of the veranda, his heart beating fast. Pegu went on, his voice slightly salacious now, the officer letting his hair down among his men after a few drinks. 'He really liked the tribal women, *really* liked them.' There were a few titters from among the men. 'That's why he would go up to Dirang when he got the chance. Then there was a Bodo woman, from one of those villages ahead of Kolamati, she came looking for him one night.' Yes, I heard about that story, someone piped up. 'Anyway, that was Saikia sir. His wife knew about it too, about that woman he kept up in Arunachal.'

He held his body rigid in the dark, not believing what he was hearing, and also willing Pegu to go on, to shed more light on the person his father had been. There was a pause, then a loud burp, followed by Pegu saying, 'The *mal* is finished *kela*. I have a half bottle in my room if anyone wants some. But this is the last party for a while, do you hear?' Pegu stepped out of the room and down from the veranda. He saw Abhijit standing there. Both men stood still for a moment, and then Abhijit turned and ran, as fast as he could go, with Pegu's voice ringing in his ears, 'Abhijit, Abhijit!'

He ran around the office and through the open gate, then crossed the road and went right, past the government school. Gradually he slowed down. To his left were the indistinct shapes of the empty stalls of the Gabharu haat or weekly market. If he kept going he would come across the army pickets in the cantonment. He remembered the ruins of an old building in the midst of the market stalls, and made his way through them. The building loomed up before him, and he climbed though a collapsed wall into the interior, where he sat in the darkness with his back against a pillar, the insides smelling of smoke and animal fur. From another room came the sound of what seemed like a person mumbling to himself. Abhijit pulled his legs up and hugged his knees. It was going to be a long night.

A Meeting in Shillong

The very next day after the incident at the Gabharu beat office with Gautam Pegu, Abhijit made a trip to Shillong. He didn't know how many days he was going for, just that he wanted to get out of Tezpur for a while. His uncle had been very angry with him afterwards, for disappearing and not picking up his call.

'Do you think this is a hotel?' Hiren Khura had yelled when a dishevelled Abhijit had turned up the next morning. 'I was scared you might have got kidnapped again. You could have told me on the phone where you were. Why didn't you pick up? Where were you, by the way? At the beat office, or somewhere else?'

Abhijit muttered something in reply and went to have a bath in the old bathroom near the well. He could understand his uncle's concerns but at the same time the questions irritated him, for his years staying alone in Delhi had given him a habit of independence. By the time he finished his bath with water drawn up from the well, he had made up his mind. He left that afternoon, after lunch, when his uncle and grandmother were taking their naps, taking with him his trusty backpack (along with his laptop).

As he left the house, he told Julie to tell Hiren Khura that he was going to Shillong for a few days.

He caught a bus from the Mission Chariali crossroads for Guwahati, stayed the night there at a cheap hotel in Paltan Bazar, and hired a shared Sumo taxi up to Shillong the next morning. The green cloak on the hills glistened from the recent rains, and as they went up, the air got cooler. He felt a lump in his throat as he remembered travelling the same route with his mother on the red Assam state transport corporation buses, and stopping at Nongpoh for tea and oily chholey bhature. But Nongpoh was no more the small stopover of the old days; it had spread all along the newly widened four-lane highway, with commercial complexes and several new eateries catering to the increased flow of people; shiny new SUVs with Guwahati and Shillong numberplates whizzed past on the highway, and at a weighbridge trucks were being unloaded of their excess coal.

There was a long line of traffic into the city: it took the yellow Sumo an hour to crawl from Mawlai to the drop-off point before the civil hospital, while it had taken just two hours to get from Guwahati to Mawlai. Abhijit felt a certain trepidation at returning after so long: who remembered him here after all? He walked all the way to Police Bazar instead of taking a taxi, past the library, the church, the government secretariat, and the Shillong Club. Police Bazar was crowded, and Abhijit went to a hotel on the road that led toward Wards Lake, where he managed to get a room. He opened the windows to get some air: the buildings were hunkered down under grey-black clouds, and didn't help to improve his mood.

The next two days he tramped the city's streets till he was tired, walking all the way from Police Bazar to Nongthymmai, and back, besides Laban, Nongrim Hills and Bara Bazar. He avoided going up from Fire Brigade to Motinagar though, where their old house had been. His uncle had told him in Guwahati that the small and cozy Assam-type structure with its wood-plank floors and plaster walls had been torn down by the new Khasi owner in order to construct a building for a hostel. It was a sight Abhijit wished to be spared.

Out on the streets he got the impression of people and vehicles crammed together in a city that had run out of space. The Assam-type houses with their red or green tin roofs, the old jeeps, the pine trees, were all slowly disappearing, and it was becoming like any other crowded hill station. Some places he remembered from his school days were still around though, like the Chinese restaurant at the bottom of the steps in Police Bazar, and the puri sabji shop opposite the post office in Laitumkhrah. Walking down through the grimy, crowded Police Bazar one day he came across Regal, where he used to come with his mother as a child, and for old times' sake he went in and ordered a dosa and coffee. The place was crowded with families and women who had finished their shopping in the market. Now that he was back he felt like a stranger, and he could have cried for that quiet, awkward boy who used to come here with his mother. What was it she used to tell him, leaning over her dosa? 'You have to be careful, do you understand, Abhijit, people will always try to hurt you.'

All alone in his small hotel room, he turned to drink

at night. For company he had with him a slim novel by Albert Camus, his father's signature across the title page; he had seen it among the few books his uncle had in his room. That first night he went out and bought two cans of strong beer, and the next night, a quarter bottle of whisky. Maybe he was trying to prove to himself after the night at the beat office that he could drink. He also watched the news, mostly an Assamese news channel. Another round of floods had hit the state. He saw visuals of people sheltering with their livestock on higher ground like highways and in schools. They were mostly miya people. The floods were an inescapable part of life in Assam. Earlier, people had avoided living in flood-prone areas, especially by the Brahmaputra river, but those areas had been slowly occupied too. Living in Tezpur, with its natural protection against the rising waters of the great river in the form of a rocky bank, it wasn't something Abhijit had paid much attention to. On the bus to Guwahati he had seen some places that were still under water.

Late at night, with nothing left to do, he would be forced to play back what he had heard Pegu say. Was it the truth about his father? Had that somehow led him to kill himself? He pulled the curtains and switched off the lights and looked at the lights of the nearby buildings, listened to voices and the occasional shout coming from the rest of the hotel. What were Rankhw and the others doing now, he wondered. Were they still there in the forests, going from one hideout to another? And Laimwn, with her wide-set eyes; he could picture her inside the dark, smoky kitchen with the rest of her family members.

On his third day in Shillong, there was a call from Major Dev. Abhijit had got back to his room around mid-morning with a copy of the local newspaper when his phone rang.

'Namaskar Saikia ji,' the major said. 'I thought I'd just say hello. Where are you?'

'I'm in Shillong,' Abhijit said, thankful to be away from Tezpur, but then the major said, 'Oh, what a coincidence. I'm in Guwahati, coming up to Shillong tomorrow. We must meet, all right?'

There was no excuse he could think of, and so he ended up agreeing to meet the major. The next evening at 7 pm, Abhijit entered the bar at the top of a hotel in Police Bazar and took a table for two by the windows. It was a weekday so there were hardly any people around. He asked the waiter for a glass of water. Beyond the lights of the buildings he could faintly make out the dark bulk of the forested range overlooking the city.

Major Dev came in about twenty minutes later, dressed formally in civil clothes. He walked with a slight limp, which Abhijit hadn't noticed before. He extended his hand as he reached the table, and almost crushed Abhijit's hand in his.

'Very sorry I'm late, Saikia ji,' he said as he took a seat. 'What'll you drink?'

They asked for whisky, and the major ordered a plate of double fried pork.

'How can I come to Shillong and not have the pork, right?' he said with a laugh.

Abhjit agreed to that. 'Have you tried the jadoh stalls here? They make good pork.'

Major Dev made a face at this. He didn't seem the

type to appreciate jadoh stalls, Abhijit reflected. The major drank quickly as they made some small talk, and then came to the point.

'So, have those people got in touch with you? Rankhw and his boys.'

'No. Why should they?'

'He liked you enough to let you go. Suppose they wanted to talk to you again?'

Abhijit shook his head. 'No one has called me.'

Major Dev considered this, slowly nodding his head. Then he seemed to change tack.

'Tell me, what do you believe in? Do you believe in the idea of India?'

'I suppose I do,' Abhijit said.

'Suppose?' the major queried, raising his eyebrows. He drained his whisky, motioned to the waiter for a repeat, and speared a piece of fatty pork with his fork.

'You may have the luxury to say "suppose", we don't. When we're out in the field, on an operation, I can't start debating with myself. Results are what I need!'

He sat back in his chair, chewing the pork, oil glistening on his lips, his eyes boring into Abhijit, who, to cover his unease, asked for another drink as well.

'I noticed,' the major said after a while, 'that you were looking at my limp when I walked in. It's an old hip injury. Do you know how I got it?'

When Abhijit shook his head, Major Dev went on to tell him how. Kashmir in the winter, a couple of years ago. He was a captain then, leading a group of commandos on a search operation in a forested area near the border, based on intelligence gathered by him from a local source. They had left at dawn, trudging through the snow, and made contact around midday. All three targets were neutralized, with the loss of one commando on their side. Major Dev was hit in the pelvic region by a bullet, and passed out due to the loss of blood. His senior-most havildar had radioed their CO and managed to get him evacuated by helicopter, thus saving his life.

'I could have died that day,' he said. 'So to go into those sort of situations you need motivation, do you understand? That you're doing it for your country, for your fellow countrymen.'

The feeling of unease grew in him, making him feel he had to somehow counter the other man's veiled aggression. Major Dev now returned to Foothills. He told Abhijit what Rankhw's boys had been up to: extortion, kidnapping, murder—even of their fellow Bodos.

'Why don't you go after them?' Abhijit asked. 'There are just a handful of them.'

'But we operate with one hand tied behind our back, do you understand?'

Abhijit felt that he had touched a raw nerve in the major.

'If we were allowed to conduct a real operation, a *real* operation,' he said, tapping the table with a stiff index finger, 'we could finish off those buggers. But no, we are a *democracy*. Everyone has their rights.'

He smiled then, an insolent smile, and before Abhijit knew why, he found himself saying, 'He has a girlfriend in the Foothills area. In the village called Amlaibari.'

Major Dev leaned forward over the table. 'Who has a girlfriend?'

'The person you were talking about. Rankhw. You didn't know, did you?'

The major shook his head. Abhijit had the momentary satisfaction of seeing the smile wiped off his face.

'What's her name?' he asked quietly.

They got up to leave about fifteen minutes later, after Major Dev got a call on his mobile. He settled the bill with a couple of 500-rupee notes.

'It's on me,' he said, when Abhijit had taken out his wallet. 'You gave me some good info.'

The bar was starting to fill up by then and the music had gotten louder. Abhijit had taken his drinks quite fast in an attempt to keep up with the major, and was feeling tipsy, but it was nothing like the night at the beat office. They went down by the lift and came out onto the main road through Police Bazar, where shops were still open and cars passing by. What a change from his schooldays, Abhijit thought, when once it was dark the city would shut down and people would stay indoors. Major Dev was right, a part of him reasoned, you couldn't entertain doubts while doing a job like that.

They walked a little ahead where near the roundabout an SUV with an AS12 Sonitpur number was waiting. The major said bye to him and headed for the vehicle. Abhijit could make out a tall man sitting in the front with the driver, and two tribal-looking girls behind, who greeted the major as he got into the back. Then the vehicle drove off, leaving Abhijit to walk back to his hotel. Once he was alone though, he started considering what he had told the major. What had taken possession of him, to disclose Laimwn's name like that? Why had he done that?

By the time he was back in his room, he found several new possibilities emerging from that one fact he had revealed. Would she be picked up by the major's men? Would they raid the family home, looking for some sort of evidence? Would she—horror of horrors—disappear? That kind of thing had happened before, he knew. Only he had never expected himself to be caught up in something of that sort. He saw now how expertly Major Dev had led the conversation, bringing up the issue of patriotism and danger, so that Abhijit, while getting drunk trying to match the other's consumption, had finally given away a good piece of information—just to make himself feel equal to the major. He felt sick in his stomach thinking about it.

And then he remembered where he had seen the SUV with the AS12 Sonitpur number plate that Major Dev had gotten into: in Missamari, driven by the MES contractor Jagat Kumar. He hadn't had a good view of the tall person in front, but it was safe to assume that it was Jagat Kumar, with his driver beside him. It was entirely plausible that Major Dev, who was posted with his unit at Missamari, knew him. Gautam Pegu would have been wary of the major, as the beat officer was said to be running the illegal sand and stone quarries on the Belsiri river with the help of Rankhw's overground workers in the Bodo village near Ramnathpur. And as one of the largest contractors at the army base, Jagat Kumar was in touch with Pegu for his requirements of sand, gravel and stones (Dulu da had told him about this). Abhijit realized that he was caught in a tangled web, among a group of dangerous men.

Abhijit woke early the next morning. The kitchen

wasn't open, so he came out of the hotel and walked to the state transport corporation complex just below the Police Bazar roundabout, where several makeshift stalls had been set up on wobbly tables. He had puri sabji, the puris served on a torn magazine page, the sabji with Nutrela and lauki in it, along with tea in a plastic glass from the stall of a middle-aged Assamese woman who said she was there from 5 am to around 8.30 am, helped by her school-going son. Where did all these people come from, Abhijit wondered, as he went back through the morning crowd to his hotel. Breakfast had revived him, but he had already made a decision not to drink any more.

He stopped at the reception to pick up a copy of the local newspaper, and the thin receptionist in an oversized blue shirt smiled at him. As he got to the steps going up Abhijit looked back, and saw the man looking at him. In his room a new source of paranoia came upon him. Was he being watched? Was his phone being tapped? Could the major have that done? He tried calling the teacher Dilip Basumatary several times, just to talk to him, but the call wouldn't go through. In the end he switched off his phone, took a bath, and checked out of the hotel. He had no plans beyond looking for a cheap, nondescript hotel, but it was a clear sunny day, and on an impulse he withdrew some money from an ATM and hired a local taxi to take him to Cherrapunji.

It was a relief to get out of the city (though the outskirts were turning into suburbs now), and ride the winding roads up to the windswept plateau, from where he was lucky to see the waterfalls gushing down the cliffs, the watery plains of Bangladesh far below—only later, after he'd had his lunch in a jadoh shop run by a Khasi woman, did those thick white clouds come rolling in, smothering the land in their damp embrace. He took photos on his phone and felt relaxed for the first time in days, but on the way back they were stuck in a long line of traffic, mostly taxis with tourists returning to Guwahati, and that familiar black mood descended upon him again. He spent the night in another, cheaper hotel in Police Bazar. The next day he went for a walk and met a former classmate who now ran a grocery shop in the Laitumkhrah bazar. They sat in a nearby tea shop and talked about the old days and their classmates. It was nice, but he could feel, as with his neighbours in Tezpur, that too much time had passed and there was too much distance between them now. When he got back to the hotel in the afternoon he decided he would return to Tezpur the next morning.

Rafiqul Ali

Abhijit returned to Tezpur, taking the Assam state transport corporation bus which left Shillong at 8 am from Police Bazar and did the entire journey, stopping at Guwahati to pick up more passengers. The Foothills area was still on his mind, but he hesitated to set out for it again. He didn't want to come across the beat officer Pegu, after the incident that night, and he had no way of knowing if the army major and his men had paid a visit to Laimwn's house.

Abhijit called the teacher Dilip Basumatary, told him that he had been out, and that the project would be delayed by a few days. After making some small talk he asked the teacher how his family members were. They were all fine, Basumatary said, and Abhijit couldn't query further without making the other man suspicious. After he had hung up, he wondered what the major was up to. Had the girl been kept under observation? He would come to find out that his guess wasn't too far from the truth.

The weather in Tezpur was cooler now, with a slight chill in the air in the early mornings and nights. Abhijit lay low for a few days, reading, doing a bit of writing on his elephant story (which the newspaper had agreed to take as a long form for their website), helping out with the purchases from the haat. He thought of calling Pegu and Major Dev, but didn't. Then Saurav Saha called him one day. Saha didn't seem to be worried about the project in the Foothills area getting delayed, and told Abhijit to take his time. He then gave him a number: Abhijit had forgotten that he had asked Saha to enquire from the journalist Padma Bora if he could find out the whereabouts of the retired forest guard Rafiqul Ali. Abhijit thanked him, and called the number. He got through after a couple of tries. The line was patchy and he had to raise his voice to be heard by the elderly man on the other side. It took him a while to understand who was calling, and then he told Abhijit that he stayed with his family members at Bhomoraguri, near the bridge, just beside the river.

'Come and meet me if you can,' Rafiqul Ali said, 'I haven't seen you for so long.' The next morning Abhijit set out, catching an auto from Mission Chariali which was headed for Soolong on the other side of the Brahmaputra. As they left Tezpur behind, fields of yellow ripening dhan came into view, along with tin-roofed huts and large fish ponds and lean, dark men in blue and green lungis. He remembered open, desolate fields here in the Panch Mile area, when he had once gone as a child with his parents to the ferry ghat at Bhomoraguri to catch a ferry to the other side (before the bridge had come up). They had gone to Kaziranga and then visited a relative of his father's in Jorhat. Men were ceaselessly spreading upon the earth, and soon there would no unpopulated stretches, no mystery left at all.

He got down where the approach road to the bridge started climbing up through the sal trees, and took a dirt track on the right that curved down toward the riverside, past huts and shabby vegetable gardens and groups of children in dusty clothing who stared at him. The track led to a couple of small shops in a clearing by the riverbank, and a thin man with his pants rolled up to below his knees came out of a tea shop to meet him. He was Rafiqul Ali's son, and his father had asked Abhijit to accompany him to their house. The son, whose name was Rubul, led the way past the shops and then right along the top of the riverbank. Down below were porcupine structures of wood and bamboo to protect against erosion when the river rose; now there was a small stretch of sandy bank till the river, with a couple of fishing boats and larger diesel-engine driven boats moored there.

Rubul told Abhijit that he owned two engine-driven boats. It was hardly any distance to the village up on the riverbank. Rafiqul Ali, older, balding, a little bent, clad in a patterened blue lungi and a half-sleeved shirt and a white prayer cap, stood outside his hut. Behind it, there were two more huts.

'Abhijit beta,' he said, holding him by his hands, 'when I last saw you, you were a small boy.'

Ali led him into the small front room crowded with a double bed and an old sofa set with a table. There were posters on the plaster walls, including one of a bridge with 'Bangladesh' printed below. Ali's wife came out to see Abhijit, then went back inside and returned a while later with red tea and chanachur, and tamul pan in a xorai, a quintessentially Assamese tradition.

'If only your baba were here too,' Ali said, sitting beside him in a chair. 'Sometimes I think about him a lot. Do you remember this?' he clasped his hands together and blew onto the ridgeline of his knuckles to produce a bird cry. 'You used to always ask me to do that.'

The years seemed to fall away, and he found himself telling his father's old assistant about all that had happened: how his mother had taken him to Shillong, his time in Delhi, his mother's demise, returning to Assam and to Tezpur, his trip to Foothills and Kamengbari, even the episode with the insurgents. Ali was surprised at what he had been up to, but Abhijit also felt that the former forest guard had somehow understood his motives. There was something almost spiritual in the old man's calm demeanour.

'You must feel like knowing,' Ali said, helping himself to a piece of betel nut, 'what really happened. How your life turned out to be like this.'

'Yes Rafiqul Mama,' Abhijit said. 'That's why I wanted to ask you a few things.'

Ali nodded. 'Just wait. We'll go out in a while.'

Abhijit understood. From the inside of the hut came the sound of women and children's voices, and a television show. Ali now filled him up on *his* life: he had stuck on in the forest department after Saikia sir's death, being transferred from Chariduar reserve forest to Nameri and Manas and other places, and finally retiring in 2006.

'Two of my sons stay here, their houses are behind mine. One has two boats, the other does *kheti* on our land in Panch Mile. Another son is a mistry in Guwahati, and the fourth one is working in the army camp at Thakurbari. My four daughters are all married. Now I spend my days with my grandchildren and meeting people at the masjid.'

He called out then, and several children of different ages trooped into the room, laughing and giggling as their grandfather introduced them to the guest. Looking at the friend of his childhood, Abhijit felt something stirring within him—in another life, his father might have been like that, retired and content, maybe with grandchildren around him.

Ali shooed off the children, took another pan and tamul, and stood up.

'Come, let us go out,' he said. 'I want to show you something.'

They went back the way Abhijit had come, and Ali entered the dark interior of the tea shop where his son had stepped out from, and came out with another young man. Ali led the way down the riverbank to the sandy shore that had appeared with the river starting to recede. His movements, Abhijit noticed, were still quick and surefooted. There were a couple of boats moored by the river, and the young man scampered up the side of one and then let down a wood plank for Ali and Abhijit to climb aboard. It was a fair-sized boat, with a couple of plastic chairs piled up at the side. Ali took out two chairs for them as the youth fiddled with the grease-blackened diesel motor. This was one of his son's boats, Ali told Abhijit, and they would be going to a nearby sor or sandbank. The boat ferried tourists who came to see river dolphins in the winter, and passengers, and once work started on the second bridge across the Brahmaputra there would be continuous work for both boats.

Abhijit sat back and watched the placid brown-green waters flow past, deceptive in appearance, for the river flowed deep and strong, all the way from a glacier in distant Tibet. Though the river had shrunk with winter approaching it was still vast. The distant roar of buses and trucks crossing the 3-km-long bridge came across to them as a gentle breeze stirred. Ali said that the river was increasingly cutting toward the northern bank, where their village was, where Tezpur was, and it was only the rocks under the riverbank along this stretch that was saving both places. The boatman called him, and Ali stood and went to the prow where he pulled out a long bamboo pole and pushed the boat out into the water. Then the engine came to life with a *dhat dhat dhat dhat* sound and belched out black smoke and they were on their way.

They went under the bridge and headed for a sandbank closer to the southern bank. It had a beach-like sandy expanse rising up to a grassy plateau with trees and shrubs where cattle or goats seemed to be grazing. In the distance, upriver, the horizon and the river came together in a blue-grey haziness, the riverbank a thin, inconsequential strip. It felt like being in a different world. They passed a small fishing boat which was headed back to the ghat, and then a large raft of bamboo poles drifting downstream, with a small room on it with three or four men inside. Ali shouted over the noise of the engine that most fishermen went out in the evening, two or three men in a boat, fished at night and returned at dawn to sell their catch to traders who would take the fish to the chowk bazar at Tezpur. The bamboos, he said, were being taken from further upstream, maybe Golaghat, down to Guwahati, where bamboos were in high demand.

They were near the sor now and the boatman cut the engine, letting the boat drift ashore to the sandy beach. For a few seconds, Abhijit could feel a phantom beat of the diesel engine in his ears. Suddenly a glistening brown-grey shape leaped out of the water ahead of them and disappeared with a splash: a river dolphin or xihu. The boatman let down the plank for the two of them to get down, but didn't get down himself. Abhijit followed Ali up a small rise, from where, standing with his feet in the warm sand, and a breeze ruffling his shirt, he could see the long thin span of the Koliabhomora bridge far away across the river. Ali took out a packet of bidis and lit one.

'I had told Saikia sir so many times, come with me, we'll go on a boat and I'll show you the river dolphins. It never happened. That's why I wanted to show you. There!' he said, pointing at a splash some distance away in the river, 'another dolphin.'

'I think my father preferred the mountains and the forests,' Abhijit said.

Ali nodded, then looked around and picked a spot in the sand to sit down. Puffing on his bidi, his lungi-clad knees drawn up to his chest, he motioned for Abhijit to sit beside him.

'People who live by the river and people who live in the forests and the mountains are different. I know because I've lived both lives. Those people might be tougher, but we are more adaptable.' He pointed ahead, slightly to the right, where, near the sal-tree covered Bhomoraguri hill, was a rocky outcrop in the river with an iron pole sticking up from it. 'During the rainy season we see only that pole, and boatmen know they have to avoid the spot because of the rocks. In the cold season more rocks will appear from the river. One of the rocks has a hollow in the shape of a large footprint...the people here say it was made by Shiva's foot. We'll go and see it when we return.'

They sat for a while in silence, the wind in their ears. The boatman was sleeping at the bow, near the engine, one arm flung over his face. A pair of brown-black birds flew over the river with a *ka ka* call. Ali said they were called sakoi sokua in Assamese; later Abhijit would find out that they were ruddy shellducks. Ali then asked him what it was he wanted to know.

'He committed suicide, didn't he?' Abhijit asked. 'My father. Tell me the truth.'

The former forest guard sighed, and looked away, at the distant bridge.

'I suppose you're old enough to know,' he said. 'Yes, he died by his own hand.'

'My mother told me he was shot in the forest by the insurgents.'

'That's what we staff from the office told her. We thought maybe it would hurt her less. But she knew he had done it himself, I don't know how. He had his lunch that afternoon and then went out in his jeep. I wondered where he had gone, as he usually rested after his meal. In the evening we got the news from the Kolamati gate camp. An Arunachal Pradesh state transport bus that had left Doimara that morning had stopped for a few hours in Kamengbari with engine trouble. They finally set out around 3 pm, and came across Saikia sir in his jeep near the second-last wooden bridge on the road through the forest. They came and informed the people at the Kolamati gate camp. By the time we arranged another vehicle and left it was dark.'

Ali fell silent, and Abhijit had to ask him, 'Where did you find him?'

'He was inside the jeep. His rifle was between his legs, the barrel pointing up. In the chamber was an empty cartridge. The bullet had entered from under his jaw. There were insurgents in those forests by then, but if it was them, the rifle would have been taken away.'

It was as Abhijit had feared, the monstrous truth. He looked away, blinking his eyes.

Finally he asked, 'Did you find anything in the jeep? A note?'

Ali shook his head. 'Only his Charminar cigarette packet and a matchbox. There were several cigarette ends outside the jeep and the packet was empty.'

'But why would he have done something like that?' Abhijit cried out. 'Why?'

'We cannot always understand what the One above has in mind for us, beta.'

'I heard Pegu talking about my father, at the beat office that night. He mentioned a Bodo woman from one of the settlers' villages. Also a woman from Arunachal. What did my father have to do with them?'

Ali snorted, and lit another bidi, cupping his gnarled hands around the match.

'Pegu? That man isn't right. You won't make out when you meet him, but if you see his deeds you'll know. We old staff know the true story about that Bodo woman. She came in the middle of the night with her two children to the Kolamati gate camp, blood all over her dokhona. Her husband was trying to kill her, she said. Your father was there that night. He made the forest guards heat water for the woman and warm up milk for the children. The next day he took them to the civil hospital in Tezpur and paid for her treatment out of his pocket. The Bodo settlers liked him, and small-minded people like Pegu didn't like this.'

Hearing that gave Abhijit some solace, for it matched the story Rankhw had told him.

'And the woman from Arunachal? Who was she?'

Ali shook his head. 'There was nobody. Pegu must have made up some story.'

'Why did he go to Bomdila and Dirang then?'

'He went on work. There were some discussions with the Arunachal forest department about the Eaglenest sanctuary that falls within the forest coming down from Tenga valley to Foothills. And he had friends there. Those people were simpler then. Now they have money and have changed.'

'I remember him telling me something on that last night I was with him. That the Chariduar reserve would disappear one day. How did he know that such a long time back?'

Ali nodded. 'The Bodo people have something known as the dewani system. We miya people have it too. One person goes ahead looking for new land, and then comes back and informs the others. Then the people collect money to buy the land. There were people from Lakhimpur and

Golaghat coming and looking at the forest land then. They were in contact with some Bodo politicians. And once the Bodos would come, the Adivasis would follow.'

'Ok. And you're sure that my father committed suicide and wasn't murdered?'

'He wasn't murdered. The only thing I don't know is how your mother knew what had really happened. But she told you what we had told her, to protect you.'

How had she known, indeed? Something moved within him then, like the floaters in one's eyes, but he couldn't bring it into focus.

'You father knew all about the history of the Kameng area, the Foothills area,' Ali went on. 'Even then, there were very few officers like him. He would ask me about our area too,' and here Ali's left arm rose and made a wide sweep, 'and I would tell him, how I was born on the other side of the river, in Borghuli, where my father was born too. My father's father, my Dada, had come from Mymensingh during the time of the British, before Hindustan and Pakistan were created. The whole family came by boat and then walked for days. When they reached, their legs were swollen. They cleared the forest and started cultivation. But my Nana, my mother's father, returned to Mymensingh before 1947. He said, here there is land, firewood, fish and we are living well, but there will be problems in the future, so better to return and face hardship in our own land. He left with some others, and there has been no contact since then.'

But the poster of the bridge would have been brought by someone, Abhijit thought.

'Last year during the rainy season a couple of deer came to this sor from Kaziranga. Sometimes a tiger or an elephant swims across, and might even cross to Tezpur. Yes, it's happened,' Ali said, looking at the surprise on Abhijit's face. 'And this past winter, some twenty to twenty-five families appeared on this sor from somewhere downriver. They were real Bangladeshis, didn't know a word of Assamese or Hindi. The Nepali people who keep buffalos on the other side of the river told us, and we chased them away. But some people say they went and settled somewhere inside the Panch Mile area. Our political leaders do all these things.' Ali looked up at the sky and got to his feet. 'It's getting hot, we should move. Come, I'll show you Shiva's footprint on those rocks over there.'

Tales of Insurgents

His research into the human-elephant crisis had shown Abhijit that there were links to the issue of deforestation, and to the groups involved in the struggle for a separate Bodo state, or even country, and which were all in a way connected to his father's death. He had come across the stories of several people, for instance of the Bodo police commando Haphang. Another one was of an insurgent by the name of Ananta (alias Ankhwma), associated with the eastern group fighting for independence. Over time, from talking to people and following newspaper stories closely, Abhijit managed to build up a picture of Ankhwma.

He had been born into a poor Bodo family in a nondescript village toward the west of Assam, in Chirang district. The family was dirt poor, sometimes with not enough food for them as Ankhwma grew up. Two of his sisters were sent to work as maids in Shillong (they were a Baptist Christian family). One account had the small children crying themselves to sleep at night because there wasn't even rice to eat. The father was something of a wastrel; he lost the small plot of family land and then deserted his family. The mother moved to Kokrajhar where she found work in a rice hotel.

Ankhwma did a bit of schooling, then sometime in 2004 disappeared from home. He was with a group of boys who had joined the insurgents, and the new life in the forests above Kokrajhar, while tough, gave him a new sense of direction. He was taught how the Bodos, the original inhabitants of Assam, had been steadily marginalised by the Assamese and other communities. His teenage angst, sharpened by years of deprivation, found just the right path, as the people who had encouraged them to move to the camp in the forest had anticipated, and as was the case with countless other youth across the North East with other insurgent groups. He declared he was ready to undergo training in Myanmar in order to fight for their own country, an independent Bodoland.

In 2005, he and another boy went to Guwahati, and caught a train to Tinsukia, a trading city in upper Assam. From there they made their way to the coalfields of Ledo, where a contact met them and took them into Arunachal Pradesh, and then a two-day trek through forested hills into Myanmar's Sagaing state, a Naga-administered area, where they waited some days at a temporary camp for other boys to join them. Several more days of trekking brought them to a camp of the insurgent group near the Chindwin river, where there were Bodo boys and girls from their area as well.

He was in the twenty-sixth batch of the outfit, and was personally received by their leader Ringkhang. Ankhwma spent more than a year there, being trained in handling guns and explosives, and taking classes in map reading and revolutionary theory. India was the villain: they would have to use force to liberate their land from India. Nearby were other camps, with cadres from groups in Nagaland and Assam and Manipur, including from the 'organization'. Twice there were visitors to the camp: fair, Oriental-looking men—but they were kept away from the recruits. Ankhwma and a few others trekked back after the rainy season the next year; this time through Mon district in Nagaland.

They were given dry rations in backpacks, to supplement whatever they were served in the Naga villages along the way, and an assault rifle each and ammunition. Cadres from the Naga group operating in the Konyak area took them across, after which they had to leave their guns with them. The guns were later routed to Dimapur, from where they were picked up by sympathizers (including government officials like ADCs and SDOs posted in the BTAD) and transported to the north bank and BTAD areas in their official cars. Ankhwma and the others, singly and in pairs, came down to Assam and went to Guwahati, from where they made their way up by train to Rangapara near Tezpur.

The forest villages above Rangapara were where cadres from the early batches of Ankhwma's group had been trained by a few members from a powerful Naga insurgent group, then undivided. Ankhwma and the others regrouped in the forests on the foothills along the inter-state border (including above the Mansiri river, where the phandi Dilwar Saikia had once seen the gun-making camp), and here they set up camp and started operating. Ankhwma rose to become an area commander, looking after the places above Rangapara. They had in place an extortion and taxation racket (including on timber), which, along with kidnappings, saw the group collecting several crore rupees a year from Sonitpur district alone—this money was taken to Dimapur to be delivered to the group. Over time Ankhwma became a dreaded name, and many boys joined the group inspired by his story.

However, unlike cadres such as Thulunga, Ankhwma came overground at one point, following a series of blasts carried out by the insurgent group in Guwahati in 2008: after that it had split into two factions. Very soon he was working with the Assam Police and the Indian army in tracking down boys from the other faction, while they were only too happy to let him carry on certain 'collection' activities, such as from the supply of sand and stones, boulders from the rivers near his village running down into Assam from Bhutan.

Abhijit never went and met Ankhwma: some details of his story were given to him by Krishna Brahma, an ex-cadre from the independence group who had worked alongside the Naga trainers above Rangapara. This was the same Krishna Brahma who had long ago taken the phandi Dilwar to the gun-making camp up in the hills above the Mansiri river.

Abhijit first met him in Udalguri, the headquarters of the district of the same name which was immediately to the west of Sonitpur district, when he had gone there while researching the elephant story. Padma Bora had put him in touch with a journalist from Udalguri called Bijon Das, and it was through Das that he managed to contact Brahma. They met at the Deputy Commissioner's office in Udalguri. Das had arranged a room for Abhijit at the circuit house, beside the DC's office, and before those two concrete structures, their walls discoloured by the rain and humidity, there was an overgrown field (where presumably the grass was cut and events held on 15th August and 26th January every year) gazed upon by a forlorn statue of Mahatma Gandhi.

Brahma the ex-insurgent would have been in his late forties, with short grey-white hair. Abhijit noticed the spring in his step (he was wearing a pair of old Chinese sneakers) despite the gentle paunch under a faded polo shirt, and the air of fitness and athleticism about him, similar to that which good sportsmen seem to retain even with age. There was a tribal easygoingness and cheerfulness to the man. It was during that trip that a group of them—the journalist Das, Brahma, Abhijit, and Tarun Boro, the former bodyguard of an important Bodo student leader (Abhijit was meeting him for the first time as well)—went up from Udalguri past the tea gardens to the Khalingduar reserve forest which stretched north to the border with Bhutan. Here too there was deforestation by settlers and loggers, but nothing on the scale of what had happened in neighbouring Sonitpur district (Udalguri was one of four districts which made up the BTAD). Abhijit found himself observing Brahma and Boro, ex-cadres of the sovereignity group and the statehood group respectively, but they were easy around one another, as if the passions of that earlier phase of life had now been spent.

They landed up at the Nonoi forest beat office, and the Bodo ranger sent two forest guards (one with a .315 rifle, the other with a shotgun) and the department Gypsy along with them. A recent thunderstorm had felled a large number of trees so they soon had to abandon the vehicle and proceed on foot through the forest. It was an uncommonly muggy and humid day, and after a while three of the group decided to turn back, while Abhijit, one of the guards and the ex-bodyguard Boro decided to press on to Jalimukh on the border. That was when Boro told Abhijit about their journey from Kokrajhar to Udalguri on foot more than twenty years ago along the forest belt at the foothills of the mountains, carrying with them several carbines which they had obtained from somewhere near Siliguri.

Khalingduar had thick forest cover then, he said, but that had been reduced over the years with loggers chopping down valuable trees like segun, xal, titasopa, and bonsum. The loggers were now at work in areas of Khalingduar like Xarmati and also up in the Bhutan hills, using power saws of late.

But there were still signs of wildlife all along the trail: two separate elephant herds calling out from deep within the forest, besides their foot impressions in the muddy ground, and the bark worn high up on a tree where an elephant had rubbed his tusks, even marks—which the forest guard pointed out—where a herd had crossed the trail. The two men with Abhijit read the forest in a way only those who had spent their lives within it could do: signs of wild pigs having dug up the ground in search of edible roots, marks made by mithun hooves. They saw a pair of giant hornbills as well, flapping away from the tree tops as the men approached. The reserve forest still had a population of deer and tigers, the forest guard said.

They walked for about three hours that afternoon in the

humid, energy-sapping heat till they reached a vast grassy area ahead of which the misty hills of Bhutan rose up one behind the other, their tops wreathed in golden-tinged clouds as the sun went down. Boro pointed to the hills and said that the insurgent group fighting for an independent Bodoland had their camps there, even the 'organization' had set up camps there, after they had fled from Bangladesh. In 2003, a joint operation by the Indian and Bhutanese armies had put an end to that chapter. There were still boys from the eastern group up there, but in small groups, like how Rankhw's group were moving around in the Arunachal hills.

The forest guard, a grizzled Assamese man from Tangla not too far from Udalguri, told Abhijit that during the time of the British they had created stone bunds with the help of wires (hence the name Jalimukh) to control the flow of the Nonoi river down toward Mangaldoi, but later people had opened up the wires and stolen them and the bunds collapsed. These half-forgotten stories were exactly what he had come looking for, but at that moment he was distracted by what they had seen just a while ago, on the trail that led out from the forest to the grassy plain. There was a large border-marking stone on the trail, and near it in the grass a couple of bones and some rags, which, when Abhijit stopped and looked, he realized with a shock were the remains of a human being, possibly a woman.

He had to hurry to catch up with the forest guard and Boro (who had with them the rifle and shotgun), and when he told them what he had seen the forest guard told Boro casually that those were the remains of the pagoli or mad woman who had been seen near the beat office some days back, and that she must have come wandering this side before being trampled to death by an elephant herd.

In that case where was the skull, Abhijit wondered? And the rest of the bones? Had a tiger come upon the body? Or, did it hint at something darker altogether? In any case, there was no time to ponder on those remains, or gaze at the nearby mountains, as it had started growing dark, and his companions decided to return by another route so that they stayed out of the path of the two herds that had been calling from within the forest. This meant cutting a wide arc east along the Nonoi river, which in that area was really several fast-flowing streams coming down from the Bhutan hills. Their shoes were soaked as they crossed and re-crossed the meandering streams, and soon it was pitch dark, with a boulder-strewn ground before them and a vast, faintly grey sky overhead. They kept moving, but it felt to a weary Abhijit as though they were stuck in one spot.

Finally, some six hours after they had started the trek, they met the rest of the group who had been out looking for them. Brahma had fashioned a trap in a stream with sticks and caught a few small fish, which he put into a small plastic bag. As they walked back to the forest beat office nearby, Brahma told Abhijit that when they set off on their operations in the old days, they would come down from the Bhutan hills and walk along the streams in the dark, and while returning he would always trap some small fish to carry up to their camp.

The range officer, a Bodo person from Kokrajhar, had several quarter bottles of whisky waiting for them at the beat office, and they sat outside at a table (the three of them who had walked all the way had their wet shoes and socks off), seized logs and rusting vehicles lying nearby under the tall sal trees. The range officer told them how difficult it was to deal with the 'public' in incidents involving deaths caused by wild elephants, as everyone was ready to blame the forest department. But when a wild elephant died, from whatever reason, the villagers would still scatter flowers on its body, out of an old reverence.

It was past 10 pm when they finally left, with Krishna Brahma driving the Bolero from the DC's office, and they sped back to Udalguri along the darkened roads, trees and old houses appearing in the headlights in the humid night. They dropped off the former bodyguard Boro and then the journalist Das along the way, before Brahma brought Abhijit back to the circuit house. There, in the porch of that large building blazing with lights and eerily quiet at that hour, he finally shared some memories of his past life, when he had been in his twenties: an ambush on the Assam police, travelling to Calcutta to collect funds from the head offices of the tea gardens there and then depositing that money in new accounts; how before kidnapping a person they would study his movements for several weeks; and how the cadres up in the camps in Bhutan underwent 'study' sessions—Abhijit took this to mean self-criticism of the Maoist sort, something their original Naga trainers would have picked up from the old China returnees.

The next day, Abhijit was supposed to meet Brahma. But before that the journalist Das took him to meet an ex-tea garden labourer to the north of the district (which was to the west of Sonitpur district), again close to the border with Bhutan. The man was in his late forties, small, wiry and dark, from a village called No.2 Kosubil. He was an Adivasi, whose ancestors had been brought from central India during the time of the British to work in the tea gardens. Sometime earlier that year he had been in a patch of jungle near the Corramore tea estate, where he had formerly worked, collecting leaves for a puja, when he realized a wild elephant was standing right beside him.

The adult male struck the man down with his trunk, then stamped on his right leg, breaking the thigh bone. As he lay in agony on the ground, thinking he would surely be trampled to death, a few more wild elephants appeared. A female elephant charged and butted the male elephant away from the fallen man. The man said she tapped him on his back, as if warning him to stay down, even as she fought off the male elephant, which then backed away. 'Maybe a human being had been kind to her earlier, given her food or rescued her,' the man said.

He had taken six months to walk again, but was luckier than the twenty-two people, mostly Adivasis, killed by wild elephants just in Udalguri district that year alone. As for the elephant coming to his aid: this was something Abhijit was to hear over and over again from people familiar with the pachyderms, that they were remarkably human-like in their behaviour. Even while driving there in the journalist's car, through Nonoipara tea garden, an undulating carpet of green on either side of the road in the midst of which were regular lines of shade trees, just before the ex-labourer's whitewashed quarters in the labour lines beside the road, they had come upon a herd moving through the shaded tea bushes. They stopped and got down to take a few photos. The huge bulk of the elephants, the vulnerable-looking baby elephants with their small trunks, and the adults herding them along: Abhijit had felt he was watching something recognizably human. As they were looking at them, they became aware of a lone elephant to their right and behind the herd. As it moved, Abhijit could make out the fold of skin under its tail that marked it as a male, and then it turned, flapped out its ears and began moving toward the two of them: Das said it looked like a rogue, an outcast from the herd, and it was better they moved on.

Later, a senior manager at the Bhooteachang tea estate told Abhijit that they had counted up to 350 elephants in a single herd in the nearby Paneri tea estate in the early 1990s. Elephants had always entered the estates, he said, but now the herds were fragmented, with thirty to forty in a herd at the most. The one they had seen would have been about twelve to fourteen strong, including three or four calves, and the lone male would have been hanging around them, but wasn't allowed to be part of the herd. Traditionally large herds would come down from the hills in the winter and make their way down south to the Brahmaputra river, toward Singri Hill where there was an old Shiva temple. Now there were roads, traffic, towns, spreading villages and cropland, and the herds were confused, had shrunk in number, and preferred the relative quiet of the tea gardens, which due to various first-world trade certifications, were compelled to shelter them, and not chase them away.

Abhijit met the ex-insurgent Brahma in the offices of the main students' group among the Bodos—it seemed he was now helping them campaign for a separate state. They talked in the darkened, deserted library and meeting room, surrounded by books in bookcases (the office had a hostel too, for Bodo students from interior areas), and Abhijit could sense he wasn't in a mood to go into the former role of the Nagas with their sovereignty movement, beyond the fact that they had supplied them with arms. Brahma was more forthcoming though on what Abhijit really wanted to ask him about: the beat officer Khagen Saikia.

Brahma was surprised Abhijit knew about that old incident, and was even more surprised to know how Abhijit was connected to the late beat officer. Abhijit had asked him, what did *he* know about the incident? He had just joined the group then, Brahma said, and they were moving along the forests in the north bank, from Bhairabkunda to Foothills and Kamengbari to Bhalukpung (and here Abhijit remembered the camp Pegu said they had come across near Foothills in the Chariduar reserve forest, with the 'off size' planks), and they had heard about Khagen Saikia, a strict officer, but the Bodo people liked him. He had helped a Bodo woman who was almost killed by her husband, and then something happened, and he went into the forest one day in his jeep and shot himself. Abhijit asked Brahma if he was sure it was a case of suicide, and not murder, and he gave a similar reasoning to what the retired forest guard Ali had given Abhijit.

'In those days, the only people inside those forests were the boys from our group, some settlers, and a few forest guards. If we had killed him, wouldn't we have taken away his rifle? He shot himself with his own service rifle. A very sad case.'

Which still left Abhijit with the question: if his father had taken his own life, then why had he done it?

An Encounter in the Marketplace

The police commando Haphang had kept in touch with Abhijit over the phone. He was mostly in the field or otherwise at home with his family. He called early one morning and asked Abhijit to come to the Sadar thana in town. When Abhijit got there, Haphang asked him to wait in one of the rooms in the newly-built block. There were aluminium-framed doors and windows (less wood was used that way, someone had told him), rexine or glass-slab covered desks, locked trunks on some of those desks, dusty files and piles of paper, and on one wall, a map of Tezpur town with the Jamuguri, Rangapara, Thelamara, and Nagaon areas marked around it, as also the sandbars in the Brahmaputra. A balding ASI in a brown jacket sat telling a constable about the nerve problem in his left leg.

Haphang came bustling into the chilly room with his partner, both of them in plainclothes, and then Abhijit was with them in a Bolero without numberplates heading out of town, Haphang driving, his small, quiet, watchful colleague from upper Assam sitting behind.

'I asked you to come along as I needed some help from you,' Haphang said, his eyes on the road. 'I'm meeting a source at the Bindukuri haat. I just want you to tell me if he was with Rankhw's group in the jungle.'

Abhijit wasn't surprised at the request; he had seen something like this coming. But unlike the earlier incident with the major, he didn't feel demeaned in any way. Rather, there was something exciting about it, an adventure.

'But we have to be careful,' Haphang said, 'there might be some boys looking for the source as well.'

As they took a left at Mission Chariali, Abhijit wondered if Haphang knew about his meetings with the army major. Was Haphang checking *him* out? It didn't matter, he decided. He asked Haphang about his family: his son was now four and his daughter nine, they were at the house in the police reserve area. Haphang apologised if the car was smelling, saying he had picked up a few kusia or eel from the Balipara haat the previous day while returning from his parents' place in Gohpur. Abhijit told him it didn't bother him. Abhijit felt there was something shaky about Haphang that day; who knew what tensions and threats he had to deal with as a result of the operations he led and the men he had killed?

He asked the police commando about the eastern group, and Haphang spoke freely, something which Abhijit appreciated. A high-ranking insurgent commander who was hiding in Bhutan now but kept coming down to the Manas and Chirang areas had called Haphang four times recently, saying that Haphang had ruined the Bodo jati or race, killed all their people, and was solely responsible for the Bodo people's dhonxo or destruction, and that he would kill him and cook him and eat him one day.

'I told him, I don't know what you're talking about,' Haphang said, laughing, 'I told him, I haven't done anything, I just sit in an office in Tezpur.'

The special branch, which had a post in Tezpur, Haphang said, had all the phone numbers, including those across the border, which is why the cadres coming over from Myanmar of late tried not to use phones too much—even when they changed the SIM card the phone could be traced (through the device IMEI number).

Haphang took a right from BP Tinali. As the paddy fields appeared, the faint mist he had seen earlier started thickening. Up ahead the road—which came out near Rangapara—started crumbling and Haphang swerved past giant craters as they crossed small village houses, yellowing paddy fields, ghostly skinny cows, and the large new FCI godown somewhere in the distance. Just before they came to the haat at Bindukuri, Haphang stopped the car at a turning beside a bamboo grove and asked Abhijit to get down and walk, for his own safety—he would be meeting the source at a tea shop.

'There is a gelamal shop in front,' he told Abhijit. 'Wait there. Look at the boy carefully. When I look at you and put my hand to my nose, you put your hand to your head if you saw him at the camp, otherwise if you haven't seen him, turn your back to us. Got it?'

Abhijit nodded and got down, and as he did so, Haphang turned and asked his colleague for his pistol and cap. He shoved the 9mm into the back of his jeans and pulled the cap down low.

'Will there be any shooting?' Abhijit asked, trying to sound lighthearted.

'Just a precaution,' Haphang said. 'The linkmen might come looking for the source.'

The haat was spread out over a large open area, a spreading ahot or ficus tree rising out of the mist in the middle, and the place was starting to fill up with sellers. The Bolero was parked discreetly to the left, beside several mini pick-up trucks, usually hired by miya farmers pooling together. They were already spreading out their large, fertilizer-boosted cauliflowers, brinjals and other vegetables on plastic and jute sack-cloth. Some distance away, ahead of the big tree, were several Bodo butchers, selling blood-smeared pork from under their makeshift plastic and bamboo shelters. In one, a couple of Adivasi and Bodo men were already drinking white-coloured country liquor. Beyond them was a small stream, and fields under a light mist.

Abhijit wheeled to the right, towards the dry goods section with the pungent smell of gela tamul or fermented betel nuts. Men and women with dark, cracked skin on their feet and hands were selling coconuts, matimah, and tamul. Beyond this were a few thatched huts selling tea, and tekeli pitha and puri. He spotted Haphang's cap: they were standing outside one of the huts. Abhijit moved toward a wood-plank shop near a tree, the gelamal shop, and, to quell his nervousness, bought a cigarette and lit it. In his sandals and jeans and old jacket he knew he didn't exactly stand out. Still, he felt anxious looking at Haphang and his colleague.

A young boy came up to them. He looked like he was still in his teens. Haphang spoke to him, and then looked towards Abhijit and touched his nose. Abhijit focused his attention on the young man, and then, slowly, turned his back to Haphang. He smoked his cigarette before stubbing it out with his foot. When he turned back, he saw the three of them inside the hut, sitting together on a bench, their glasses of tea before them on a long, narrow table (the sort of bench and table Abhijit would have seen inside the old lady's tea shop at Gulai Centre).

A thin man in a threadbare coat was telling the owner of the shop that he had to give his cow a bundle of hay after she had eaten her husk, to which the owner said that he should wash the stalks, and the man in the coat said he cut the paddy stalks from higher up, whereas the miyas cut it from below and the stalks had mud on them.

As Abhijit listened to this rural exchange, he became aware of three young tribal men moving slowly through the dry goods section towards the tea shops. They were a few feet apart, but all three, for the speed at which they were moving, weren't looking down at the items on display, but rather toward the tea shops. He could also see Haphang and his colleague and the boy getting up, and Haphang paying the woman who ran the shop. Abhijit took out his phone, thinking to call him, but there was no network there. He looked on as the three men advanced through the betel nuts and coconuts, and on the other side—like something out of a Western—the three men started coming out of the tea shop.

Abhijit thought of calling out, but found himself frozen, transfixed by the movement of the two groups of men. Haphang stopped outside the shop and lit a cigarette.

His colleague said something to him and he smiled. The young boy took out a phone and looked at it. Then he looked up, and Abhijit could see him taken aback by the sight of the three men coming toward him. The three of them, who had seen the boy now, were trying to spread out, moving through the sellers and the goods at their feet. Then the boy bolted, towards his right. It took Haphang and the other policeman two or three seconds to realize this, by which time the three men were pushing people aside and moving toward their left. Beyond the dry goods section and the thatched tea shops were fallow fields shrouded in a thickening mist, and Abhijit could see the dark blue jacket of the boy as he stumbled over the uneven field. Then the three men were after him, and, behind them, Haphang and his colleague, their pistols in their hands. They disappeared into the mist.

All of this had taken place in silence, and only a few people had noticed it and were looking. Abhijit started moving toward the tea shops. Suddenly there came the sharp flat popping sound of a pistol, followed by another, then another. Now people's heads turned. Abhijit hurried up to the last tea shop and strained his eyes against the white mist. What's happening, he could hear people say. But no one was moving forward. Then, out of the mist, a figure appeared, coming back toward the haat. It was Haphang, pistol in one hand, phone in the other, trying a number. He saw Abhijit as he came closer, and jerked his head, as if telling him to go and see. Some of the more curious ones were moving forward now in a low hubbub of voices and Abhijit went along with them.

The earth in the fields was lumpy and uneven amid the remnants of old dried paddy stalks. He could feel the wetness of the mist in his nostrils, taking him back to winters in Delhi, residential colonies early in the morning, men with buckets wiping cars parked outside on the road. He had a brief sense of time being compressed, and then there was one body face down, one of the three men, a dark stain on the back of his t-shirt. A little ahead of him Haphang's quiet, watchful colleague stood over the body of their source, lying on his back, his eyes and mouth open and frozen. He was very young. For some reason Abhijit found himself thinking of Haphang's small son during their first meeting, when he had come and asked his father to get him a toy jeep. Where are the other two, he asked Haphang's colleague, and the man made a gesture with his pistol toward the mist, as if to say they had disappeared in it.

Two police Gypsys arrived with police commandos in uniform, and they took the two bodies away (wrapped in woven bamboo mats), Haphang's colleague going with them. Abhijit waited, having two or three glasses of tea in the same tea stall, the market still going on but with a sort of hush fallen upon it. The lady who ran the stall was a stout Bodo woman in a green dokhona. She kept saying to whoever would listen, even as she bustled about her duties, 'Our boys will just go on dying like this.'

After a while Abhijit was in the unmarked Bolero going back to Tezpur with Haphang. Abhijit had thought he might be angry, but instead he seemed subdued. He had got one of the linkmen with one shot, he said. The other two would have run toward Bahbari. But the police knew who they were. Abhijit asked what information they had got from the source, and Haphang said it was something to do with Rankhw.

'I should have called out when I saw those men,' Abhijit said. 'But I don't know what happened to me. My body seemed stuck.'

Haphang looked at him, then back at the potholed road. 'You did your job. The rest of it was up to us to handle.'

A tractor trailer had stopped on the road ahead of them, and a bent, old woman in a clean white sari got down from the trailer along with two black goat kids tied with a rope. Haphang stopped to let her cross the broken road, dragging the kids behind her. Then he drove on. The mist was lifting off the fields as the sun rose behind cloud cover. There was an air of unreality to what had just happened. Abhijit could picture a headline in a local newspaper the next morning: 'Two dead in marketplace encounter'. As with trying to write about his kidnapping, he felt the inadequacy of words to describe the situation.

So Abhijit went back to his questioning. Did the army know about these linkmen? Yes, Haphang said, but the army while operating had to take along people from the nearest police thana. They weren't that effective, he said, but once they got hold of the surrendered boys or got sources they had more slush funds to spend than the police. Abhijit felt there would be times when there was competition to catch or kill people—which might be seen as a positive thing by some higher ups. But what sort of stress would it breed in the men who had to do such work?

Since he was operating in the Foothills area, Abhijit

asked Haphang if he knew about what had happened in the Chariduar reserve forest. It turned out that he knew quite a bit. The Foothills area was opened up by the western insurgents, he said, and people came by train from Chirang, Udalguri, Dhemaji, Silapathar, Golaghat, Gohpur, even Karbi Anglong and Dimapur. The measurement was done and people were given one seet or 12 bighas of land for around 1,000 rupees—gaon buras or headmen were appointed from among the settlers, a sort of dewani system (which the retired forest guard Ali had told Abhijit about). There was besa kina or selling and buying of the land, and current rates were apparently around 25,000 a bigha, so 3 lakh for a seet—a three hundred fold increase in a space of roughly twenty years. He said there weren't many settlers around 1994–95—it increased from 1998–99 onward. 'That is how the Chariduar reserve forest disappeared,' he said.

Haphang said ultimately roads and facilities would come to those areas. But the forest official had told Abhijit that only people who had extended the fourteen original forest villages in Sonitpur district were supposed to get user rights. The insurgents levied a house tax of 400 rupees a year, Haphang said, and tax on timber chopped in the forest: 15 to 20 rupees a CFT. There were still people going up into Arunachal and cutting trees, bringing back the logs, carrying or dragging them, or drifting them along the rivers, and then they stockpiled it at one place to sell to traders from places like Dhekiajuli or Rangapara, or to small sawmills running illegally, where the wood was turned into timber. According to him, if earlier 90 per cent of Bodos supported the insurgents, now it was 50 per cent. But he also said 50 per cent of the work for Bodoland was done, 50 per cent remained, which Abhijit took to mean the stretch from Udalguri to the east to Gohpur, an area not under the BTAD at present.

Abhijit looked at him as he drove, turning the steering quickly to avoid the potholes. It struck him that he had never seen Haphang smoking a cigarette before today. He had the feeling the policeman's vices would be strictly controlled: a matter of survival. What was notable was his humility and politeness, but when he spoke on the phone in Bodo there were times Abhijit could make out the direct roughness associated with action. As they neared BP Tiniali Abhijit asked him how many kills he had. Haphang thought a while and said about thirty. Did he keep notches on his AK, Abhijit asked, and he smiled. It wasn't like that, he said, he didn't even think about it anymore, it just happened, his finger pulling the trigger (when Abhijit shook his hand it was relatively soft). A year later, with widespread operations on against the insurgents, the mild-mannered police commando's tally would cross forty.

In reply to a question from Abhijit he said he had never been double-crossed by a source: in such instances he always tried to keep the source close to them. Other times they would find out later during interrogations: you fled, how did you know we were coming, and then the person would say who it was that tipped them off. He had always worked with good, reliable sources. Two of his batchmates had been killed though, in Tinsukia and in Haflong. It was difficult in the hills, with ambushes from above on vehicles. The conflict would keep on going this way, he said. Some boys joined to fight for their land, some for money, some for adventure. There were no fixed timings for their work, easy patrolling during easy times, and harder jungle marches during more active times.

Abhijit asked him about the Nagas. They had trained the eastern group initially in the forest villages above Rangapara, he said, and were involved in the bank dacoities a long time back in Dhekiajuli and Rangapara, the former in 1994, the boys fleeing along the Batasipur road. Later two Naga boys were arrested by the police.

Such was the drama being played out in those areas. The Bodo people as a whole, from what Abhijit had seen, were a simple race, easily stirred, and had been left with the short end of the economy in Assam. They had found it difficult to adapt to the present-day economy, along with the divide among them between the moving and settled cultivators.

In his enquiries into the settlement of the Chariduar reserve forest, Abhijit came to hear about the settlers being given receipts by members of a committee. What committee was this? At the Tezpur DFO's office, the person who was supposed to deal with Chariduar RF said he hadn't heard of anything of that sort. Abhijit thought he was just trying to be careful. At the suggestion of a colleague of his, he told Abhijit to go and talk to a local journalist and RTI activist from Dhekiajuli by the name of Uttam Nath.

So he took a bus going to Dhekiajuli on the crowded highway heading west from Tezpur, with tall simul trees at the sides. At Thelamara he saw a large hoarding of a young female Bodo boxer from the area who had won gold at an international meet. Dhekiajuli was 35 km from Tezpur, and the range office was on the right just after the small bridge on the road running through the town. Seized 'fanta' logs (very roughly finished logs) and sawn logs from storm-felled trees, besides smaller timber, were lying out in the open before the small Assam-type office buildings. Nath, who had called Abhijit there, was a lean man in a dark-brown half jacket and jeans, with a well-kept sedan car. He was from Hugrajuli, and he talked a lot, reminding Abhijit at one point of the journalist Bijon Das from Udalguri. They were of the same type: small-town reporters who knew all the important officials and could call in favours for lesser mortals. Abhijit explained why he was there, to find out how the forest had disappeared. Nath said he was in an NGO. 'I have written a lot about the encroachment, kept clippings, written to the President and the CM,' he said. 'I am a lone man fighting against 2 lakh encroachers. Sonitpur West has 40,000 voters in the encroached areas, there are thirty-eight schools in Sonai Rupai, and the same number of voter booths for elections. The MLA doesn't care for Assamese voters in town, he only cares for this block of Bodo voters who can swing an election by voting for one person.'

He said the present forest minister, a Bodo lady, had said she was for eviction from encroached areas, which was why people there were tense, but she might be removed too because of her stand. *Abhayaranyo*, the description in Assamese, meant wildlife sanctuary, and Nath said people were not supposed to enter, take photos, or even pluck a leaf, so how could people be living there? Those who claimed to be the bhumiputra or sons of the soil had cut down all the trees, there was not even a tree left for a little shade. 'If I go to those areas,' he said, laughing, 'they'll cut me up and *tel nimokh xani* (rub me with oil and salt) they'll eat me up.'

A short, elderly forest guard with a large, craggy face (he had the title Bora but looked tribal) who knew Nath had been listening, and now he told Abhijit that two 'committees' had come up in the late 1990s: in Hugrajuli and Batasipur. He said, *manuh ahisil mati bhangibo*, or people came to break ground. The committee people did the mati jukha or land measurement and gave people a seet, 12 bighas, for 750 rupees in the beginning. Nath said a Bodo MLA from Sonitpur district was the brains behind it all. Abhijit was curious about the figure of 12 bighas. Nath said that in the fourteen old forest villages in Sonitpur, all on the outskirts of the RFs, people had originally been given 12 bighas, that was why. These people still paid a bon gau or forest village revenue of 2 rupees per bigha annually. There were agents who got in touch with the families and with the committees (the dewani system Rafiqul Ali and Haphang had mentioned to Abhijit).

Nath said the Hugrajuli committee had seven people, including a Tanti (Adivasi), and a Nath (Assamese). Hearing about this, Nath people from Bihaguri started coming to get land (they would come on one particular bus), but when the evictions started and the police chased them they went away, but the Bodos 'stuck on like glue'. That's why it was the Bodos in those areas and not the Assamese, Nath said. Only they cut forests, he said, the miyas stick to the sor sapori and the Assamese to their own places. Above Batachipur the people came from Dimapur side and a lot from Jonai, some of whom were flood affected. Most came to get more land, with family members or relatives staying back in the original place: Udalguri, Tangla, Gohpur, Baksa.

Timber from the felled trees was taken by train to sawmills in Goreswar and Tangla. The valuable trees like bonsum were felled with axes, the less valuable ones were burnt little by little (covered with leaves or soil, water thrown on them) to make charcoal. Sonitpur was famous for bonsum trees: now they were nowhere to be seen. Nath said the forest department would sometimes seize logs from a morning train, and it would take them till the next day to unload the timber. There was a mountain of logs at Hugrajuli at one time. During the time of the earlier forest department official (whom Abhijit had met), the people in the new villages had set up forest rights committees of their own with rubber stamps (for example, Gulai forest rights protection committee) and had submitted applications for land pattas. All of those documents were apparently in files at the Tezpur DFO's office.

Nath then narrated how the Jhingabil IB, an old two-storey building from the British times, was burnt down in 2001 or 2002 (Rankhw had first mentioned this to Abhijit). After an eviction drive went awry, a crowd of thirty to forty encroachers attacked them with sticks and spears. A tall Bodo youth with a sword was shot right in the head with a rifle, while Nath was firing a shotgun and saved the ranger, a person from Guwahati whose knees were trembling. The forest guard held the crowd back with his unloaded rifle after his single cartridge fell down while he was trying to load. They had fled the place in a truck, driving over the dead body of the youth. After they left, the crowd burnt down the beautiful old IB.

Uttam Nath, who was old enough to remember the khachhar camp at Foothills, narrated a strange story at the end, about an elephant belonging to someone from Dhekiajuli, another Nath, which was whitewashed with *sun* or lime and taken for shooting in the film *Safed Haathi* near the Jhingabil IB. A hole was dug before it where the mahout hid from the camera and gave commands, so that it would seem like the elephant was obeying the child actor. Shatrughan Sinha came and landed in a helicopter near Hugrajuli, and they made a large cordon for the onlookers. Abhijit later looked up the movie: it was a children's film released in 1978, so Nath would have been talking about 1976 or 1977. The director, Tapan Sinha, passed away in 2009 in Kolkata. He had been a well-known filmmaker, and his son, Anindya Sinha, Abhijit learned from the Internet, was a primatologist who had discovered a new species of primate, the Arunachal macaque, in the Kameng region some years previously.

Of Men and the Wilderness

The Bodo boy who had been gunned down on the Foothills road by the police commandos, and whose body Abhijit had seen: in order to understand why he was a member of an insurgent group, Abhijit had to go back in history. The Bodos, or the Kacharis as they were earlier (and still are) known, and who are tribals, arc what the social science people call autochthons—the original inhabitants—of the Brahmaputra valley. They came down from the direction of the Tibetan plateau in separate groups along separate routes, entering what is today north Bengal and lower Assam, many hundreds of years ago. They are themselves descendants of an earlier larger migration from what is now China (the Adi tribe along the banks of the Siang river in Arunachal Pradesh are another group which moved from China to Tibet, and then down to their present abode). Could they be said to be the first people in what is today known as the North East? The Khasi-Jaintia people of the Meghalaya plateau, thought to belong to the Mon-Khmer branch of the Austric family (as opposed to the Mongoloid Bodos and Ahoms), are held by some to be those first people, seafaring people who came by boat from somewhere around present-day Indonesia—only this is now complicated by new evidence which says they might have come from the *east*, from today's central India (indeed, there are similarities between the people of the Meghalaya plateau and the Adivasi tribals of central India, not the least their old practice of erecting stone menhirs).

In the north bank region of Assam, the first people to arrive were those coming down from what is now Tibet (from where came the word Bod, or dwelling place, and from where the term Bodo is thought to derive). The detail about the seafaring race reaching the North East was mentioned to Abhijit by a Bodo person himself, a government official whose workplace he had visited in Tezpur to learn something about Bodo history and culture, a side of society usually cut off for the lay Assamese person, just like it is, say, with the Adivasis or tea tribes and the miyas or Muslims of Bengali descent.

These people entered the plains beneath the foothills of the great mountains which were part of the eastern Himalayan chain. The land then would have been thickly forested, with elephant herds and rhinos and tigers roaming unchallenged by man. These first arrivals in this Garden of Eden must have trod gingerly in their new environment, living off wild vegetables and fruits and fighting off animals. Gradually though, their mastery of fire gave them an advantage. They burnt tracts of jungle and figured out how to cultivate grain, starting an early form of jhum or swidden cultivation—something which the teacher's family members were following in a way, hundreds of years later. Slowly these people spread out across what is called the North East, and over time became separate communities, on either side of the Brahmaputra: the Garo, the Rabha, the Dimasa, the Tripuri, even the Koch and Mech, and the Morans and Muttocks of upper Assam, were all related to them, and part of a greater Bodo race, the government official told Abhijit. There might have been Rabha people present near the Chariduar forest area too, in that long ago time.

By then though there were other people who had appeared in the North East as well, woodcutters and traders from India proper starting to venture into eastern Assam, and small tribes from the north and the east, lost and isolated within thick forests on remote mountains. Slowly larger kingdoms to the west began sending missions up the Brahmaputra river. The ruins of ancient civilizations scattered over Assam, whatever remain in the humid climate, suggest that towns were established, mostly along the great river (including in Tezpur), settlements with perhaps a mixed population of local people and outsiders, but were then abandoned for some reason: war, earthquakes, disease, who knew?

There were the carved stone ruins on a hill known as Bamuni pahar beside the Brahmaputra in Tezpur which Abhijit had visited long ago. He knew that carved stone blocks, weathered with age, had been taken away by people on their cycles—indeed there were a few in the house of Pradip Deka, brought by his father, including one which showed the image of a woman, the elements having worn it down over the centuries till one could only make out the swell of the face and her breasts on the stone block. Now of course it was a protected site, and wandering through the ruins one morning—there were still a few well-preserved pieces of stone carving among the blocks—Abhijit was struck by the tribal (or Mongoloid) looking features of a carved male figure with a small pot belly, undeniably a Bodo figure. Intermingling, destruction, and then dispersal—that seemed to be the lesson from those ruins.

Around the 13th century AD, a group of people came over the Pangsau Pass on today's Arunachal Pradesh–Myanmar border and entered the upper reaches of the long Brahmaputra valley. Their exact numbers are a matter of conjecture: some say a king came followed by thousands of followers, while others say it was a village chief with a few families accompanying him. This group of people, of Shan heritage, would seem to have had a more comprehensive idea of social organization, as it is accepted that they, through a process of intermarriage and consolidation with local communities and tribes, laid the basis for a larger Assamese society in the Brahmaputra valley. The Ahoms, as they came to be known, rose in power, and the original groups of Bodo people were pushed into pockets, for example along the foothills above the Brahmaputra river. The Ahoms set up outposts on the north bank, and also settled people there, including convicts and undesirable types.

The Ahoms managed, over many decades, to get the better of the Mughals who had conquered most of the Indian subcontinent by then, including Bengal. Several battles were fought between both sides with territory in the Brahmaputra valley being lost and regained. The decisive battles were at Saraighat and Itakhuli on the Brahmaputra towards the end of the 17th century, where the Mughal army was defeated. This was the high point of the Ahom kingdom though, and fissures started to appear soon after.

The next group to enter what is today called the North East were the British, in the form of the East India Company. It is generally held that they landed up in Assam looking for sources of revenue like tea and oil. However the process of colonization was not straightforward. The first troops under Captain Welsh reached Upper Assam towards the end of the 18th century. They did not stay on though, as the province was considered too remote and insalubrious to merit occupation, and wracked by internal rebellion, raids by hill tribes, and incursions by the Burmese. The British returned a second time about two decades later, after the invading Burmese army had subdued Manipur and Assam (and carried off numerous people as slaves). What brought them back was the proximity of the Burmese army to Bengal (and the then capital of British India, Calcutta) as well as reports that the French—with whom the British had a running rivalry—after being expelled from India were plotting with the Burmese. The Yandaboo Treaty of 1826 followed, while the discovery of tea was largely due to the efforts of Scottish adventurers such as the Bruce brothers, and the discovery of oil came much later. The province of Assam was in no way central to the British Empire; indeed, most books on the subject mention Assam in a cursory way, if at all.

The Bodo Kachari groups meanwhile went about their own ways of life and tried not to have too much to do with the British, or the people they were bringing into Assam from the rest of India, mostly labour, skilled and unskilled.

Among the Bodos of the north bank region, some went to work in the new tea gardens set up by the British after clearing the forests—many among them attracted the attention of missionaries, who were out to civilize these heathens, for it was far harder to try and convert the Hindu Assamese. One of the most well-known of these missionaries was the Reverend Sidney Endle, who authored the first manual of the Bodo language in 1884, and lies buried in Bengbari, not far from Udalguri, forgotten by the outside world. Udalguri was one of the centres of the Bodo Christian community, while toward the west to Kokrajhar there was more of an earlier Hindu influence among the people. As Assam was slowly drawn into the independence struggle and then the wrangling over Partition, there were those young Bodos with a reformist mindset who were already talking about the need to protect their people from being marginalised by immigration from Bengal. This later took the form of the Tribal Belts and Blocks, where non-tribals (which meant Muslims from East Pakistan/Bangladesh, Adivasis and Assamese) were not supposed to own land, but that was exactly what happened over time, leading to land alienation among the sons of the soil.

One of the factors that led to this was the willingness of Bodo cultivators to sell their land, either to Muslim or Adivasi farmers, and move to new areas, sometimes a long distance away. This is how the Bodo population built up in the areas formerly covered by reserve forests around Gohpur and Biswanath on the north bank. Their argument was that these were their lands of yore. But an even larger influence was the strong desire, among a certain section of the Bodos, almost a sort of genetic trait, to clear the forest and start cultivation afresh. They termed it in their own language as *hadan siphainai*, what in Assamese was called *jonghol bhonga* or clearing the jungle or forest, as well as *notun mati luwa* or taking possession of new land. These virgin forest lands, as the beat officer Gautam Pegu had mentioned when Abhijit had visited the Foothills area after many years, were naturally fertile and gave large yields of rice. After most of the aforementioned areas had been occupied (which in turn led to clashes between the Bodos and Assamese in the 1980s), the only sizeable stretch that remained in the north bank was in Sonitpur district—especially the Balipara and Chariduar reserve forests to the north of the district, comprising almost 900 sq km of subtropical evergreen and tropical deciduous tree cover: some of the most impressive forests in India, teeming with wildlife.

In the decades after Independence, the marginalisation of the Bodos continued even as the numbers of other communities—Muslims, Adivasis, Bengali Hindus, Assamese—in the traditional Bodo areas increased. The Muslim farmers, descended from people who had been heavily taxed by the Mughals in Bengal, were more intensive, settled cultivators with a commercial bent, whereas the Bodos were in the nature of shifting cultivators and thus at a disadvantage. If they had been a community in the previously remote hills of North East India, like say the Khasis or Mizos, they might have got a separate state of their own. Instead there was the formation of a body called the Plains Tribal Council of Assam or the PTCA, ultimately co-opted by the ruling Congress party, which controlled politics in the state (and the North East) till the mid-1980s. The well-organized students' union among the Bodos rejected the PTCA, and made it clear that what they called the chauvinistic attitude of the caste Hindu Assamese people left the creation of a separate Bodo state as the only option. In 1985 the student-led AGP government came to power in the state. There was a falling out with a section of the Bodo leadership over the separate state issue. There were indications that the Congress party, which had earlier used its dirty tricks in Punjab and Kashmir to stifle or co-opt regional dissent, now used the services of senior politicians from Silchar, West Bengal and Arunachal Pradesh (besides intelligence agencies) to aid the extremist fringe among the Bodos, leading to strong action from an often clueless state-police force. The massacre of Bodo people (and people from other communities in retaliatory attacks) in the riots in Gohpur and Lakhimpur in the late 1980s led to a further hardening of attitudes on both sides.

Going through some old newspapers stacked in his grandfather's room, Abhijit came across several mentions of the unrest in the Bodo areas in Assam's north bank region in the late 1980s. The violence had started in Kokrajhar and Udalguri districts, and there were mentions of pipe guns and bow and arrows, bomb blasts on railway lines and bandhs. Also, in those sparse accounts of events from long ago, there were already mention of fratricidal attacks among the Bodo groups. People associated with the PTCA were killed, and its cadres killed youths from the other groups. This was around the time when Khagen Saikia had passed away. It was also the period when the 'organization' or ULFA had stepped up its activities, mainly in upper and lower Assam, to 'liberate' the state. By the time Abhijit had returned from Delhi there were more sophisticated arms circulating in the north bank areas: AK-47s and M-16s, pistols and UBGLs; more blood, more massacres, riots. Death had become a commonplace occurrence.

Among the Bodo youth involved in their community's struggle, two separate channels or streams, so to speak, had opened up. To the west, toward Kokrajhar, a volunteer force came up, in part to protect Bodo villages (especially after incidents like the gangrape of several women by the police at a village called Bhumka in the January of 1988), and then, with the acquisition (and manufacture) of weapons, morphed into an armed group fighting for a separate Bodo state within India. This process was hastened by the formation to the east, toward Udalguri, of a Bodo youth organization which soon emerged—with the help of one of the Naga insurgent groups, through a Shillong connection—as an armed group fighting for independence for the Bodos. One group for statehood, one group for independence, both groups with arms: internecine strife was sure to follow between the cadres of the two groups, especially in the remote areas toward the Assam border with Bhutan and Arunachal Pradesh.

'Those were terrible times,' a former bodyguard of a famous student leader (now deceased, and who had fought for statehood) told Abhijit in Udalguri, on his second visit there. 'People would avoid the road heading from Udalguri to Bhairabkunda (the tri-junction of Assam, Arunachal Pradesh, and Bhutan) as cadres from both groups roamed the area. Many were killed from either side.' Tarun Boro, the bodyguard, was the one who told Abhijit, with his first-hand experience of the period, that the volunteer force wasn't under the students' union as was often reported, just that with the appearance of arms the union lost control of the volunteer force; the volunteers became a separate group.

Boro said that the two objectives—statehood and independence—led to conflicts between the two groups, as each sought to take over the other, and it was only incidental that most leaders associated with the western group were Hindus while most associated with the eastern group were Christians: it wasn't as some people later wrote, that a Hindu–Christian schism had appeared among them. The former bodyguard had once made a trip from Kokrajhar to Udalguri, along the foothills of the mountains, travelling by night, crossing rivers with the help of Muslim boatmen ('at that time they supported our cause,' he said), and carrying with them several carbines which they had obtained from Siliguri. They didn't have, he told Abhijit, the Nagaland link that would later allow the independence-seeking group access to sophisticated weapons.

Their group, Boro said, began to be used by the army and the police in operations against the other group. Divide and rule: the usual strategy. In the new millennium, Boro's group was dissolved and a political party formed in its place which took over a territorial council granted by the Centre—with the finance and law wings under the charge of the Assam government. As was to be expected, the two groups kept clashing, with a renewed call for a Bodoland or separate Bodo state in the north bank. 'Divide Assam 50:50' was their demand. The independence group then split following the orchestration of serial bomb blasts in Guwahati and other places in Assam in 2008 in which eighty-one people were killed. The faction that remained carried on from its bases in Myanmar (along with bases of some Manipuri groups and the original 'organization' from Assam, now much shrunken in number), and it was the boys from this faction of the independence-seeking group that had picked up Abhijit. The boy who had been shot on the Foothills road by the police commandos had belonged to this group as well.

Abhijit also had to go back in history to find out more about how most of the Chariduar RF had disappeared. The events that led to the reserve forest, that wilderness of his childhood which had made a deep, unfathomable impression upon him, shrinking from an area of 460 sq km (almost as large as the Kaziranga national park) to just about 80 or 90 sq km, in a matter of less than two decades, was something no one seemed to have a full picture of. That led to situations where journalists could say that there were forty to fifty thousand people in those areas (under the Dhekiajuli LAC) without panchayat rights, putting the blame on the government, the state, the higher powers. They wouldn't have spoken to people like the old man Nana at Kamengbari, who had told Abhijit how he had heard on nights the *dham dham dham* sound as the big trees were felled one after the other by the new settlers.

A long, long time ago, most of the Assam valley had been heavily forested. Woodcutters from the west and settlers from the east were the first to start clearing these vast primal forests, but this area of the north bank under the Eastern

Himalayas was too remote to be reached. The Bodos, or Kacharis as they were (and still are) referred to, and who had come down in phases from Tibet, were the original owners of these lands. But they were troubled by raiders from the Bhutan hills, as a result of which the foothill areas weren't settled, the Bodos preferring to carry out their shifting cultivation (by clearing patches of forest) lower down. The Belsiri and Dhansiri rivers flowed through the Chariduar tract, and were supposed to be the names of Bodo queens of yore. In time, a group of people came down from Tibet into the Kameng area and eastern Bhutan. One of their kings, known as Japtang, from the Sherdukpen tribe, started collecting tribute from the Bodos of the Chariduar tract. Japtang's brother became a king in eastern Bhutan.

Abhijit came to know two versions of this: in one, Japtang's father, who had several wives, married an Ahom princess from Sivasagar in upper Assam, and the Ahom king later ceded the tract to his grandson; in the other, and more probable version, Japtang's father married a princess from the Koch tribe, which had ties with the Kacharis, and which at one time had a kingdom stretching up to the Darrang area, including Sonitpur. The Sherdukpens would come down from Rupa to a place called Doimara (from where Abhijit had set out on his ill-fated trek) to collect their posa or tribute (in the form of household goods).

This system of paying tribute to the highlanders was converted by the British into a monetary payment, which was stopped in 1873. By then the British were clearing large tracts of forest to set up tea plantations, where some Bodos went to work as daily wage earners. In 1878, the Chariduar tract had been notified as a game sanctuary by the British; in 1934 it was declared as a game reserve on account of its rich wildlife, including rhinos. There was a game warden camped by the Belsiri river (which was actually one of the four old duars or corridors of the char duar or Chariduar). In 1939, just before the outbreak of World War II, the English explorer Harold Tilman arrived at Rangapara train station with an entourage of sherpas from Darjeeling, en route to climbing Mount Gorichen. After spending a night at Nameri by the Bhoroli river (where he was troubled by mosquitoes, and had a clear sight of the snow-capped mountains further north), they reached the game warden's camp at a place called 'Tiger Flat', probably present-day Kamengbari, or the old army mule camp near the river, to which there was then a rough road along the foothills from Bhalukpung. The next day they set out into the hills with elephants carrying their supplies. Tilman mentions Bhutia traders going up with grain and salt who were attacked by wild elephants, and also that the few huts at Doimara were deserted (it was only occupied during the winter by people coming down from Rupa; the beat officer Gautam Pegu had told Abhijit about this).

After Independence, it was possible till the late 1960s, as the old phandi Dilwar Saikia had told Abhijit, to shoot deer inside the forest and bring it out after paying a fee at the Kolamati gate. Maybe it was something like this that people like Pradip Deka were looking for during their hunting trips at night. By then the India–China war had also taken place in 1962 (with soldiers in retreat stumbling down through the Kameng region onto the North Bank), and while after that the army presence increased in Tezpur (where the new 4 Corps had its headquarters) and in Missamari, there existed into the 21st century an unofficial central government policy of not encouraging or undertaking any large infrastructure or business projects in the North Bank area, for fear of those falling into enemy hands during another conflict. A new road was started from Balipara, passing through Chariduar (the station) and up into the hills, meeting the old Foothills to Tawang track at Rupa. It was a small road, and widening work on it had been going on for more than a decade now under the BRO. This policy of not encouraging employment generation in the North Bank would turn out to be important.

There had always been small-scale logging (with the help of elephants and trucks) and poaching in the forests along the North Bank, Chariduar reserve forest included, mainly with the connivance of the low paid forest guards and rangers. What would a truckload of timber or a pair of deer matter, they might have rationalised, when there was so much left. That the forests were common property of the state of Assam wouldn't really have been on anyone's mind. The very nature of people's existence and the political system meant that short-term gains were all people were interested in. The reserve forests were seen by most people, leaving aside some daring men, as protected areas, where one didn't venture. This came to an end by the late 1980s and early 1990s, as surrendered insurgents, by parlaying their status as people helping the police and army in fighting the 'organization', started entering the reserve forests more frequently to bring out truckloads of freshly-cut timber, for sale in nearby market towns, or sent further down by train to sawmills. Once this started happening, common people started seeing the forests as fair game in order to earn money.

The settlement of people in the Chariduar reserve forest was done by certain politicians and condoned by political parties—who ensured that the new settlers could cast their votes in both state assembly and national assembly elections—and also by the eastern group demanding a sovereign Bodoland. This started happening on a larger scale from the late 1990s onwards, when people saw that the state government could be coerced into not taking definite action. The forest department carried out numerous eviction drives, close to a hundred of them, but in the absence of support from the judiciary and other departments, gave up by the year 2002.

Another factor was the shifting cultivation of the Bodos done by clearing forest lands, an old and ingrained practice of theirs, whereby one or more sons in a family, in combination with others, would go to clear the forest, *jonghol sapha kora* as they said in Assamese, or, in almost Biblical-sounding language, *notun mati bhonga*: breaking new land. People who were familiar with the issue said that only the Bodos were tough enough to carry this out, clearing the forest and establishing new villages, it was something which ran in their blood. And by the late 1990s, the Chariduar forest was the last remaining large patch of forest in the North Bank. The western insurgent group, which had links with the main Naga armed faction, also seems to have been influenced by the 'cleansing' drives carried out by the latter in the hills of Manipur starting in the early 1990s. To control a territory, you had to have your own people on the ground.

Not all Bodos were interested in searching for 'new earth' though, especially those who stayed in the revenue villages. Abhijit was told about this by a Bodo LP or lower-primary school headmaster who had a modest house in the civilian area of Missamari. Before becoming a teacher, this person had been a halua or ploughman, and his brother was a gang man in the railways: the family was originally from Cachar. When Abhijit reached their house in the evening the headmaster and his wife had got back from a church xobha or gathering in nearby Gormara ('rhino killing', the place name, again a link to the old) and he was having a cup of tea. He had been at a nearby school for the past twenty years, and he had recently been transferred as headmaster to a school some 8 km ahead of Thelamara, toward the river, a mostly miya area. He still reached on time, cleaned up the school and had the children sing the national anthem before classes started at 9 am.

The headmaster too said that the people in the Foothills area and above Batasipur had come from other places, including Karbi Anglong and the Nagaland border and Dimapur, and that they had been settled through a sort of dewani system (the word Haphang and Rubul Ali had used) where agents went ahead and looked for notun mati, *jot jonghol bhangibo pari*, or 'where the jungle can be cleared'. He said the people in those areas, non-revenue areas (as opposed to the old revenue Bodo villages like Dhekipelowa, Rikamari, etc.), had a different mentality, and that he didn't mix with them.

'They think differently, and somewhere in their mind they are always thinking of notun mati where crops will grow well, but nowadays we have fertilizers, and there is less land available. How can people live without facilities in this day and age? They will take a long time to come up in life. As long as they don't change their thinking they will always be left behind. All those insurgents have harmed our Bodo society, even those who have surrendered can never come back to normal society, they always try to make money by intimidating people or cornering contracts.' As Mohen Doctor had told Abhijit, the older Bodo people in Sonitpur had almost become Assamese in their habits.

The settlement of people and the attendant large-scale clearing of the forest led to the development of an economy based on timber and charcoal (made by burning trees of lesser value in covered pits). Timber was sent out by the train line that ran along the North Bank from Balipara through Dhekiajuli toward the west. Individuals took small lots of timber themselves on the trains, in passenger compartments, after getting to the train line by cycle or bullock cart, while middlemen in places like Rangapara arranged for forest department TPs or transit passes to send timber to dealers and sawmills in lower Assam or even further on to Bihar or Delhi. Charcoal and firewood went into supporting the local economy of places like Missamari, Rangapara and Dhekiajuli.

As population in the North Bank increased, so too did the pressure on land. The unofficial policy of the Indian government after the 1962 war in not allowing any large projects to come up in the area meant that, apart from government jobs and the tea gardens (where most workers had hereditary jobs) and a tiny private sector, there were no jobs to be had. It was this factor, along with inter-community riots toward the west of the North Bank and floods and silt burying fields toward the east of the North Bank, that led to the region becoming the second-highest source of trafficking in India, besides outmigration of people from all communities, including Bodo and Assamese, for low-paid jobs elsewhere in India, and boys joining insurgent groups, and also, inevitably the monetization of the wild: timber and wildlife, sand and stones from rivers. Away from the small towns along the highway, a whole new form of economy based on clearing forests came into being. About half a century after the war, Delhi belatedly realized that a disgruntled populace was a larger threat than a repeat invasion, and projects started to come up. But it was too late: the forests had disappeared, and poor families had been uprooted and torn apart.

The short-term profit motives of politicians and contractors alike was both a cause and symptom of what ailed the North Bank region. By the turn of the century, there was a revenue collection stream in the forest department which went down right from the top to the level of a beat officer, who had to come up with 2 lakh rupees or so a month (and would invariably also keep a similar amount for himself). Postings of DFOs were sold for lakhs of rupees, the amount to be recouped later by further exploitation of whatever forest resources remained. In all of this, the morale of the ill-paid forest guards, the first line of defence, never high in the first place, sank lower.

With the change in the state government in 2015, a Bodo woman politician with a reputation for straightforwardness was made the forest minister. Some efforts were made at stemming the rot within the department, including some laudable work by a woman DFO posted at Tezpur. There were murmurs among wildlife NGO members and forest department staff about some sort of rejuvenation plan for the encroached forests, where the settlers would be given rights for 40 or 50 per cent of the land, and the rest would be re-forested through plantation drives. However, the entire system had been subverted for too long, and there were powerful lobbies at work. The forest minister had her portfolio removed, and the DFO was transferred to Jorhat on the South Bank.

Thus had Abhijit come to an understanding of the factors that had led to the disappearance of that great forest he had known as a child. And all of these factors came together in a sort of perfect storm just before the end of the century.

A final piece of information regarding this episode came from Lokhi, who all those years ago had been looking after Pradip Deka's camp at Foothills. They had met a couple of times, and he knew of Abhijit's interest in the Chariduar reserve forest area. It was Lokhi who mentioned something which Abhijit had overlooked, or hadn't heard about from anyone else. He said there had been a large furniture market at Dhekiajuli, which lay 35 km to the west of Tezpur on the highway. It was then that Abhijit recalled the furniture shops along the highway just as one entered that small town. To the north of Dhekiajuli was the railway station, from where sawn logs had been sent out by train, and above the railway station was the Batasipur area (where the young ASP had been ambushed and killed). A lot of timber had made its way down to the furniture market at Dhekiajuli, where, Lokhi said, people came from all over Assam, lower Assam and upper Assam, to buy beds and dining tables and almirahs, among other items, especially before a wedding. Then there were the carpenters who made rough furniture pieces and 'polished' them with a type of earth called *gerua mati*, for furniture store owners from places like Tezpur and Nagaon, because then those could be shown as 'finished' goods and couldn't be seized by the forest department or police. The pieces would then be taken apart and given a finer finishing at the final destination. Thus, it seemed like the entire state of Assam had, in a way, shared in the plunder from those magnificent forests.

There was a Nath person from Bihaguri near Tezpur who had been a big player there, when the market had been at its heyday about a decade earlier, Lokhi told Abhijit. This person had started out as a petty thief, then moved into selling timber, and finally became a sort of 'furniture king' of the area. Lokhi didn't know if he was alive or dead now.

A Link to the Past

Two days after Abhijit had got back from the Dhekiajuli range office, he got a call from a harried-sounding Dilip Basumatary from Missamari. The teacher said he had been trying Abhijit's number for several days, and asked where he was. Abhijit explained that he was in Tezpur, but had been travelling a bit, and asked him how things were. What Basumatary told him left him speechless: two boys, surrendered cadres from toward Batasipur, had come one day on a bike and asked about Laimwn. She hadn't been at home then. The next day, a team of army men had come at night, when they were all sleeping. They took Laimwn into the kitchen to be questioned, and they could hear her screaming inside. She had cried the whole night after the men had left, and then disappeared in the morning. Later a friend of hers told Basumatary that she had gone to join the insurgents, and that she wanted to go to Myanmar for training.

'My brother and his wife have lost one child,' he said. 'They cannot lose another.'

He then asked Abhijit if he knew what had happened. Though he denied any knowledge of it, his heart raced at the thought of what the teacher would ask next. Sure enough,

Basumatary demanded to know why Abhijit hadn't told him about the letter from Rankhw.

'You brought a letter from the commander to give to Laimwn, didn't you?'

'I didn't know it was for her,' Abhijit pleaded, which was true. 'I was told to give the letter to the old woman in the tea shop.'

'Laimwn saw you there, she told me after those two boys came,' Basumatary said. 'Why didn't you tell me about it?'

'I ... I forgot,' Abhijit stuttered. 'I forgot about the letter.'

The teacher's voice now rose. 'How did they know about Laimwn and the letter? How did they know where she lived? Who told the surrendered boys and the army?'

Abhijit, who was outside on the veranda, put his free hand on a pillar to steady himself. What had he got himself into!

'I don't know,' he said weakly, 'I didn't tell anyone anything.'

'Then how did they know?' Basumatary demanded, shouting now. 'How did they know? *You* came to our house!'

'I don't know, I don't know anything,' Abhijit pleaded.

'My brother told me, you should have never brought that Assamese fellow to our home!' Basumatary spat out, and hung up.

Abhijit stood there for a while, looking at the phone in his hands, then went to a corner of the lawn where he bent over and retched, bringing out some of his morning tea. What had he gotten himself involved in? Where was the girl now? What had the army men done to her? The thoughts swirled around in his mind, making him feel weak and giddy. He went back to the house, where he wandered about the rooms. He felt unable to concentrate, to decide what to do next. His uncle was out on some work, and his grandmother after having had a bath was sitting in her customary chair by the cluttered table, brushing her hair and watching Julie prepare the daytime meal in the kitchen at the rear.

'Boha,' she said, asking him to sit, looking up at him and smiling, using the formal term as though he were a visitor.

'Bohisu,' he said to her, I'm sitting, and sat down on a chair near her.

She kept looking at him, a sad smile masking her confusion. But how peaceful she was, with no idea of what the world had turned into, lost within her own memories. Where would *he* find peace now? Her gnarled, arthritic hand reached out and held his forearm. He wondered if some glimmer of recognition had seeped through. She regarded the people around her as she did the newspaper she read everyday: recognizable only as human beings, and words, with no further meaning beyond that. Now she started talking about her grandfather. Something had happened, someone had been killed after an argument over a woman, people had gathered. Abhijit didn't know the names she was mentioning, and her story was disjointed. She spoke about the kala azar fever: it had spread across the land, whole villages had been emptied by death and desertion. It seemed her grandfather and some others had taken the man to the British authorities in town and he had been thrown in jail. Then she lapsed into silence once again, her mouth quivering, as if some old memory of childhood terror had risen up. Who was the woman, he asked her, but she wouldn't talk any more.

Abhijit spent the rest of the day in a vague, confused state, both aware of the events concerning Laimwn at the back of his mind and also not wishing to dwell upon them, for hadn't he been the one who had opened his mouth and told Major Dev about her? He tried reading a book but the words didn't register in his mind. So he turned his grandmother's story around in his mind, and it conjured up for him a hazy, half-remembered world, cut off from the world outside. Wasn't it still that way, he thought: the disappeared forests, the invisible people by the great river?

He spent a sleepless night, and the next morning after breakfast went out for a walk to Mission Chariali, to buy a couple of household items, but actually to get out of the house and clear his head. Winter wasn't too far off, and it was a pleasant morning. He walked along the newly-constructed covered drain (which had been left incomplete in parts), rubbish strewn at its sides, past the petrol pump, the old flour mill, the police outpost and the shops opposite the Mission hospital. The morning traffic was just starting to build up at the crossroads. He crossed over to the shops on the other side, opposite the hotel, where there was a newspaper agent beside a bus counter, both inside one small shop. An elderly man in thick-rimmed glasses and a half sweater was leafing through an Assamese magazine, and he looked up at Abhijit as he entered. There was something familiar about the man, but he quickly left with the magazine, walking to a motorcycle and kickstarting it. Then the ticket-counter man said, to the newspaper boy, 'Mohen Doctor came after a long time, didn't he?' Abhijit stepped out, but the motorcycle was already gone.

He went back in and asked if they knew where Mohen Doctor stayed. They weren't sure, but the ticket-counter man said he could find out, so Abhijit gave him his number. Late in the afternoon, when Abhijit was reading a book (about the British officer in the North Eastern Frontier, the same book he had been reading by the river above Doimara), the man from the counter called him with Mohen Doctor's address—the former homeopathic doctor stayed in a house near Goroimari, on the highway from Tezpur to Balipara. Abhijit thanked him, and thought about it for a moment: the doctor had been a good friend of his father's and Pradip Deka's. He got ready and left the house. He caught an auto from the main road headed to Goroimari, and reached the tiniali or tri-junction about twenty-five minutes later and got down. There were small shops all around, and one road went right toward the air force station, where the Sukhoi fighter jets were stationed.

From the tri-junction he had to walk beside the busy highway where cars and trucks sped past. The shops quickly fell away, and houses appeared, modest dwellings in large compounds. Finally he came to the address, a single-story house built lengthwise down the property with a tin roof overhanging from the sides, similar in style to most neighbouring houses. Abhijit walked through the overgrown grass to the iron-grille-enclosed veranda and pressed the bell. In one corner of the veranda, which was bare save for the old motorcycle parked there, was a cardboard box with a sack inside it, possibly for a dog. He pressed the bell again but no one appeared. Stepping onto the grass, he looked down both sides of the house, but there appeared to be no one among the betel nut and coconut trees behind the house. Just then he heard the gate open, and turned to see the man in the half sweater and thick glasses, holding a brown desi dog on a leash.

Abhijit stood there explaining who he was, as the dog sniffed and barked at him. Finally the doctor understood and tied the dog to the veranda grille and opened the door to the sitting room, asking him in. The French beard was gone, Abhijit noticed, that was why the doctor looked different, older and slower too, like all the people his father had known. The sitting room smelt musty, occupied by a cane sofa set, a bed and a table with an old desktop computer covered in plastic—a room untouched by the hand of a woman, it seemed. Mohen Doctor sat on a chair near Abhijit and said that he was surprised to see his old friend's son after so many years, where had he come from? As the daylight faded in the small room Abhijit told him everything: the years in Shillong, believing his father had been killed, the years in Delhi, his mother passing away, his own travels around the Foothills area trying to gain some understanding of why his father might have taken his own life.

'I read about your mother passing away,' Mohen Doctor said in his soft voice, 'there was a small item in one of the Assamese newspapers. And several times after that I would wonder where Khagen da's son was. So you finally found out what happened to him?'

'It's true, isn't it?' Abhijit said, his voice quavering. 'But why did he do it?'

The doctor looked at him for several moments, then stood up and went into the house, returning a while later with something in his hand. He handed it to Abhijit and asked him to read it, even as he pulled the curtains and switched on the tubelight in the room and then went into the house again, saying he would make tea for them. It was an old envelope, the ink-blue coloured ones marked 'Aerogramme', and on the front, in his father's handwriting, there was his mother's name and the address of the Tezpur house. Abhijit opened the folds of the letter with a trembling hand. The first thing was the date in the top right-hand corner: a few days after he had left his father at the Gabharu beat office and returned to Tezpur by bus. It was addressed to his mother, with his father's name at the end, a short letter. He took a deep breath and looked away from the letter. Beside the old desktop computer was a table-top calendar of a nearby wine shop, with foreign scenery and an inspirational quote. Abhijit started reading the letter.

He read it several times, following his father's neat cursive in blue fountain-ink, now faded with time. Only when he stopped and looked up did he realize that the doctor was back with a tray on which were two small cups of tea and a plate of nimki and pitha. What he had read, at once so simple and yet containing the turmoil and dilemma of a man's life, spoke to him across the years in a direct way. The anger he had sometimes felt toward his father lifted, to be replaced by a deep sorrow.

'It was addressed to my mother!' he cried out. 'Why

didn't she show it to me? And how did this come to be with you?'

The doctor handed Abhijit a cup of tea, took a sip from the other cup, and said, 'I hope the tea is okay. I do all my cooking myself. Never got married, you see. You're asking how this letter ended up with me? Now that you've read it, what do you think your mother must have felt when *she* read it?'

And he could see it now, not just how his mother must have felt, the blow the letter would have given her, but also how the letter would have pushed her to abandon her in-laws, Tezpur even, to try and put all the memories of her husband behind her—and for that, she would have had to tell him, Abhijit, that his father had been shot in the forest by the insurgents.

He nodded slowly. 'Yes, I think I can understand what she felt.'

'She got the letter, then she tried calling the beat office. It was already too late by then. When I went to your father's house she showed me the letter. She told me I could keep it, along with a small photo of them, taken just after their marriage. She said,' here the doctor took a deep breath, 'she said otherwise she would throw them away. Later I heard she had taken you and left for Shillong the next morning. She didn't want you to light his pyre, she told me that.'

He was aware of the tears running down his cheek then, and the doctor got up, laid a hand on his shoulder, and then graciously went inside the house. He had recovered by the time Mohen Doctor returned, along with the small black-and-white photo of his parents, which the doctor said he could keep, besides the letter.

'I have read that letter and looked at that photo so many times they are imprinted on my mind,' the doctor said. 'Now it's time they go with you. Do not judge your parents too harshly Abhijit, every life has its own share of problems. I am just glad that your father and I were friends once upon a time.'

Abhijit asked how they had become friends, and the doctor told him. Here there was another surprise awaiting Abhijit, for he had somehow always assumed that Mohen Doctor had come to Tezpur from upper Assam. But the doctor told him that he was originally from there itself, actually from near Balipara further ahead. He knew, the way people do in small places, who Khagen Saikia and Pradip Deka were, but he really got friendly with them while he was doing his timber business, from around 1975 to 1985, bringing in timber to a sawmill near Balipara from the Nameri area, the trees felled by woodcutters and dragged out by elephants and loaded onto second-hand Shaktiman trucks.

Then he had left for upper Assam, where he worked for a while in a tea estate even as he picked up the practice of homeopathy from an elderly Bengali homeopath with whom he had become friendly. But by the early 1990s not just the army and the 'organization', but also surrendered members of the organization were troubling people, and he had returned to Tezpur—later Abhijit would feel that it might have had something to do with money. He had set up a homeopathy practice in Tezpur, and then become an overseer for Pradip Deka's MES projects up in the Tawang area of Arunachal Pradesh. All that came to an end after the contractor's death, caused, like so many in their group, by the bottle, and he had moved into this house, which had belonged to his father, and then opened a pharmacy at the nearby Goroimari tiniali, where he still handed out homeopathic medicine to those who wanted it.

When he had been working as an overseer for Pradip Deka, he had stayed in the Dirang and Tawang areas for months at a time. One time he was flown to Bomdila by a drunk sardar helicopter pilot, with the helicopter touching the tree tops, and once in Dirang the local Monpas showed him a house where there were stacks of skeletons with dog tags which they claimed were from the 1962 war, and another time a minister wearing shorts and carrying a dao walked into an office where Mohen Doctor was waiting. When the clerk didn't pay any heed to him, the minister thrashed the clerk and another fellow.

It was oddly comforting to hear about the peripatetic existence of his father's friend, living his own small modest life now. He asked the doctor about life in the forests, about working with Pradip Deka, and how the vast forests along the border with Arunachal had disappeared.

'I lead a simple life. I don't have many possessions. But I had an interesting life, and saw many things, from the forests to the tea gardens to the mountains. From what I saw from my first business,' the doctor said, 'the people who stayed in the forest and did that work became jungli in a way, firing guns and drinking, but some of them were educated people too. We would drive around late at night back then with no worries. From the Assam Agitation days the troubles started. Encroachment in the forests was always there, but it picked up from the late 1980s. There was logging by surrendered cadres from the 'organization', by criminals, by insurgents, the forest guards abandoned their posts in fear, and timber was being sent out by train from Rangapara and Dhekiajuli stations.'

'And my father knew all of this was going to happen?'

'Yes, he had an idea of it. I remember him telling me that what had happened above Gohpur and Biswanath Chariali would also happen above Rangapara and Missamari and Dhekiajuli. And besides, I think your father was suffering from depression. Nobody knew what it was back then. But I've spent a long time thinking about him ... if it was today he could have maybe seen a psychiatrist and been prescribed medicines.'

'But would that have solved his problem up in Bomdila?' Abhijit asked.

'You know about that too?' the doctor said. 'Of course, it was in the letter.'

'Yes. Who was she?'

'That I don't know,' the doctor said, and started clearing the table.

Abhijit asked him when he had last visited Foothills, and he said it had been about a decade ago, to a place in the jungle where at one time people had been sacrificed, Erang Terang or something like that, maybe an old name for Shiva and Parvati. Abhijit mentioned the ruins of the small shrine near the Gelgeli beat camp, and the Guxani beel inside the jungle, and he said that could be it. They had gone to the beel to sacrifice four goats, for a minister who was standing for re-election, and they had taken him along too. They saw boys from the western insurgent group eating food by the beel. One Hazarika from Rikamari bazar did the puja and the sacrifices.

'But the dao kept bouncing off the fourth goat,' Mohen Doctor said, 'and then the pujari went into a trance and started muttering, there were gusts of wind, the sky grew dark, and a loud sound like that made by an elephant, and the forest ranger with us said there might be one coming our way, but then we saw the largest hornbill I have ever seen, flying over us in the middle of the jungle and crying out.'

It was time for Abhijit to take his leave. They walked out into the evening, still talking. Mohen Doctor told him about how the miyas had been stopped from going further in the area by the tea gardens. Then there were Nepalis who had been affected by floods and settled in the area. There were old Bodo families too who had become almost Assamese now: *namot he Bodo hoi ase etiya*, he said, or, they are Bodo only in name now. He mentioned the massive new plant being set up in the nearby industrial estate by a famous religious baba's company.

'Look at the traffic on the road, go and see the rubbish all around the market,' he said as he opened the gate. 'People are the problem. No one cares nowadays. I think it's better to just be ignorant—if you know things, it makes you think, and that makes you miserable.'

Abhijit looked back as he walked toward the gaudily-lit tiniali, and saw Mohen Doctor raise a hand to bid him farewell. He got on to a minibus headed for Mission Chariali. Looking at the vehicles with their lights streaming past on the busy road, he remembered what his father had said on that last night, about animals having limited wants. The letter might have been written the next morning, while Abhijit was sleeping. He took it out along with the photo from his shirt pocket and went through it again. Having read the letter yet again, he looked out into the night, and in the short distance to the Mission Chariali crossroads, he felt as though he had turned a corner in his life.

He knew now what had happened, something simple and terrible, and the knowledge had set him free. No longer did he feel the need to go to Missamari and Foothills. If he went, it would be to try and atone for whatever sin he may have committed, by visiting the contact he had been told about at the Dhankhana Centre, the linkman Jaikhlong, to try and get in touch with Rankhw, to explain what had happened with the major. Rankhw would understand, he knew. One last trip to see the old forest beat office. He thought about love and forgiveness, and the short time given to people to live their lives, and for the first time in weeks he thought of the one whom he had so cruelly banished from his life. She deserved better, yes, and he would call her and tell her. And Delhi, was it such a terrible place after all? It had given him a living, once upon a time. How long would he remain stuck in the past?

He remembered a relative he had gone to see once in Tezpur, not long after he had arrived. The middle-aged man related to his father was lounging in a chair watching television, and he spent almost an entire hour talking only about his car accident and his injuries and how he couldn't do anything now; there was no desire to find out where

Abhijit might have been or had been doing, and as he returned home, Abhijit realized his relative's life had shrunk to a point where he had no curiosity about other people and the outside world, only his own little life—and he had an intimation of what awaited him as well in the future. No, it was time he acted, it was time he outgrew his passive self.

He got down from the bus (as it had turned left, going to Soolong beyond the bridge), and, feeling the sudden need for a cigarette, walked over to a nearby paan shop. There was an elderly Assamese man sitting cross-legged behind the display, a gentle-mannered man making a few paans for a customer, and as Abhijit waited, the radio, which had been playing a Bhupen Hazarika number, now changed to *Kohuwa Bon*. It seemed to him that life had come full circle for him: he had got down here a few months ago a very different individual to what he was now. He bought a single stick and lit it, savouring the tobacco smoke and the slight headrush it brought on, then moved aside and dialled a number on his phone, praying that it hadn't been changed.

A few rings, and that familiar voice on the other side, 'Hello? Abhijit?'

He swallowed down the lump in his throat. So much had happened!

'Debolina? How are you?'

'I'm...I'm,' she cleared her throat, 'getting by...I suppose.'

'I wanted to call you...'

'After more than a year...'

'I wasn't sure you would answer...'

'Yes, maybe I shouldn't have!'

She was crying now, and he waited with his heart hammering, by the side of the busy crossing. Finally, she regained control of herself, and asked, 'Where are you?'

'Tezpur, in Assam,' he said, and added, 'at my father's house.'

'Oh...so you've...settled there?'

'No, no. I...' he had to take a deep breath to continue 'I was actually thinking of coming back to Delhi.'

After a long silence he asked, 'Can I come and see you?'

She said quietly, 'Yes.' And then, 'Why do you have to ask?'

'I thought things might have changed...Anyway, I'll be coming soon. There's just one last trip I need to make...'

Their said their goodbyes soon after, and he took a last drag on his cigarette before walking back to his father's house.

After he got back he had washed up, and was sitting in the back veranda with a cup of red tea he had asked Julie to make for him, thinking about the conversation he had just had, when his uncle came hurrying out from his room.

'Have you seen what they're showing on the news?' he asked, seeming agitated.

Abhijit followed him, wondering what the matter was. It turned out that there had been a massacre of Adivasi tribals, by members of the western insurgent group. On an Assamese news channel, cameras lit up rolled bamboo mats with the bodies inside in the back of a battered pick-up truck standing outside the police station at Biswanath Chariali, 65 km east of Tezpur. Some distance away an old man in tattered clothing squatted on the ground, his dark, aboriginal face expressionless, just another unfortunate event in a lifetime of deprivation. One infant had been shot as it was suckling at its mother's breast. There were four locations, the others near Dhekiajuli (to the west of Tezpur), and in Chirang and Kokrajhar districts, with many Adivasi people killed, labourers from the tea gardens who had moved out and established villages.

Abhijit sat down in a chair, shocked. The true reality of what he had gotten involved in came to him then. Walking free from Rankhw's group had in a way bolstered his confidence, but the encounter with the major, then the phone call from the village teacher, and now this news, showed him how far he had drifted off course while trying to find out about his father.

'Do you see what they've done?' his uncle asked, his voice quivering. 'You're not going to Foothills again, do you understand?'

Abhijit nodded. In a way he felt relieved, for now the decision had been taken out of his hands, almost. He needn't go looking for the linkman in Dhankhana in order to get word across to Rankhw. This was something big. Things would be different from here on.

That night after dinner he spent a long time looking at the old photo of his parents, before he had been conceived, and then going through the letter again and again. There were just two paragraphs to it:

'What have I done in this life? What have I given you and our son? I have never fitted into this society. I became a forest officer thinking I would be able to escape it all, but there is no escape for me in this life. You know about the woman from Bomdila, so I need not tell you about her. If I cannot be with her, then I cannot be with you either.

'My son I hope will make up his own mind about me when he grows up and finds out what happened. I feel there is a great storm coming, one that will scatter our small lives all over the place. Better to accept this fact and get ready. Take care of Abhijit. By the time you read this I will have shot myself in the forest. Do not think of me. I myself do not know what I am: a beast or a god.'

The last five words were from a quote by Aristotle, which Abhijit found using his phone: 'Anyone who either cannot lead the common life or is so self-sufficient as not to need to, and therefore does not partake of society, is either a beast or a god.' It seemed to him a good description of himself as well. His parents were gone from this world, and he was all alone. As he turned off the light and lay down on the bed, the recent images from the massacre went through his mind. He too felt that there was a great storm coming.

Journey to Tawang

In the morning there was more news, in the newspaper and on television. The death toll was close to eighty Adivasi men, women, and children. Tempers were running high, and Adivasis were targeting Bodo villages, burning them down, killing a few, while in towns like Dhekiajuli they had gathered and were turning violent. There were reports of a massive crackdown being imminent. Abhijit's uncle sat watching this and bemoaning the fate of Assam. It was time for him to move on, Abhijit thought. But he had a few things to take care of before that, starting with finding out who the woman in Bomdila had been.

Later that day he visited Lokhi in his modest house in Kolibari, past the huge red walls of the district jail. Lokhi was in his fifties now, lean and spare with his short hair turned grey. He had given up drinking and smoking after surviving an illness, and his quiet, thoughtful nature had moved toward contemplation and spirituality as he grew older. Abhijit had met him twice before. Lokhi didn't really say anything about his days at the camp at Foothills, rightly viewing them as something that had passed a long time ago. That day though, after Abhijit mentioned that he would be going back to Delhi soon, Lokhi started talking unbidden about his first visit to the camp near the Belsiri river.

'It was sometime in 1987 or 1988 I think,' he said, sipping the tea he had made as they sat out on the veranda. 'I remember it was a gloomy, overcast day, and the forest was dark and damp. Pradip Khura showed me the camp: this is your room, put your bedding here; this is the kitchen, cook your food here. Then he drove off in his Gypsy. I felt like I had been abandoned somewhere at the end of the world. Slowly I got busy with the work, and made friends with the Monpa people in both the lower village by the river and the upper village. Sometimes we would go for picnics and they would dam the river and toss in bleaching powder to kill the fish, then burn them in a fire and eat them, or they would throw dynamite into the river, scooping up the stunned fish later. Nowadays I've heard they use a generator.'

The camp had folded up by 1992, he said. The eviction drives had stopped around 2002, by which time people had come and taken over the land in even larger numbers. Lokhi said when he had returned once in 1996 to the upper village (the lower one by the river had been abandoned by then), most of the forest was still there: this tallied with Abhijit's estimate (confirmed by Google Earth's satellite view) that most of the reserve forest had been cut down in the five years from 1997 to 2001. Lokhi was a circumspect person, always had been, and didn't seem to feel the need to draw any conclusions from his experience at the camp. He had lived through it, and that was good enough for him.

Abhijit then told Lokhi what he had found out about his father.

'The news spread that the insurgents had killed him,' Lokhi said. 'But there was more to the story. You heard the doctor, didn't you? Pradip Khura knew about it, but he would never bring it up, except sometimes while drinking. If Khagen da was there he would start teasing him about going up to Bomdila and Dirang. You know how he was, loved teasing people, pulling their leg.'

'She was a Monpa woman? Up in Bomdila?'

'Yes. I think she was posted in Dirang in some government post. Khagen da would go to meet her. Things were okay, but I think he wanted to leave your mother for her. You know how our society is, they would never accept it. Some tribal woman from the hills! Your mother came to know about it and said she would leave him. And after that...you know what happened.'

'But did she like him? This woman from Bomdila? What was her name?'

'I can't remember her name now, I just heard it once or twice. She liked him, I think, but maybe she had problems of her own, who knows?'

'If I could only find out who she was...'

'Do you remember Nyima, Pradip Khura's friend?' Lokhi said. 'He might be able to tell you.'

'Yes, I remember him. I have his number.'

'One more thing. I got a call sometime back from Pori. You remember her, don't you? Pradip Khura's eldest daughter.'

'Of course.'

'She'll be coming from Guwahati in a couple of days. You should go and meet her.'

'I will. I haven't been back to their house yet.'

The old man Nana at Kamengbari had given Abhijit his son-in-law's number, and after trying it and not getting through for several days, Abhijit finally got lucky one day. Nyima's voice sounded as hoarse and forceful as before and he told Abhijit that his father-in-law had mentioned him, and that the phone network had been down in the entire Rupa area for three days. Abhijit was lucky to have got through as he was going down to the dam project on the Kameng river, where he was doing some contract work, and from there he would go all the way up to Tawang to pick up his sister's son from the monastery. Abhijit could join him if he wished.

So early the next morning, Abhijit went out to the main road and caught a Sumo taxi heading up to Bomdila. Squashed in the back seat with three labourers headed up to some construction project near Tawang, he looked out at the blue skies, the yellow to dark brown paddy fields spreading in area after crossing Balipara, where they got onto the Tawang highway. He saw stands of thin trees, possibly planted by the army's Eco Task Force, and a few isolated large trees which had somehow survived amid the villages and market centres, part of the old Balipara reserve forest, as well as Bodo people starting to harvest paddy in the fields. There were pairs of army men patrolling along the highway all the way from the forested approach to the Nameri sanctuary to Tippi on the inter-state border. Amid the villages after the 12-Mile Centre they came upon the AR camp by the blue waters of the Bhoroli, which was the Kameng river after reaching the plains of Assam, with dark green mountains looming in the distance; populated thinly by some Aka, or Hrusso, tribals along with Monpas and Nyishis. It was where the dam project was located.

Abhijit got down at Bhalukpung, before the check-gate where the Arunachal police checked inner line permits, and walked past the gate to the dismal-looking Tibetan restaurant where Nyima had asked him to wait. The border outpost had grown into a scruffy town, and there was a large red-and-black 'international' hotel now, looming over the small shops and petrol pump. Nyima turned up about 45 minutes later: an accident between a dumper and an army vehicle on the road from Kimi had held him up. The Monpa tribal had aged (and described himself a Sherdukpen now), his hair having grown thinner, a pair of glasses on his face, but otherwise he was still the stocky, pugnacious figure from Abhijit's childhood with his broken Assamese and Hindi. They had a hurried meal of chicken chow before setting out in Nyima's pick-up truck, which had seen better days.

About 10 km out of Bhalukpung was Pinjori, where the road climbed up sharply to the left; Nyima pointed to the right where there was a Bailey bridge and then a kutcha road snaking along the side of the mountains: the road to the hydro project site at Kimi.

As they drove up through the still-green forests of the Kameng area, Nyima told Abhijit what he had been up to all these years: after the short-lived video hall business in their old village by the Belsiri, he had moved on to hiring out a truck he had bought, to the army and forest departments. He'd had to leave their old village after being served an extortion notice by the insurgents, so he'd gone up to Rupa with his family, where he'd set up an electrical goods shop and did a little walnut and orange farming. Now there was his contract work with the dam company, supplying them with stones and cement and bamboo. There was enough for the family to get by, besides his children were settled, the daughter married to a boy who was in the government service in Bomdila and the son a teacher in the KV school in nearby Tenga valley. That was his life now.

Abhijit, who had mentioned on the phone that he was working as a journalist, gave Nyima a brief sketch of his own life: Shillong, Delhi, journalism and publishing, coming back to Tezpur, where he was doing some research. Faced with the other man's vigorous and straightforward manner, Abhijit hesitated to ask him what he wanted to find out about his father, and resolved to bring it up later. Nyima made no mention of the kidnapping incident—maybe he hadn't heard of it, or didn't associate Abhijit with it—and so he kept quiet about it. They did end up talking about Khagen Saikia, Nyima telling him a story about how his father had once faced down a lone wild buffalo in the forest on his own. He said, in his rough, broken Assamese, 'When I pass through the Foothills road once in a while, I remember that old forest, and people like your father. I was just a youngster then, but he treated me with respect.'

They had to wait for a couple of hours as a landslide was cleared by a BRO excavator at a stretch below Jamiri where the eternal road-widening work was going on. To pass the time Nyima showed Abhijit photos on his phone of the project site at Kimi: the jade green waters of the Kameng in a rocky gorge with the dense green forest of the Pakke tiger reserve on the other side; a flat-bed truck on the dirt track carrying a single large steel pipe segment called a ferrule, for the pipe that would bring water down to the powerhouse from the dam; a dusty new residential and office complex spread out on a hillside (and the older project colony with their small Assam-type houses). The gigantic scale of the powerhouse, a cavernous expanse with people at work down below in the cavities for the turbines, was apparent even from the phone photos. There were four entry pipes on top of the powerhouse, one for each turbine, carrying water from the two penstock pipes which in turn were connected to the tunnel which came down from the dam through the mountains. How strange it was, Abhijit thought, the sight of such a huge thing being constructed in the middle of the jungle. The photos of the place, from the construction sites to the storage yards to the shabby but well-stocked shops (with piles of dusty beer bottles beside them), suggested a sort of rough frontier feel. Here, too, man was altering the environment, as he had done in a more elemental way in the Chariduar reserve forest.

They reached Tenga valley in the evening, and Nyima decided to halt the night at home in the small town of Rupa. He had a well-made wood plank house with a cabbage patch and high prayer flags in front. After dinner with the rest of the family Abhijit went to bed in a guest room, and they set out early the next morning in Nyima's battered pick-up truck, with Abhijit shivering in the chilly cabin till the sun came out.

The Tenga valley with its river and high, enclosing cliffs

was like something out of Switzerland, but nearly all of the valley (and the areas around Rupa) were occupied by the army base. Nyima said the defence authorities were going to pay out a few hundred crores to compensate the landowners whose land had been taken over after the 1962 war with China. They drove up to Bomdila, which was scruffy as ever, with rubbish thrown down the mountainsides before the town, and then crested one range, talking about times past as they went along to Dirang with its dun-coloured fields and wooden houses. Nyima stopped for a while at a relative's place in the colourful Dirang basti with the old Tibetan dzong overlooking it, then came the newer town above the river flowing through the valley, where several shops had been burnt down in a recent fire. The flames had leapt from one side of the small road to the other, pushed by the wind, Nyima said.

They talked about the Foothills camp and Pradip Deka and all the old people along the way, and Abhijit purposely turned the conversation toward Khagen Saikia. Nyima, with his direct manner, said that the beat officer had shot himself, but he didn't know what had led to that extreme step, even when Abhijit mentioned that there had been rumours of his father's involvement with a woman from Bomdila.

'*Kune koise? Pagol niki? Sob misa*,' Nyima said in his rough Assamese: 'Says who? Are you mad? All lies.'

Abhijit let it go, for the moment. They had a passable lunch in a Nepali-run 'hotel' after Dirang at a stop called Padma, one of those incongruous place names in Arunachal which are the legacy of BRO road camps, before climbing up the narrow road past the Baisakhi army station all the way up to Sela at 13,000 feet. Here there were icy blasts of wind coming off the lake as the afternoon sun started waning. Now the road turned rough as it went down through a small valley, huge rockfaces towering overhead and CI-sheet cabins by a stream. Nyima stopped at a frozen stream of water by the road to relieve himself, after which he opened a small bottle of brandy to warm himself up.

It was downhill from there, past the settlement of Jang, and then, after crossing an iron bridge over a large river, uphill again along the side of high mountains as it grew dark, passing stands of coniferous trees. Listening to Nyima's talk of contract works, and grants from Delhi, and ministers selling hydropower rights of rivers in their areas, Abhijit had a sense of a state and a people that had changed irreversibly over the past thirty years, just as in the 1980s they had changed from what they had been just after India's independence. Though they had still been much simpler people back then in the 1980s. They passed the settlements of Lhau and Bomdir, the giant Buddha statue looming in the darkness as they drove up to Tawang, where the shops were already starting to close at 7 pm.

Nyima took them to a friend's hotel at the upper end of Tawang, near the monastery. It was a three-storey building, and the concrete rooms were freezing even with the room heater on. After an early dinner of rice and yak meat curry Abhijit bundled himself up in one of the single beds and put on the television while Nyima went out looking for some alcohol (the brandy was long gone). He returned with a bottle of rum and an electric kettle and urged Abhijit to get out onto the balcony. When he stepped out into the cold night, he saw, magically, soft white flakes swirling down from the dark sky and carpeting the roofs and trees and cars and the sides of the road. He forgot the cold, and they pulled the curtains and turned off the lights, watching the snow coming down as Nyima drank the rum with hot water, the howling of packs of stray dogs faintly rising up from the market area down below. Nyima sat on a chair with both his legs folded up as he had a 'lock' in his vertebrae from jumping down a cliff to get away from a wild elephant in the forest above Doimara; a lama in Bomdila fixed it for him from time to time.

Nyima started reminiscing about the old days, about the time he had spent in Tawang around 1990, when Pradip Deka had a contract for constructing sheds for the Bofors guns, and Nyima and Mohen Doctor had stayed in an old inspection bungalow near the MES office in the lower part of Tawang. The doctor would pass the time by playing solitaire. The project site was somewhere near a village on the way to Zemithang, but they would take a shortcut in Deka's Gypsy, on a track so steep that things kept on the dashboard would fall onto their laps. After the other man had poured out his fourth drink, Abhijit brought up the topic of Khagen Saikia once again. And this time Nyima nodded in acknowledgment.

'Yes, there was a woman. You're his son, I suppose you should know. Her name was Lobsang. She was from near Bomdila, her father was a village headman and she had gone to college in Guwahati. When Khagen da met her in Dirang she was working in the social welfare department. They became friendly, and he used to visit her sometimes, driving up in his jeep from Kamengbari to Rupa and Dirang. I know they would post letters to each other. Lobsang was supposed to marry someone, but he had died in an accident some years before that.' Nyima paused, and looked at the glowing heater through the rum in his glass. 'It was a love story, but a tragic one.'

It took Abhijit a long time to fall asleep that night, and not just because of the other man's snoring. Nyima's account was a confirmation of the letter, which Mohen Doctor had given him. But what played on his mind were the letters they would have written to one another, addressed to the social welfare department in Dirang and the Gabharu beat office. What had they talked about, where were those letters now?

Abhijit awoke before Nyima the next morning (to be fair he had been driving the whole way), and stepping out onto the small balcony saw something which took his breath away: the town below and around them was carpeted in a blanket of snow, the sky a deep, dark blue with light coming from the west, the high grey-black cliffs above Tawang flecked with snow. The sun rose (his phone showed it was –2 degrees, but there was no wind) and Abhijit stood watching, breathing in the cold air deeply and feeling strangely alive after a long, long time. Down on the road furry stray dogs wandered about among snow-caked Sumo taxis, and people were walking to the nearby monastery, their shoes crunching the ice on the road. Blue sky and white snow, and vapour rising up as the sun rose higher. Fragrant smoke wafted up from juniper branches being burnt in the incense burner by the hotel owner's wife, and old women were throwing the snow over their house walls. A memory came to him: winter mornings in Shillong, condensation on the inside of the window panes, getting out of the warm bed and washing his face with the ice-cold tap water, his mother getting his breakfast ready in the small kitchen, sometimes suji, at other times dry chappatis torn into pieces and dunked in milk with sugar.

After Nyima got up they had some tea and got ready, then walked over to the monastery, which was just down the road. There were men, women, families, and elderly people going into the monastery to pray, a glimpse of living faith, especially the red-robed young monks coming out of their whitewashed two-storied stone huts below the monastery, like a scene out of a medieval town. While Nyima went in search of his nephew, Abhijit entered the main hall where rows of monks were already at prayer, and offered his own silent prayers to the immense, serene Buddha looking down at them: may his parents be safe, wherever they were now. Outside, to one side of the courtyard, a monk was feeding the monastery dogs a sort of rough khichdi. Abhijit found Nyima waiting while an elder monk helped the six-year-old nephew change from his red robes into jeans and a jacket. He was small, tough and shaven-headed, and Abhijit felt sorry for him, but once they were out of the monastery gates he was like any other child, pestering his uncle for chips and chocolates.

As they drove out of Tawang, passing elderly men and women in the market dressed in their heavy traditional red felt coats with gumboots on their feet, past stalls selling crackers, shoes, clothes, decorations, and arrows, the child sat in the middle of the pick-up truck between them playing games on Nyima's mobile till he fell asleep on the way up to the Sela Pass. His name was Sengey, Nyima's younger sister's youngest child, and it was a great honour for the family to have him at the 336-year-old monastery.

Abhijit asked Nyima about the old forests, and his people, as they came down from Tawang and climbed up to Sela. They had come down long, long ago from Tibet to what was now Rupa, he said, and later some of them moved to Shergaon. Another group had come down to Thembang (near Dirang). There were three royal classes (like the Thong), three general classes (like the Khrime), and five commoner classes (like the Mijiji), the last being the actual inhabitants of the area when the Sherdukpens arrived from up above. The word for their community came from 'Shardrukpon': king of the eastern lands. The Monpa were simply those who stayed in Monyul, the southern lowlands (below Tibet), while the plains of Assam were Gyagar.

Earlier, Nyima said, Doimara was above the spot where the Khellong and Belsiri rivers met, where an older stone chorten and a newer one from the 1990s stood. The museum at the Rupa gompa had many strange things, including an iron sword tied into a knot. The Ahom king Rudra Singha had given the Dirang people two small *top* or cannon which they used on Thembang during the ten-year feud; now they were rusted and in the museum.

Abhijit asked if they still hunted in the hills. Nyima said they killed only three or four animals, including the barking deer and wild pig, and only during the two months before

Losar or the Buddhist new year. The Eaglenest sanctuary area was about 280 sq km, and the Sherdukpen area out of that was about 200 sq km, but Nyima said the impression nowadays was that only the Bugun people were into conservation. He knew the AR major at the Kamengbari camp, they conducted operations at night where they killed whoever they came across in the jungle, because anyone around then would be either a poacher or an extremist. They killed them and buried them in the jungle. According to Nyima, the whole Eaglenest area had been marked as a possible hideout if the 'organization' and the eastern group had to flee their bases in Myanmar.

In the old days his people had collected tax from the area stretching from Garubandha to Mazbat, and during one puja they would have to wait till the tamul arrived from down below. Rock salt from above was traded for rice and silk cloth. It was mostly Rabha people in those areas earlier. The Peri La was the highest elephant corridor, where snow fell, and the animals were smaller and more compact than the plains elephants, while the Sopai area had the highest number of hornbills earlier. Their old migration from Rupa to Doimara (and then to the plains, by the Belsiri) was known as besme, a way of fixing borders, he said.

Nyima said money from the timber trade didn't last: there had been a Marwari, one Agarwal, who would hire an entire goods train for transporting timber from the saw mill at Doimara and from the Chariduar forest, loading the wood at the Belsiri or Missamari stations, to be sent to Delhi. Ultimately, he lost all his money, and he was presently in Tipi near Bhalukpung running a saw mill or something of that sort. It was an allegorical tale: you couldn't run a house and a family with that kind of money.

After lunch at Padma again, this time at a different 'hotel' (where the nephew ate as much rice as the two of them), they approached Dirang, and after Rama Camp, Nyima stopped at a long, two-storied wooden house with three shops below. He spoke to a girl behind one of the counters, who yelled out to someone above, and presently an elderly lady came down the steps and talked to Nyima and his nephew, sharing some gentle banter in their language. She was slightly bent, wearing a maroon woollen coat over a sweater and a wraparound skirt, and a woollen hat, rosary beads in one hand, and her eyes behind her glasses still held something lively in them. They set off again, and after a while, as they made their way on the narrow road through Dirang town, Nyima pointed up a hillside to an old block of quarters: beside the now dilapidated small wood-and-plaster houses were newer ugly cemented blocks.

'Whose quarters were they?' Abhijit asked, and when he looked at Nyima found him smiling to himself. Nyima just shook his head when asked why he was smiling, but Abhijit kept persisting, and then, as they sped downhill toward old Dirang or the basti, Nyima said, 'You didn't know who that old lady was? Lobsang. Your father's friend once upon a time. He would visit her in her quarter, I just pointed it out to you.'

For a while Abhijit was too surprised to say anything. He thought of asking Nyima to turn back. But what would he say to the elderly woman? Would she like a stranger coming and opening up a past episode of her life?

'Why didn't you tell me when you stopped there?' Abhijit asked Nyima at last, to which he replied, 'You would have started asking her questions! But you got to see her, didn't you?'

Which was true too, in a way. Abhijit looked at the dry green hills around them in the cold gloomy afternoon. Across the gorge of a small river was what looked like an abandoned entrance tunnel for a hydropower dam's water-diversion tunnel. Nyima told him she had never married, and, after retirement, stayed with her brother's family. The girl in the shop he had called out to had been adopted by her several years back.

'Did she find out what happened to my father?' he asked, to which Nyima nodded.

'Much later. She would hardly talk to anyone for a long time. Then she adopted the girl, who had been abandoned in town by someone. After that she started getting better.'

There was a lot more Abhijit wanted to ask, but he held his tongue. Maybe it was enough to have been given a glimpse of her, as Nyima had said. By the time they reached Bomdila it was almost dark, and the town was enveloped in thick fog. When they got to Rupa, Nyima's family was waiting, including his sister and her family who'd come up from Kalaktang for the family puja. Abhijit even drank the hot ara liquor made from maize along with the rest of the men and chewed on khabse and fried yak meat. He wouldn't remember most of what they talked about, except for the sister's husband insisting that the Foothills area actually belonged to the Monpas earlier, as they were paid tribute for it by the Kacharis. The next morning, Nyima took him down to a taxi counter in the town from where he caught a Sumo to Tezpur. He said he would look Abhijit up if he came to Tezpur.

All the way back, as they went winding down and down along the mountainsides towards the plains, Abhijit thought of the elderly lady with her lively eyes, and the forest officer who'd wanted to leave his wife for her, and that great forest between them. Abhijit had found out what had happened to his father, had found out how that forest had nearly disappeared, but where had that got him? As Mohen Doctor had said to him, maybe it was better to remain ignorant. The more you thought, the more you suffered. And how much would his mother have suffered, knowing what his father had told her, and at the same time keeping that knowledge from her son? It could be said that his father had killed her, as her brother had said. But guilt and innocence no longer held any meaning for Abhijit. He thought of the Buddha statue he had sat under the previous morning at the monastery. Life is suffering, he now dimly understood.

After the 12-Mile Centre, where the road curved up into the trees from the straight stretch (and where the hydropower project manager had been lifted from), he saw by the roadside an old Bodo man standing beside stacks of firewood and sacks of charcoal for sale. He got home in the afternoon. It took him a few days to forget those mountains; the snow and red-robed monks and the medieval monastery, and get used to life back in the plains, among people who were supposed to be his own.

Killers at Dawn

The feeling that a phase of his life had come to an end grew stronger within Abhijit. To stay on in Tezpur meant risking turning into another version of his uncle in the long run. Besides, he had solved the mystery of his father's death, so to speak, the main reason he had returned, and that had freed him in a way. He tried to keep Rankhw, Laimwn, and the teacher Dilip Basumatary out of his mind, and put the finishing touches to his article on the human–elephant conflict. At the same time he called up people to see if he could visit other areas of the former Chariduar RF, in a last attempt at gathering material. Abhijit called Haphang's number too, but it was out of reach: the police commando was probably up in the hills, looking for Rankhw and his group before the army or AR could get them.

One evening there was a call from the Sonitpur SP, Santanu Bora, who asked if Abhijit would be free to join him that evening at the Tezpur Station Club. The invitation came as a surprise, and Abhijit said yes partly out of curiosity. He reached the club above the Ganesh ghat at 8 pm, and had to wait for a while for the SP to arrive.

'Sorry, I had a lot of work,' he said as he got down from his car. 'Come, let's go in.'

It was a weekday, and the small club was nearly deserted, apart from two men drinking at one of the small round tables, and two more slowly playing a game in the billiards room. They sat at the bar, its wood dark and stained, under ancient fans, and were served slightly cold beer by the equally ancient barman. The club was close to the SP's office, the DC's office, the courts, the old train station, and the two ghats in town by the Brahmaputra—it wasn't too hard to imagine a British planter coming into the club for a gin on a hot day as he waited for his factory's tea chests, which would have reached there on the train line, to be sent down to Calcutta by river steamer and from there on to London by ship.

'Do you know when this club was started?' Bora said, after he had checked his phone and taken a sip of his beer. He answered himself, 'In the year 1875. It started off with just a billiards table inside a thatched hut. You have to admire the British.'

'I didn't know that,' Abhijit said.

'You must be wondering why I called you. Well, you've seen the outside world, haven't you? And you have a mind of your own. Otherwise you wouldn't be roaming around Foothills.'

Abhijit nodded, not sure where this was going. He hadn't touched his beer.

'The other day I got news of a suspicious death. A man had been knocked down by a heavy vehicle on the road from Kolamati Gate to Dhankhana Centre. Do you know what my first thought was? That it might have been you.'

'Who was it?' Abhijit asked.

'Somebody from a nearby village. Might have been drunk. The OC at the Missamari thana entered "road accident" as the cause of death. You would know about heavy vehicles plying there, I guess?'

'The tractor trailers which haul sand, gravel and stones from the Belsiri and Gabharu rivers?' Abhijit ventured.

'Yes. And how much do they usually carry?'

'Four cubic metres I heard. Roughly four tons.'

'Correct,' said the SP. 'An illegal trade, but taking place nonetheless. So you understand why I thought it was you? You've found out quite a bit about those areas.'

'Yes,' Abhijit said, wondering what exactly the SP knew.

'Well, at least you know what happened there. There are journalists here in Tezpur who keep writing about 50,000 people in those areas without land pattas. They probably think those people have been living there since the time of the British. Ah, here comes my guest. You know him, I guess?'

Abhijit turned, and saw Major Dev walking towards the bar, with the barely noticeable limp, and dressed in jeans and a polo shirt.

Bora introduced Abhijit, and he had to endure a crushing handshake from the major.

'Hello Abhijit, we meet again,' the major said.

'Oh, you do know each other,' Bora said, helping himself to a handful of fried peanuts.

'Old friends,' the major said, and grinned.

The night in Shillong came back to Abhijit, and he reminded himself to keep his mouth shut. The SP glanced at him then, and looking into those calm eyes Abhijit suddenly understood. The barman poured out another beer and handed it to Major Dev.

'He's been trying to find out more about his father's death,' the SP said to the major. 'His father was...'

The major set down his glass. '*Pata hai*, a forest officer. But what the place was then, it is no more now. He was picked up by Rankhw's gang too. Weren't you?'

Abhijit nodded. The SP said, 'Picked up, let go. Maybe they didn't find it worthwhile to kill him.'

'Or maybe someone sent him to meet Rankhw?' the major mused aloud.

'You should know about that,' the SP said, checking a message on his phone.

The major looked at Abhijit and shook his head, as if he were tired of the present conversation. He said to the SP, '*Aur batao*, what is your lethal weapon doing?' in what Abhijit guessed was a reference to Haphang.

'We're working on it,' the SP said, smiling at the major. 'This Rankhw is a very slippery fellow.'

'*Ek achhi* lead *mili thi hume*,' the major said, looking at Abhijit. 'We found out a girl close to him. But she wouldn't open her mouth. Tough people, these Bodos, that I must admit.'

Santanu Bora and Major Dev then discussed cadres of the eastern group who had fled after the massacre, and where they could be. How could they be tracked and lured back? The major said he had a couple of cadres in his custody at present.

'Some people kill them, but I don't,' he said, looking at Abhijit.

Many had been killed in the recent operations, and some even shot while trying to surrender, he said. His voice softened: there was no development in those areas, no roads, people led a hard life. And it was difficult terrain to operate in, with paddy fields and mosquitoes. Both the overground factions and the surrendered boys were afraid of the cadres who were still in the forests. Arms were still coming in, cadres too, from Myanmar, female ones included. 'We are using the surrendered boys to get results,' he said, then added in a reflective tone, 'but do we know what pitting Bodo against Bodo will do to their society in the long run?'

A colonial-era club, two security officers who were part competitors, part collaborators: Abhijit thought of Rankhw and his group, still holed up in those forests, who knew for how much longer? It struck him that Haphang and his colleagues had more in common with them than the two men he was with. The major was showing the SP photos on his phone of a Bodo woman in one of the villages near Foothills who had been beaten badly with sticks by some cadres of the eastern group, after she had refused to cook for them, breaking one of her arms in the process.

'Rankhw wouldn't do that,' the SP said, 'maybe it was Thulunga.'

'Whoever it was, I'm going to get these guys,' the major said. 'We're going to be transferred in a few months, I don't know where, Siliguri, Rajasthan. But I'll get one big kill before I leave, that I guarantee you!'

Santanu Bora smiled, ate some peanuts, and said, 'Hasn't Jagat Kumar been able to tell you where they are? I thought he was paying them for the sand-gravel he needs at the Missamari army base.'

The major was startled, but only momentarily. 'Boss, you tell me what the poor guy will do? Buy sand-gravel from Rangapara or Tezpur at a higher cost? *Kisi ko toh milne hi hai paise*. Someone has to get the money. And here it is that beat officer.' He motioned to the barman, who was half asleep in one corner, to fill his glass, then turned back to them. 'Pegu is making a lakh and a half minimum each month from those tractor trailers. Those boys will naturally collect something from the people lifting the sand-gravel, *hai na*? It is how this country works.'

Later, after the major left in a private car—his unit was at Missamari, but he had come over to the army base at Salonibari near Tezpur—the SP took out a packet of cigarettes from his vehicle and lit up.

'I sometimes feel like having one,' he said, blowing out a stream of smoke over Abhijit's head.

'Thank you,' Abhijit said. 'So you know about the major and me?'

'It's not a problem, Abhijit. We need to keep an eye on what these guys are up to as well. Achha, we have some news about Rankhw. Something should happen soon. There are just two or three boys left with him. They're moving about all the time now.'

'What about the girl, Laimwn?' Abhijit asked. 'Do you know happened to her?'

'Must be hiding out somewhere. Maybe they'll send her to Myanmar, to the camps.'

So that was how it would end, he thought. A short-lived romance, and now the net tightening around the Foothills commander. Not for the first time, Abhijit thought how it was almost like a Western, with the sherrif in town getting ready to go after the Indians.

He soon found out that the SP had been correct. The journalist Padma Bora, with whom Abhijit had been in touch, called him early one morning. *Khobor eta ase*, he said: I have news. Bora had known of Abhijit's interest in Rankhw and his men. Now he told Abhijit that he had heard from a source that a police team had finished off Rankhw and a couple of others. Abhijit immediately thought of Haphang. Bora didn't know about Haphang; Abhijit felt he wanted to impress him with the news. Abhijit then called the SP, who confirmed it.

There had been an encounter somewhere above Rangapara he said. Three killed. Later, he sent a couple of photos to Abhijit's phone. There was a disturbing banality to them. They showed a small, rough shelter in the middle of trees, made of wood planks (the 'off size' Pegu had mentioned) hoisted on logs and covered with blue plastic sheets. The backs of a couple of police commandos in tan uniforms could be seen. A tall, lean youth, good-looking, wearing only a pair of shorts, lay on the ground, small neat bullet holes in his torso and arms around which were drops of blood, his head thrown back—the commander Rankhw. The other two were shorter, wearing t-shirts, curly hair on their chins from not shaving, the bullet holes and blood not easily visible on their dark t-shirts. One was Phanjit, the youth who'd told Abhijit he wanted to make a Bodo video film based on their lives. His dream had died with him: this was where the road had ended for them.

In spite of the ordeal he had suffered at their hands,

Abhijit felt a deep sadness at their deaths, as if they were his friends. And there was something else, which came to him later in the day: they were more like outlaws than anything else, living and dying by the gun. Then there were people like Haphang, hunting people where once people like Pradip Deka and Karuna drank and hunted deer. Abhijit felt it was really a curtain call for that sort of life in the wild: people and farms were spreading, roads and electricity were being demanded, the true wilderness was about to disappear for good and along with it the men who had lived and hunted in it. In a way maybe it was fortunate that his father wasn't around to witness it.

Abhijit met Haphang a couple of days later, for the last time. He was a busy man, and they had nothing in common, only Abhijit's interest in his work, which he shared up to a point maybe because Abhijit had knowledge of the terrain he traversed. He had been in the service almost twelve years, with more than a decade of operations, and had another fifteen years to go. In a few years maybe he would take up a desk job, he said.

Abhijit asked him if they had eliminated Rankhw, and he said yes, it was his operation. It had taken place ahead of Paharpur, above Dopdopi near Rangapara: the same Dopdopi the elephant phandi Dilwar Saikia had mentioned. Rankhw and two of his guards had moved eastward after the operations started, and were staying and eating with a group of *kath phala manuh* or woodcutters operating up in Arunachal, and these woodcutters had betrayed the trio for money (Haphang didn't say for how much).

'We started at midnight,' he said, matter of fact in his

narration, 'and went up through the jungle, across streams and rivers, climbing up into the hills, without using torches. At one place a herd of wild elephants went ahead of us and we followed. They didn't trouble us. Elephants don't like the smell of gunpowder. There were a couple of us, five police commandos including me, five Cobras from the CRPF, and a source of mine who was leading me there. I think we walked about 5 to 6 km up into the mountains, and then as it grew light we spotted the camp on top of a hill. I went ahead and checked, all three were sleeping. When I yelled and woke them, they tried to run in shock, and we shot all three of them. The Cobras fired from the back. Later I shouted at them. They could have hit me from behind. Some army and CRPF men are afraid of going into the jungle. For us it's something we're used to.'

Haphang said a couple of cadres of the eastern faction had been gunned down just before the massacre, two of them at Gulai Centre itself, and another two toward Kokrajhar, and the group started suspecting informers from among the Adivasi community. According to him though, the massacre had been planned by a few local cadres, not by the higher-ups in Myanmar. There had been some radio chatter picked up prior to the attack, but in the remote, lightly-policed belt along the top of the state, matters were left as they were.

Abhijit would come to read in the newspapers an occasional report about boys from the insurgent group being killed or arrested—no surrenders were being accepted. He would call Haphang once, and the police commando would tell him there were only a handful of insurgents left in the areas ahead of Missamari. Prior to the massacre there were around fifty to sixty cadres in the Karki and Gulai Centre areas, even venturing till Garubandha and Dhankhana. About twenty cadres had been killed and the same number arrested, and there were just a few left in hiding now. Several had run away to south India where they were working in factories, Haphang said. Some of them had been caught by the police there, some had been lured back by the army or Assam police and locked up. And as for the girl by the name of Laimwn, Haphang said he had no information about her.

After that last meeting with Haphang, Abhijit called Pori, Pradip Deka's elder daughter, on the number Lokhi had given him. She was in Tezpur for a few days, and asked him to come over, so Abhijit went to the old house one afternoon. It wasn't too far from Ketekibari, where Abhijit's grandfather's house was, on the road headed into town, but ever since he had returned Abhijit had seen the line of three shops before the house (which hadn't been there when he was a child) and and had somehow felt dissuaded from entering. Also, there was no one living there. On that day however he unlatched the old gate beside the shops and walked down the overgrown grass toward the house, half-hidden by untrimmed shrubs and trees. He realized the place was smaller than what he remembered. Parked before the house was a new SUV with an AS01 Guwahati registration number. Abhijit had heard that Pori's husband was a contractor from there.

The lanky girl with a ready laugh he remembered from his childhood had turned into a stolid, heavyset woman. She led him through the dark musty-smelling sitting room and an 'office room' to the inner courtyard, where the cement had cracked in several places and the moss had crept into the crevices and climbed up the corners. They sat on old chairs and she asked the worker, a girl who had come with them from Guwahati, to make tea. She filled in Abhijit on her life, and what had happened to the family. After both of them had got married and left Tezpur their mother had followed them. Things had changed after her father had passed away. Tani was married to a boy who worked in Bangalore, and their mother spent a few months in a year with them, otherwise she was in her flat in Guwahati's Six Mile area, in the same building where Pori and her husband stayed. Pori had a daughter, and her husband was a government contractor and supplier.

A caretaker (who lived behind the house with his wife) looked after the place. Pori and her husband were here to meet a lawyer and sign some papers: they were planning to tear the old house down and build an apartment complex there. Her husband's firm would handle it. The daughter and husband wandered out of the house as Pori spoke, and she introduced them to Abhijit. They looked at him incuriously and drifted away, busy with their phones. She asked Abhijit what he was doing, and he gave her a brief history, including the fact that he was doing some research on the Foothills area.

'I heard all the forests have disappeared over there, isn't it?' she said, and got up to go check on the tea without waiting for Abhijit's answer.

He reminded himself that not everyone would share

his obsession. Still, he would have thought Pradip Khura's daughter would have shown some interest. She remembered her father though, and told Abhijit how hard things had been toward the end, before he had died.

'I sometimes feel that people like him should have been born much earlier,' she said. 'When they could have lived as they pleased. Don't you think so?'

Abhijit just nodded, surprised to have his own feelings relayed back to him.

'He would talk about you sometimes,' she said, in a reflective mood a while later. 'Khagen's son, I wonder where he is, he would say. I told him you were studying in Shillong and had gone to Delhi. Mother's cousin who was in Shillong told us. He always said you were a serious boy and that you loved being in the forest.'

Sitting there in the crumbling courtyard of the old house drinking his tea, Abhijit felt as though he was within touching distance of something intangible that he had been searching for. The moment passed. It was time to go. Pori and her family were going out shopping. They were to return to Guwahati the day after, and her husband hoped to start the project during the winters. Abhijit asked her if he could have a look around the house, and she said he could and went inside.

The garden behind was overgrown, a semi-wilderness. The caretaker and his wife both worked elsewhere during the day and obviously didn't have time to look after the house. Plump yellow starfruit lay rotting under the starfruit trees, while the pineapple patch had disappeared. Abhijit went back in to the courtyard and let himself out through the sitting room, where in the shadows hung old framed photographs. He had seen enough. From the gate he looked back once, trying to imprint in his mind an image of the house with its plaster walls and tin roof, a last reminder of his father's old friend, soon to be torn down. Pori had told him she would tell her mother that she had met Abhijit, and on his way back he tried to remember more about the thin, slightly nervous-looking woman from his childhood and found that he couldn't. Who knew what her life had been like, he thought.

It was dark by the time he got back to the house. His grandmother was watching the television in Hiren Khura's room, Julie was in the kitchen squatting and cutting vegetables before a fire in the hearth, and his uncle was sitting by the table in the rear veranda re-reading the day's newspaper. Abhijit sat near him and told him where he had been and the family's plans for the house.

'Imagine, flats coming up in Tezpur,' his uncle said, putting the newspaper aside. 'Anyway, there's no one staying there now. The house is more or less abandoned.'

'Who had built it? Pradip Deka's grandfather?'

'Yes. Do you know he used to supply the British with pineapples?'

Abhijit shook his head. He remembered the backyard garden he had seen earlier.

'Strange, isn't it,' his uncle said, 'where people come from, where they end up. Do you know about our family tree?'

Abhijit said he didn't, and so his uncle told him: there had been a handwritten bongxobali or family tree which their father, Abhijit's grandfather, had kept. It was found much after his death, crumbling into dust, and it no longer existed. But Hiren Khura remembered what their father had told them about it. Long, long ago, possibly in the second half of the 17th century, a certain Maniram had left Kannauj after Aurangzeb had decreed that the Hindus were to convert to Islam and come to Kamakhya (in present-day Guwahati), where there was the famous old temple. From there Maniram ended up in the court of the Ahom king in Garhgaon teaching music, where he was given the title of Saikia. The battles of the Ahoms with the Mughals came and went. Then one of this man's descendants crossed the Brahmaputra to Tezpur in the early 19th century, fleeing the devastation wrought by the invasion of the Man or Burmese, and four generations later, the three brothers Romen, Khagen, and Hiren had been born to Jogeshwar Saikia (the family tree traced only the male line, as was the practice then). One of their ancestors in Tezpur had even been asked to come up by the raja of the Akas (now known as the Hrussos) in Kameng, to teach his children, and this man had gone and never returned, becoming a part of their society in the mountains. 'So that's it, the story of our family,' Hiren Khura said to Abhijit.

The Economics of Settlement

Abhijit had wanted to see, before he left Tezpur, something of the settlements that had sprung up elsewhere in the now denuded Chariduar reserve forest. Little did he know that he would finally come across someone who would openly tell him how they had come and settled on forest department land, how the entire process had been carried out. Padma Bora put him in touch with the Bodo students' association, which had a widespread network. By then Abhijit had sent off his long-form article, and had booked a flight ticket online for Delhi on the cheap. In the time he had left he started visiting those places in the shadow of the hills.

He met a general secretary of the association at their office in Dhekiajuli town; a low wall, cows grazing in an overgrown field, large mostly empty rooms. The secretary pointed to the battered gate—a mob of Adivasis had come looking for them after the massacre. Laughing, the secretary said he had fled from the rear. He had a ready smile like most of them, and was polite. Only when Abhijit said their statehood demand for Bodoland was problematic because of the mix of populations, did he see something like a flash of anger. It then struck Abhijit that they saw it as *their own* land. Adivasis were a large segment of the population around the town, the secretary said, but not so much beyond the train line to the north. Darrang district next door was full of Bengali Muslims, in the char and chapori areas, and they were still arriving by boat from Nagaon, and Borsola beside Orang national park was full of Muslims as well.

A stocky young LP school teacher took Abhijit around on his bike in the 'field'. North of Dhekiajuli were villages, paddy fields, a tea garden, then came Batasipur, a huddle of shops on a small winding road, and the nearly empty Dhekiajuli Road station, above which was a kutcha road with large stones and muddy pits. The landscape was similar to that ahead of Kolamati Gate: rice fields, scattered huts, thick, dark mud from the forest soil, and no remainder of the forest except the occasional tree stump. The teacher, like the secretary, said people had moved into the forest areas from 1996. He himself had studied in Lakhimpur before moving here as a LP teacher at a place called Moinajuli. He was married, with a five-year-old son, while his parents were back in Lakhimpur. He said to Abhijit, 'We Bodo people have this habit of moving from place to place.'

They passed a Bathou mandir with its siju tree and pagoda-like roof, a Brahma mandir with a hall (inside it a hanging drum or kham), and then a couple of gravestones with wooden crosses near an Adivasi village, victims of the recent massacre. The paddy was ripening under a grey overcast sky, while groups of children played in small streams and pools, their clothes specked with mud. The teacher pointed out the dry kheti: chillies, kosu, ginger and turmeric.

There were small rubber and tea patches, a plantation of gamari trees. The rice yield without fertilizers, the teacher told him, was 20 to 25 mun per bigha: comparable to that at Foothills. There were mud-plastered houses with tin roofs set back from the road, two or three dwellings to a plot, surrounded by patches of cultivation and bamboo groves. The muddy road would have been an earlier forest trail; once again, Abhijit felt a disbelief at how the vast reserve forest had disappeared, and so many people had moved in.

They stopped at a house belonging to the teacher's friend. The woodwork suggested Buddhist influences. A friend of this person, who was with the sahitya sabha of the Bodo community, came by on his bike. He said they had received news of the movement of a group of twelve insurgents back from Myanmar somewhere above Rangapara. The villagers had been told not to give them anything as they would be in trouble later.

The teacher's friend pointed out the patches of rubber and tea being planted beside his compound, and said the three of them and a few others had recently acquired a plot of 10 bighas with a view to opening a fishery and planting tamul trees (they would start getting returns in five years). They were sitting on the raised, covered area of his house with a breeze blowing, litchi and chilli growing in his front garden, and a framed photo of Sarvapalli Radhakrishnan in the porch. The teacher said they grew everything they needed here, except salt and kerosene, which had to be bought. They started telling Abhijit about the bad roads, lack of teachers and schools, lack of support from the government, that they should have got land pattas based on the Forest Dwellers Act 2006, so that they could have panchayats. That was why the area was backward, and people suffered, it was hard for children to study, but still they managed to get to class 10 and high school, a few even going to college. The situation was slightly better now, it had been worse earlier, the common people caught between the demands of the insurgents and the army's questioning. It was a tale of a strange, hard life, of a community which had woken up late and was now trying to catch up.

The four of them drove ahead toward the inter-state border on the two bikes, past houses where people were sitting outside, others working, a primal environment, and Abhijit could imagine the boys with their guns walking through the paddy fields. They crossed a tea garden, the flat-looking Sopai river flowing through the high garden land, in the distance the dark-green bulk of the Arunachal Himalayas, where Nyima and his men still went hunting. Then came the school at Mauriapur, with some buildings (but occupied by the BSF, with tin sheets outside, and a guard post), and a bamboo grove after that between the road and someone's plot (a hut could be seen through the trees), the slight depression in the road, the place where the police party had been ambushed, killing the ASP and the informer. A breeze rustled the bamboo grove from where the firing would have come. They had set off from the army camp at Batasipur at night, the teacher told Abhijit, and made the mistake of returning by the same route.

Laodangi, when they finally came to it, the Centre, was a collection of small shops on either side of a dirt track: general stores, clothes shops, tea shops, and a mechanic.

A tractor trailer stood before the mechanic's shop in the midday heat. Up ahead were the empty sheds of the weekly market, trees, and across a low grassy plain rose the hills, two smaller ones within Assam, where people had started cultivating, and beyond that the larger peaks, flecked with white clouds. Again, a Western came to Abhijit's mind: the frontier settlement, waiting for the gunslingers. He saw four police commandos nearby, dressed all in black, carrying AKs with folding wire stocks, and when they left, a Bolero and a Sumo arrived with a police officer and some more personnel in black.

In a tea shop they had milky tea in small cups. A few large, well-built men were sitting there, different in build from the skinnier boys one saw in tight jeans and chappals. It seemed the Sopai river had changed course to the west after coming down from the mountains, about five years ago (though Gautam Pegu had told Abhijit that the settlers had themselves diverted the river by moving boulders in the winter). Foothills wasn't too far, maybe 10 to 12 kilometres in a north-easterly direction. They had heard about the old Monpa settlement beside the Belsiri river, and knew about the AR camp at Kamengbari. They were surprised when Abhijit mentioned the Sopai forest IB; how did you go there, they asked, walking? He told them it had been a long time ago, when he was a child.

Kolamati Gate and Kamengbari to the east, Batasipur and Laudangi in the middle—and then Abhijit got a chance to visit the western side of what used to be the Chariduar RF (and still was on government maps): Hugrajuli and Khaobla. Tarun Boro, the former bodyguard, and who was now dabbling in politics, called Abhijit one day and told him he was coming to Hugrajuli from Tangla to visit a friend's rubber plantation near the Arunachal border, and Abhijit could come along.

Abhijit was keen to see a rubber plantation in the former reserve forest, so next morning he caught a bus headed westward to Dhekiajuli. In that morning's English-language daily from Guwahati he had read an article by a journalist from Tezpur about the people in the new villages in Chariduar RF. They were portrayed as age-old residents of the area, facing hardship in their villages from malaria, insurgents, wild elephants, and harassed by the forest department and the army, making it seem as though the settlers had lived in those areas from time immemorial and it was the forest department and the security forces who had recently encroached upon the forest areas leading to a loss of habitat for wild animals. Abhijit noted that the piece ignored how four-fifths of that vast forest had disappeared recently, in a matter of just a few years.

He got down past Dhekiajuli at Sirajuli, where Tarun Boro had been waiting for him outside a pan shop. The former bodyguard had come on a friend's Bullet. The road going north from the highway was good, narrow but smooth, and the Bullet chugged past neat villages and paddy fields, mountains looming up ahead. Abhijit noticed Nepali and Assamese and Adivasi people, and then Bodo people as they neared Hugrajuli station (which came after the Missamari, Belsiri, and Dhekiajuli Road stations on the line headed west).

They crossed Rowmari Centre, a small place with

shops of satai bera or split-bamboo walls. Roumari, nearby Oxurmari and Raikoxmari, then further ahead Jingabil and Hatiputa: elemental place names. The road turned into a bumpy kutcha track ahead of the station, and they passed rice fields, rattled over wood plank and bamboo bridges, passed a school, an APBN post (tin sheets around a school building), the local office of the Bodo student organization, then came Khaobla Centre, shops scattered around a tiniali, where they entered a tea shop—smooth old tables, earthen floor, oily snacks in a cabinet, sweet tea in small glasses—and Tarun Boro said the Bodo people made big singaras in their tea shops.

From there a muddy, uneven track through patches of rice fields and kosu cultivation led them up into a village called Udangsri with a wide track running through it, and where the villagers were digging a ditch by the track to divert water coming down from the hills. Clusters of huts, some well-built and some slightly shabby, set in large, open plots, solar panels on straw or tin roofs, pigs and chickens, small children running about, clumps of bamboo (big and slender), patches of tamul trees and tea shrubs, women weaving on the loom or hisansali in the verandas of the huts. Abhijit saw the rubber plantation, and in the distance the high, folded mountains of the Eastern Himalayas, clouds drifting past them. They entered an iron gate with bougainvillea flowers above it, and after them came two tractor trailers with sand and stones from the nearby Pachnoi river. The drivers and labour were Adivasi; the sand and stones were for a building being constructed in the compound.

Beside it was a long hut with a kitchen, and a covered shed. Boro took Abhijit to show him the plantation, with some 6000 trees, which would be ready for tapping later that year, six to seven years since his friend had planted them. Orderly lines of slim rubber trees ran into the distance. Their girth had to be 18 cm or more for tapping. A few trees had come down in a recent thunderstorm, a loss of a lakh per tree. An elephant had entered once and tried to cross through but was stopped by the razor-blade fencing and went back bleeding. Boro said his friend had bought the land at Rs 1 lakh per seet from older settlers (with another 20,000 per seet to the insurgents), and had more than 100 bighas (each seet was 12 bighas), about 8 to 10 seet in all. Tapping would start later that year, and he would be sending out his rubber to companies. Rubber was going for 200 rupees a kilo at one time, but had come down to 120, but that was all right as the production cost wasn't too high, Boro said.

They came back and sat in the open shed. Tarun Boro handed over some money to his friend's helper, and asked his wife for some rice beer. She poured him a glass and said she would cook some pork for them. Boro told Abhijit how the paramilitary people, the tribal ones, would come to the villages to drink as part of their training, and ask for deer meat, and then get the names of the hunters. Later those people would be picked up by the paramilitary or army with their guns and passed off as insurgents.

Boro mentioned something Abhijit had become aware of: the split in Bodo society between the settled class of people and those still moving about looking for trees to cut and new land to break. He said that the Bodos were the most contented people, having wrapped up their harvest and filled their granary, they were free to relax the rest of the year, meat and vegetables in their own yards, while from time to time they would sell one or two tins of rice to pay for salt and oil. Living naturally, they seldom fell sick. Abhijit agreed. Travelling those inner roads, made by the people themselves out of the forest, it once more felt like going back in time to a more primal state of affairs.

The helper at the plantation, also from Tangla, seemed to have a Nepali touch to him, in looks and speech. He was thirty-six years old, a dark, stocky man, and told Abhijit he had arrived there to clear the jungle fifteen years ago, in the year 1999. And just like that, Abhijit finally had before him someone who spoke openly about how the settlers had come. There were three 'committees'—in Belsiri, Batasipur, and Hugrajuli—which gave people land at Rs 750 per seet (Haphang's figure had been Rs 1000 per seet), and so they came and cleared the land: trees were cut and burnt for charcoal, and the good timber was sold for Rs 100 a CFT with another 15 to 20 rupees for the insurgents. Behind the committees had been Bodo politicians, he claimed. The 'fanta' or large rough logs were tied onto cycles and taken out.

The helper and some others stayed under plastic sheets initially, sowing mustard, then cultivating rice. They saw elephants and deer but not tigers. The worker was blasé about the whole thing: they had come and settled there, that was all. Then his wife had come, leaving their son behind with a relative in Rangiya. Malaria had been present and many people had died. Nowadays, depending on the land, a seet would go for Rs 2 to 5 lakhs. People grew kosu, chilli, til, matimah, and mustard on the land. They got about Rs 500 to 700 per year from one tamul tree. The land was a bit sandy for tea though. Abhijit realized that this one person's experience, multiplied a few thousand times, was the story of how the Chariduar reserve forest of his childhood had disappeared.

Tarun Boro said his friend had come back from Mumbai and had first set up a tea garden in Tangla. When he started the rubber plantation, he had been threatened over the phone from Myanmar and by the local commander of the eastern group: they had wanted Rs 25 lakh over and above their tax. But his friend never paid up. He said the surrounding people initially thought he was a fool, but now that tapping was approaching and the money would start coming in, they had already started changing their ideas.

'My friend keeps telling me,' Tarun Boro said, laughing, 'that there's so much cleared forest land lying waste around here, we should bring the miyas to grow boro (winter crop) rice.' From an ancient forest to settlers on the cleared land to plantations with cash crops and assessing the commercial potential of the land—that too was a cycle of humankind.

After a lunch of rice and pork they left, driving back through Khaobla. Boro stopped at one of the tea shops, where they met a former district president of the students' body, along with a policeman from the nearby camp. A father and his son sat drinking tea, while a fair girl in a green dokhona with a heart-shaped face and marks on her neck served them. The former president, a stocky, round-faced youth, said he had come in 2008. Their people didn't have facilities he said, mentioning an RTI activist from Dhekiajuli who had stopped electricity and other amenities from coming to them: this was Uttam Nath, whom Abhijit had already met. He said they were still trying for the land pattas, to which Tarun Boro said, 'It is all political, so if it happens, it could happen overnight.'

The ex-president said the situation was very bad at one time with the insurgents and the army troubling the local people. Many boys had to go outside to Bangalore and Gujarat for work. Now things were better, but elephants were troubling the people. Boro told him about measures that could be taken, like building a fire with dry chillies and sada or tobacco. The policeman mentioned a group that had gone up into the hills to cut trees when they came face to face with a tusker, and then used their 'Honda' or chainsaw to drive it away.

They left as the sun set beyond the craggy, misty magnificent mountains in the near distance. Tarun Boro dropped him off at Dhekiajuli, and Abhijit got on a bus to Tezpur through the evening traffic. His tour of the Chariduar reserve forest was done. What remained with him at the end of the day were the Adivasi men shovelling sand and stones from the two trailers as a mobile phone played a song in Hindi, the singer describing how Yeshuwa had given his blood to save him, which was why he now sang Yeshuwa's praise. Descendants of people from the Chota Nagpur plateau who'd been brought to work in the tea gardens of Assam by the British, listening to a Christian hymn in Hindi while working for a Bodo man in a former reserve forest, the tune itself a cross between an American country song and a Bhupen Hazarika number. No matter how much he explored, there was always the feeling of somehow missing the larger picture.

One last excursion was yet to come. The journalist Padma Bora, perhaps inspired by Abhijit, had begun doing some environmental stories, and one day he took Abhijit along with him toward Rangapara. They had seen a small elephant herd in Sonajuli tea estate above Rangapara, a group huddled around their calves under the shade trees as Adivasi youths stopped their cycles and bikes on the road and rushed through the tea bushes to jeer and throw stones at them. Bora was fuming when he saw this.

'Who are the animals here?' he asked Abhijit. 'Who are the animals?'

They carried on to Tarajuli tea estate, which lay above Sonajuli and to the east of the Gabharu river (to the west of the river was the road to Foothills). They had gone in from the highway through Ghoramari, past the air force base to the west of Tezpur, passing village huts and a 'centre' that had come up because of the renewed activity in the industrial estate next door. They passed rice fields and Adivasi villages and, far away, beyond a dark ridge line, were the snow-capped peaks of the Gorichen range.

On the way to Tarajuli past Sonajuli, Bora pointed out the colours on top of the thin, white-painted cement posts strung together with wire fencing: green for Williamson Magor, red for Apeejay, blue for the Tata group. And in the interior of Tarajuli, where the plantation ended, and from where one could see the Gabharu river to the left and the foothills of Arunachal further ahead, they saw a piteous sight: a small herd of eight or nine adult elephants, with two or three calves, moving slowly among the tea bushes, the adults looking emaciated, their bones jutting out of their hides at the top. Clearly there wasn't enough for them to eat in the forest. Bora took a few photos of the herd with his camera.

They had come through the labour lines of Tarajuli, and a labour supervisor, or 'line sardar', known to Bora followed them on his bike. He wore jeans, and had a dark, weathered face, his hair cut short, his teeth discoloured from chewing tobacco. Bora had stopped among some trees by a track skirting the plantation. In the distance, beyond a stream where two men were fishing, patches of grass with cows grazing, and some paddy cultivation, were small hills, scarred with landslips, which rose into the larger mountains. One hill in Assam had been cleared for tea cultivation by Bodo villagers—they sold the green leaf in the Tarajuli factory.

To the north-west was Sonai Rupai (Abhijit could see the haat on the other side of the fast-flowing Gabharu river), whatever little forest remained of it, to the north-east were Urohiloga, Mainasree, Akabeel and other Bodo villages. The sardar said the cutting down of the forests along the foothills—from Kokrajhar in the west through Foothills to Gohpur in the east—for the settlement of people had pushed the elephants further down, into gardens and villages. He was born in 1975, and for his first fifteen years he had never seen a wild elephant. They started appearing as the forests started disappearing. His community were Odiya people, originally from Koraput, and with the other bagan communities such as the Munda and Oraon they spoke the bagani pidgin, but among themselves they still spoke in Odiya.

'I saw that whole jungle disappear before my eyes,' the sardar told them, pointing ahead of him. The British had set up a small forest village of Kachari people, Urohiloga, above Tarajuli tea garden around 1910. Over time a second Urohiloga came up. The villagers got along with the Adivasis in the tea garden. Then in the 1990s the new settlers appeared from everywhere in Assam, in trains, carrying babies, they couldn't even ride cycles properly, the sardar said, their women rode men's cycles. The trees were all chopped down, and then shipped out by train or sent to towns like Rangapara or Dhekiajuli to be sold. Then boys from the insurgent group appeared and started troubling people, collecting taxes, burning girls' jeans in their courtyards for not wearing the traditional Bodo dokhona. Even the forest guards had to take permission from the insurgents to go up into the foothills. The sardar said almost half of the original Bodo families of the two Urohiloga villages had moved out, to Rangapara and elsewhere, where they could live in peace.

On their way back Bora told him a story about when he had been chased by a rogue tusker in Addabari tea garden, not too far from Tezpur. It had learnt to take out the women pluckers' tiffins from their bags and open them by throwing them to the ground. It had eaten some seventy or eighty tiffins one day when the forest guards had reached there with a hired elephant to chase it away, but this elephant took fright and bolted, and the tusker had chased Bora and the others, till the guards managed to ward it off with gun shots and fire crackers.

'I looked back as I ran, and it was coming closer and closer,' he said, laughing.

As winter approached, Abhijit's days in Tezpur drew to a close. The newspaper to which he had sent the article replied, saying that it was a good piece and they would carry it soon. They asked him to consider sending them more such pieces. Abhijit told them he would think about it. Some nights he would lie awake at night listening to the Sukhoi fighter jets from the nearby Salonibari IAF base as they flew their training sorties, the whooshing roar of the engines increasing and then fading away. When the planes flew lower than normal the roar was even louder, while at other times they flew high and quiet, two lights visible, one red, the other white. These fighters were equipped with supersonic missiles which could travel hundreds of kilometres, a deterrent against a repeat of the 1962 debacle. While down below on the ground, elephants, and humans, continued to die: 250 elephants and 950 people in a decade.

The beat officer Pegu during one of their meetings told him about the body of a middle-aged farmer they had found trampled to death in his own paddy field by a herd that had come down from a nearby hill. Not too far from him lay the carcass of an elephant, killed when its trunk came in contact with an 11 kilovolt overhead wire. The elephants were poisoned, or died from being hit by trains as they walked along the tracks, or were electrocuted. Humans had chopped down the forests and spread over the landscape, and now the elephants were running out of places to call home, raiding human settlements in search of food and entering tea gardens, which couldn't do anything openly against these giant animals for fear of losing their Rainforest Alliance affiliations or similar first-world trade agreements.

And not just elephants in the forests—Abhijit had also slowly come to realize how certain everpresent elements of his childhood, like the foxes and fireflies, even bats and vultures, had all but disappeared from Tezpur. Meanwhile, he had read there were to be survey operations for constructing a train line from either Missamari or Bhalukpung up to Tawang. Everything would be mapped, measured, fenced, and protected, leaving nothing of that old wilderness.

During the time he had been in Tezpur, he had noticed several buildings coming up on both sides of the road headed from Mission Chariali towards the town, buildings for showrooms, restaurants, hotels. And at night he could hear, sometimes till one or two in the morning, heavy trucks passing through the Chariali crossroads, coal trucks from Upper Assam headed down, supply trucks for the Lower Subansiri hydropower project headed up, both instances of the landscape at the upper end of the Brahmaputra valley being altered by the hand of man (the tea gardens and the oil wells being early examples of this).

And what of the state itself? More and more Abhijit found himself coming around to the view of a historian from Nagaon, across the Brahmaputra from Tezpur, who had written a history of Assam during the middle of the British period: 'The absence of an uniform administrative and social system covering the entire valley before the coming of the English had its effects on the people...under the veneer of an unbreakable Assamese society there were... some unbridgeable differences.'

And then one day it was his last day in Tezpur. The day before he had sat with his grandmother for a long time. He mentioned a couple of place names to see if she remembered anything—Chariduar, Balipara, Foothills, Udalguri—and was surprised by what she told him.

She started talking about old history, or rather myths: the attack to rescue Krishna's grandson Annirudha from the Ban Roja, supposedly a Kachari with his kingdom at Bhalukpung, the monkeys on the trees attacking the troops that came (hence the name Bandarmari), Krishna sounding the horn for war—so the place became Harisinga (near Udalguri), where Hari or God had blown his xonkho or conch. She told him about the man who had fled with his beloved dheki when the news came that the Man or Burmese had attacked, and where he finally dropped it and ran away became Dhekipelowa (near Missamari). The name of the Gabharu river, she said, came from Habru, the Bodo word for mud. And Missamari, according to her, got the name from an old pond that had existed near the present shopping centre in the army base where people used to catch prawns or misa mas.

On that last night he could make out that both Hiren Khura and Julie weren't looking forward to seeing him leave. His uncle bought some mutton from town and Julie made a spicy curry of it with potatoes which his grandmother, and the rest of them, greatly enjoyed. Abhijit told his uncle, when asked about it, that he hadn't packed and would do so in the morning. He would have breakfast and leave in a taxi to be at the airport at Guwahati by midday for his afternoon flight. Debolina had messaged him, and he replied to her before going to bed saying that he would let her know once he had left the house.

He lay awake till late at night thinking about his mother, about his father and Pradip Deka, about the Monpa woman Lobsang, about that great forest from his childhood. In time people would forget about the forests that once covered the Chariduar and Balipara areas, like in other parts of Assam. Farmland, haat markets, 'centres', and towns would come up. It was a cycle of mankind. The moors of England, for instance, were once covered with temperate rainforests, but as population increased, trees started to be felled in greater numbers to make space for cultivation and then fires were started which swept through the landscape, killing off most of the wildlife.

Earlier in the day he had been reading W.G. Sebald's *The Rings of Saturn*, and in it he had underlined the following passage: 'Our spread over the earth was fuelled by reducing the higher species of vegetation to charcoal, by incessantly burning whatever would burn...From the earliest times, human civilisation has been no more than a strange luminescence growing more intense by the hour, of which no one can say when it will begin to wane and when it will fade away.'

That night he dreamt of a plane taking off from Guwahati airport and banking, and the view below from his window seat of the Brahmaputra river and the sprawl of Guwahati city, before the plane climbed up above the clouds. In the seat ahead of him, a boy of four or five sat with his face pressed against the plastic window, lost in wonder at the changing scale of the view outside. When he woke in the morning, Abhijit thought about the house caught in the past where he now found himself, and the woman who was waiting for him in Delhi. He was reminded of the sudden storm in the forest which Mohen Doctor had told him about, with the large hornbill flying over the beel and crying out, a solitary remnant of a bygone wilderness.

The mysteries of our childhood fade, even as man continues on his inevitable march to bring the earth (and everything in it) under his control.

He got out of bed and washed up. He collected the bags for the haat from the kitchen. His uncle asked him whether he had packed and had called for the taxi. Abhijit said he hadn't, and his uncle nodded, as if he had been expecting it. The ATM which Abhijit usually visited to take out money wasn't in order, so he had to go further ahead to the Mission Chariali crossroads, where he had got down months ago from a bus. It felt like another lifetime now. Then he walked to the haat where he started looking around for vegetables and fish for the house.